VIKING SOCIETY FOR NORTHERN RESEARCH
TEXT SERIES

GENERAL EDITORS

Alison Finlay and Carl Phelpstead

VOLUME IV

TWO ICELANDIC STORIES

Edited by Anthony Faulkes

TWO ICELANDIC STORIES

HREIÐARS ÞÁTTR
ORMS ÞÁTTR

EDITED BY

ANTHONY FAULKES

SECOND EDITION

VIKING SOCIETY
FOR NORTHERN RESEARCH
UNIVERSITY COLLEGE LONDON
2011

© VIKING SOCIETY FOR NORTHERN RESEARCH

ISBN: 978-0-903521-73-4

First published 1967 with the help of a gift to the University of Cambridge in memory of Dorothea Coke, Skæret, 1951

Reprinted with minor additions 1978
New edition with corrections and further additions 2011

Printed by Short Run Press Limited, Exeter

GENERAL EDITOR'S PREFACE [1967]

This, the fourth volume to be published in our Text Series, comprises two remarkable Icelandic tales. The first, *Hreiðars þáttr*, is in an ancient narrative form. It is one of the oldest Icelandic short stories preserved and its archaic style adds greatly to its interest. The story also gives an insight into medieval humour, very different from that of today.

The second tale, *Orms þáttr*, differs greatly in age and type from *Hreiðars þáttr*. It is a late composition and reveals a taste that grew in Iceland in the late Middle Ages, a taste for stories of adventure, magic and feats of strength.

The spelling of both texts has been normalised. In the first case, since the text is archaic, an archaic spelling is adopted. In the second, the spelling used by the editor approaches that of Modern Icelandic.

It is hoped that these two texts will provide an introduction to Icelandic narrative prose of different ages, and be especially of service to students who are not satisfied to read snippets in standard handbooks.

I wish to thank Mr Richard Perkins, who read a proof of the Glossary, and Mr David Thomas, who has given great assistance in the production of this book. On behalf of the Society I must express our great gratitude to the Managers of the Dorothea Coke Fund of the University of Cambridge for the kind consideration they gave to our request for financial help towards its publication.

G.T.-P.

ACKNOWLEDGMENTS

I owe my thanks to Professor G. Turville-Petre for his help and guidance at all stages of the making of this book, and to Professor P. Foote for his many useful suggestions and corrections; to the Arnamagnæan Institute for kindly lending me proofs of the text of *Hreiðars þáttr* from the forthcoming edition of Hulda prepared by Miss Jonna Louis-Jensen; and to Gestur Þorgeirsson of Stórólfshvoll for showing me round the neighbourhood of Ormr's former home in most inclement weather.

A.F.
[1967]

PREFACE TO SECOND EDITION

For this new edition the text has been entirely reset and numerous additions and corrections made, as well the binding being restored to something like that of the original edition.

A.F.
[2011]

CONTENTS

General Editor's Preface	v
Acknowledgments	vi
Abbreviations and Manuscripts	viii
Introduction	
The *þáttr* in Icelandic literature	1
Hreiðars þáttr	5
Orms þáttr	20
Hreiðars þáttr	41
Orms þáttr	57
Textual Notes	79
General Notes	81
Glossary	102
Index of Proper Names	166

ABBREVIATIONS

Flb.   *Flateyjarbók* I–III (ed. Guðbrandur Vigfússon and C. R. Unger, 1860–68).
ÍF   *Íslenzk fornrit* I– (1933–).
Ln.   *Landnamabók* (ed. Finnur Jónsson, 1900).
Msk.   *Morkinskinna* (ed. Finnur Jónsson, 1932).
NN   E. A. Kock, *Notationes Norrænæ* (1923–44). [References are to the paragraphs.]
Skj.   *Den norsk-islandske Skjaldedigtning* A I–II; B I–II (ed. Finnur Jónsson, 1912–15).
Ǫrv.   *Ǫrvar-Odds saga* (ed. R. C. Boer, 1888).

MANUSCRIPTS

A   AM 66 fol. (*Hulda*).
B   AM 567 4to.
F   GkS 1005 fol. (*Flateyjarbók*).
H   GkS 1010 fol. (*Hrokkinskinna*).
M   GkS 1009 fol. (*Morkinskinna*).
S   GkS 2845 4to.

All Icelandic quotations, including those in the textual notes pp. 79–80, are given in normalised form.

INTRODUCTION

The þáttr in Icelandic literature

The primary meaning of the word *þáttr* (plural *þættir*) is 'a strand' (in a rope), but it early developed various metaphorical meanings with the basic sense of 'a subsidiary part of something'. When used in medieval manuscripts of pieces of narrative writing, it refers to episodes or 'strands' of a story subsidiary to the main theme.[1] Since many such episodes were themselves originally independent stories, the word has come to be used by modern editors to describe a particular kind of short story in Icelandic prose. Just as the word *saga*, meaning simply 'something told, a story', has also acquired the more particular sense of 'a narrative in Icelandic prose of certain dimensions', so the word *þáttr*, from its older sense of 'episode', has come to be the name of a particular genre, 'a narrative in Icelandic prose of limited dimensions'. The two words, as they are now used, indicate a difference between two genres similar to that between the novel and the short story in modern English literature.

Icelandic short stories, therefore, came to be called *þættir* because many of them are preserved as episodes in sagas, chiefly Sagas of Kings.[2] Indeed hardly any *þættir* exist as independent stories in

---

[1] e.g. *Flb.* I, 558, II, 176 (headings of extracts from *Orkneyinga saga* included in the sagas of Óláfr Tryggvason and Óláfr the Saint); I 299, 533 (extracts from *Hallfreðar saga*). Cf. the prologue to *Flateyjarbók*: . . . *frá Óláfi konungi Tryggvasyni meðr öllum sínum þáttum* &c. The word *þáttr* is not used in the headings of any of the many episodes in *Morkinskinna* (*c.* 1275). Note also the words *þǫttr* and *bragþǫttr* in *Lexicon Poeticum*, rev. Finnur Jónsson (1931).

[2] The most important collections of this kind are in *Flateyjarbók* (GkS 1005 fol.) and *Morkinskinna* (GkS 1009 fol.).

manuscripts older than the fifteenth century,[1] though there is little doubt that many of them were originally independent, and some may be older than the sagas into which they have been incorporated. There is often reason to think that the texts of such stories were altered, particularly by being shortened, when they were included as parts of larger works.

Some *þættir* are probably older than the oldest Sagas of Icelanders. They are often about the dealings between some Icelander and one of the kings of Norway. They are therefore to be considered an offshoot from the writing of Sagas of Kings, though as the genre developed, *þættir* also came to be written on many other subjects, including themes similar to those of the Sagas of Icelanders and the Heroic Sagas. But in the first place they seem to have been written to assert the position and importance of the Icelander at the court of Norway (the heroes of many of them are court poets). They may therefore have facilitated the transition from the writing of stories about the kings of Norway to the treatment of purely Icelandic subjects.

The distinction between a *þáttr* and a saga (in the modern senses of the words as names of literary genres) is not primarily one of length. It is also a question of subject-matter, treatment and style.[2] The saga, like its equivalent in verse form, the epic, is a leisurely affair, that can delve deeply into motive and spend many words on circumstantial description and details of subsidiary importance (such as, for instance, genealogy). The *þáttr*, like the epic lay, must make its effect with bolder strokes, and must be content merely to suggest complexity of motive with subtle outline, although

---

[1] Among the oldest are GkS 2845 4to and the parts of *Flateyjarbók* written in the fifteenth century. The older parts of *Flateyjarbók* also include a few independent *þættir*, but not a random collection.

[2] See J. C. Harris, 'Genre and Narrative Structure in some Íslendinga þættir', *Scandinavian Studies*, 44 (1972), 1–27.

this does not mean that the form precludes the same profundity and insight into character as can be achieved on the larger canvas.

Most of the stories now classed as *þættir* contain only a single-stranded story, often a single episode or group of closely related episodes about one man, while the sagas usually tell the whole life-story of a man or group of men, or the history of a family or even a district. The Sagas of Kings mostly relate the events of a reign or dynasty. The heroes of *þættir* are often historically unimportant men (sometimes they are not even named), and the events related historically insignificant, but the sagas tell of the great deeds of great men, of the heroes of Icelandic antiquity or the kings and jarls of Scandinavia; or else they tell of the lives of holy men. Most of the Sagas of Icelanders relate to the period from the end of the settlement of Iceland in 930 to the death of St Óláfr in 1030, and although they are not lacking in humour, they are on the whole devoted to a serious reconstruction of this heroic age of Iceland. Many *þættir*, however, relate to later periods, and many are humorous stories obviously written purely for entertainment. Although these differences may in part be due to the accidents of preservation, there do seem to have been traditional restrictions about the proper subject for a saga which did not apply to the *þáttr*. The *þáttr* seems in many ways to have been a less formal sort of composition than the saga (the closest equivalent in English is perhaps 'anecdote') and could with some justification be considered to stand in the same relation to the saga as the *fabliau* stood to the more formal romance in other parts of Europe. For this reason the *þættir* cannot be thought of as the raw material for sagas, or the sagas as expanded or amalgamated *þættir*;[1] they are two distinct genres.

---

[1] This view is revived by Wolfgang Lange, 'Einige Bemerkungen zur altnordischen Novelle', *Zeitschrift für Deutsches Altertum*, LXXXVIII (1957–8), 150–59.

Many of the *þættir* contain a high proportion of conversation, and in accordance with the lighter tone of many of them, the style often gives the impression of being colloquial, in contrast to the more formal style of the sagas. This is probably a deliberate attempt by their authors to achieve a style closer to that of oral story-telling. It is not likely that any of the *þættir* that survive are literal transcriptions of oral tales, although like the sagas, some may be based on oral sources (especially those that contain old verses may be based on oral traditions in prose handed down as accompaniments to the verses). But the *þættir* as we have them are literary works, bearing all the marks of careful composition and deliberate artistry. Most of them are concerned with the portrayal of character, and such a preoccupation with character is not typical of oral story-telling. Oral tales undoubtedly existed in medieval Iceland, but nothing at all is known of their form or style, and little of their subjects. The word *þáttr*, which is the name of a highly-developed literary genre, must not be applied to them.[1]

---

[1] On the *þættir* as a genre, see J. Lindow, 'Old Icelandic þáttr', *Scripta Islandica* 29 (1978), 3–44; J. Harris, 'Theme and Genre in some "Íslendinga þættir"', *Scandinavian Studies* 48, 1–28 (1976). On folk-tale parallels see John Lindow, 'Hreiðars þáttr heimska and AT 326', *Arv* 34 (1978), 152–79. [AT 326 (*Folklore Fellows Communications* 184, 114–15) = Grimm No 4, The story of the boy who went out into the world to learn fear; cf. p. 14 below]. Cf. the folk-tale parallels to *Hróa þáttr*, discussed in Dag Strömbäck, 'Uppsala, Iceland and the Orient', *Early English and Norse Studies Presented to Hugh Smith* (1963), 178–90. [*Hróa þáttr* is based on Senex cæcus in the collection of Märchen known as The Seven Sages; also in The Thousand and One Nights and in Indian, Arabian and Near Eastern Collections. Cf. the Middle English (15th century) Tale of Beryn.

INTRODUCTION 5

Hreiðars þáttr

There is nothing in the story of Hreiðarr that could not actually have happened. Unlike many medieval stories, it has no supernatural elements, and it does not assume in the reader a particular religious or moral outlook. The only thing the modern reader might find somewhat foreign is the joke that is the climax of the story, Hreiðarr's gift of a silver pig to King Haraldr. This is a reference to the king's father's nickname (*sýr*, 'sow'). The humour of this is somewhat different from the adult humour of today. But although this may seem to us a childish joke, it is noteworthy that its point is not made over-obvious: the reference is not explained and the name *sýr* is not even mentioned in the *þáttr*. To understand it the reader is required to have some intelligence as well as some special knowledge.

The story is entirely human, and both externally and psychologically realistic. Exception has been taken to the unlikely manner of Hreiðarr's escape from King Haraldr in Uppland,[1] but although he appears to escape rather too easily, there is nothing impossible in the actual fact of his escape. If the author lets the incident pass without trying to make the details more convincing, it is only because he is more interested in the reactions of his characters to events than in the events themselves.[2] More serious criticism is invited by the conclusion of the story, where King Magnús rewards Hreiðarr for a eulogistic poem with an island off the coast of Norway—a most unlikely payment—and then immediately buys it back from him. This is both historically and psychologically inappropriate, but it is the only part of the story

---

[1] See *ÍF* X, xciii.
[2] On similar features in the narrative of *Auðunar þáttr* see A. R. Taylor, 'Auðunn and the bear', *Saga-Book* XIII (1946–53), 78–96, esp. 90.

that is unsatisfactory; like many later authors, the author of *Hreiðars þáttr* found it difficult to wind up his story convincingly.

Otherwise the story is outstanding in its realism; in particular it is worth noting that although Hreiðarr, like many other story-heroes, is said to have exceptional strength, he never does anything requiring supernatural strength. Neither his manner of killing King Haraldr's courtier nor his ability to keep up with galloping horses (being ridden by fully armed men) are beyond the bounds of possibility.

The realism of the story is due entirely to the art of the author, for there appears to be no historical basis for it. It is a work of fiction. Although it is set against the real historical background of the period of joint rule of King Magnús the Good and Haraldr harðráði ('the harsh') in the year 1046, none of the characters apart from the two kings seems to have existed. There are only eight personal names in the story (other characters, for instance the courtier killed by Hreiðarr, are nameless). Besides the two kings, the only character whose existence is confirmed from other sources is Glúmr (line 3), if this really is the same man as the hero of *Víga-Glúms saga*. But the incident referred to is not mentioned elsewhere, and was perhaps invented to connect the hero of *Hreiðars þáttr* with a known historical character. The geographical references in the *þáttr* are also vague; there is only one to a definite place (Bjǫrgyn), the others are only to localities. The island King Magnús gave Hreiðarr is not named. Nothing of the poem composed by Hreiðarr in honour of the king survives, and probably neither the poem nor the poet ever existed.

The historical background of the story is based on the tradition of the uneasy joint rule of the half-brother and son of St Óláfr. King Magnús's reputation as a good king (and his nickname) seems to derive partly from the story of his rebuke by the poet Sigvatr in his 'Outspoken Verses'[1] (in which the king is compared to Hákon inn góði) and his subsequent reform as a ruler, and partly from the fact that by his early death he left as sole ruler of Norway the forceful but unlucky Haraldr; Magnús's memory was evidently made the sweeter by contrast with his successor. But Haraldr's reputation for harshness is probably equally undeserved: although there is some support in early verses for the view that he was a difficult man to deal with,[2] there is no evidence that his nickname is older than the thirteenth century.[3] In the Sagas of Kings and scaldic verses generally he is represented as a strong and courageous ruler, and almost the only criticism expressed of him concerns his ill-fated expedition to England in 1066.[4] But the contrast between the characters of the two kings seems to have been magnified in oral tradition, which must have been reinforced by Adam of Bremen's patently biassed account of King Haraldr,[5] influenced mainly by the fact that Adam's sources were Danish, and so hostile to Haraldr, and also perhaps by ecclesiastical rivalry

---

[1] *Bersǫglisvísur*, *ÍF* XXVIII, 26–31; *Msk.*, 26–30. See M. Olsen 'Om Balder-digtning og Balder-kultus', *Arkiv för Nordisk filologi*, XL (1924), 148–75, esp. 155–7.

[2] e.g. *ÍF* XXVIII, 123, verse 114 (Þjóðólfr).

[3] See *ÍF* XXVIII, xxxix, note 1. But Saxo Grammaticus, *Gesta Danorum* (ed. A. Holder, 1886), p. 371, gives him the cognomen *malus*. The nickname *Harfagera* given him in the Old English Chronicle D (*Anno* 1066), thence into other English histories, indicates confusion of the two Haraldrs, rather than knowledge of the second Haraldr's nickname.

[4] *ÍF* XXVIII, 190, verse 159 (Þjóðólfr); *Skj.* B I 324, verse 13 (Arnórr jarlaskáld).

[5] Adam of Bremen, *Gesta Hammaburgensis Ecclesiae Pontificum* (written about 1070), lib. III, cap. xiii ff., esp. cap. xvii (ed. B. Schmeidler in *Scriptores Rerum Germanicarum . . . ex Monumentis Germaniae Historicis* (1917), 153 ff.).

between the Norwegian Church and the archbishopric of Bremen. There is also a possibility that Haraldr, after his stay in Constantinople, favoured the Eastern Church in the disputes that at that time existed between it and the Western Church.[1]

The older histories[2] have nothing to say of any friction between these two kings, but in the stories composed in Iceland in the early thirteenth century there develops a thriving literary tradition about it, and it becomes the background for many episodes in Sagas of Kings. There is an apparent contradiction between the pictures of Haraldr in some of these stories: some are sympathetic to him, while in others he appears as arrogant, arbitrary and cruel. In fact there is no real contradiction. They simply reveal two sides of a many-faceted personality. In tradition, Haraldr had soon become a heroic figure of stature comparable to the heroes of Germanic antiquity—in one early poem he is directly associated with Sigurðr the dragon-slayer[3]—and this was partly the result of his romantic expeditions to Russia and Constantinople and the probably fictional but nevertheless fascinating stories that grew up around his adventures there. There is scarcely any other Norwegian king about whom more stories are told. In these stories he always has something of the aura of romance about him, and his character is cast in the traditional heroic mould; he is depicted as fearless, strong-willed, inspiring immense personal loyalty in his followers, but harsh to his enemies and to those who offended him. His sense

---

[1] Cf. *ÍF* XXVIII, xxxix ff.; Magnús Már Lárusson, 'On the so-called "Armenian" bishops', *Studia Islandica* XVIII (1960), 23–38; Sigfús Blöndal, *Væringjasaga* (1954), pp. 165–6.

[2] i.e. Ágrip (*c.* 1190) and Theodoricus, *Historia de antiquitate regum Norwagiensium* (*c.* 1180).

[3] *Skj.* B I 354 (Illugi Bryndœlaskáld). Cf. also *Rauðúlfs þáttr*, in *Saga Óláfs konungs hins helga* (ed. O. A. Johnsen and Jón Helgason (1941), p. 676, where the same association is made.

of humour is broad but unreliable: in a story that shows him in the best possible light, he still appears as a man it is dangerous to offend.[1] His character is more rounded and true to life in Icelandic stories than that of any other of the early Norwegian kings, though it probably owes more to the romantic interpretation of story-tellers than to the man himself.[2]

The author of *Hreiðars þáttr* has used this traditional interpretation of the characters of the two kings (though he seems to have added some personal details of his own invention), but it is uncertain whether he had any literary sources for it. The tradition does not appear in the older synoptic histories, and it is doubtful whether any version of a *Haralds saga harðráða* existed before the compilation of the sagas in the *Morkinskinna* collection about 1220—that this could have been known to the author of the *þáttr* is unlikely. He may have known some of the other *þættir* concerned with Haraldr. There are three other stories that include references to the king's sensitivity about his father's nickname. Like *Hreiðars þáttr*, these are all included in *Morkinskinna*, and they were probably all written in the early thirteenth century. One tells how King Haraldr insulted King Magnús's half-brother Þórir with a satirical verse against his father. On the suggestion of King Magnús, Þórir retaliates with a verse satirising Haraldr's father, in which the insulting nickname *sýr* is introduced.[3] Another story concerns the Icelander Halldórr Snorrason. Haraldr forced Halldórr to take a sconce that Halldórr considered unjust. Halldórr said: 'It may well be that you can force me to drink, but I am quite sure that Sigurðr Sow would not have been able to force Snorri the Priest to do it.' He is here implying that his father Snorri was both

---

[1] *Stúfs þáttr* (*ÍF* V, 281–90).
[2] Cf. the account of his character in *Sneglu-Halla þáttr*, *ÍF* IX, 263).
[3] *Msk.*, 109–10.

of nobler breeding and of stronger character than Haraldr's farmer father Sigurðr.[1] The third story concerns another Icelander, Stúfr Þórðarson. King Haraldr made an obvious joke about the nickname of Stúfr's father, Kǫttr ('Cat'). Instead of replying, Stúfr merely laughed. Haraldr guessed that Stúfr was thinking of the corresponding joke about his own father's nickname, but on this occasion he takes no offence, and the whole episode is kept on a plane of bantering and good humour.[2]

There is no evidence of a literary relationship between these four stories. They may all derive independently from an oral tradition (which may be genuine) about the nickname *sýr* and King Haraldr's sensitivity about it.

The oldest manuscript that contains *Hreiðars þáttr* is *Morkinskinna* (GkS 1009 fol., M), written about 1275. This manuscript contains a collection of Sagas of Kings of Norway from Magnús the Good onwards which is thought to have been first compiled about 1220. The surviving version in M includes many episodes or *þættir* about Icelanders who had dealings with kings of Norway, among which is *Hreiðars þáttr*, but it is uncertain how many of these were in the original compilation. A version of the sagas of Magnús the Good and Haraldr harðráði survives in *Flateyjarbók* which is derived from the same original compilation, but here many of the *þættir* in M, including *Hreiðars þáttr*, are lacking. The authors of two other collections of Sagas of Kings, *Heimskringla* and *Fagrskinna*, also used a version of the *Morkinskinna* compilation that must have been older than M, but they did not

---

[1] *Halldórs þáttr Snorrasonar* (*Msk.*, 149, ÍF V, 269).

[2] *Stúfs þáttr* (*Msk.*, 252, ÍF V, 283–4). *Halldórs þáttr* and *Stúfs þáttr* can be read in *Stories from Sagas of Kings*, ed. Anthony Faulkes (2007). Punning on personal names is associated with King Haraldr also in *Hemings þáttr* (ed. G. F. Jensen, 1962), pp. 12–13, where there is also possibly an implied reference to the nickname *sýr*.

include any of the *þættir* about Icelanders, though there is evidence that they knew some of them.[1] This may mean that the original *Morkinskinna* compilation included fewer *þættir* than the surviving version in M, though the inclusion or omission of various episodes may also reflect the different aims and methods of the writers of these books. Snorri Sturluson, certainly, was more interested in the political history of Norway than in any well-told but slight anecdotes about Icelanders. But it is likely nevertheless that some at least of the *þættir* in M were added to the compilation after it was first made, and many were almost certainly originally independent stories, in some cases older than the sagas in which they are preserved as chapters.

The style of the text of *Hreiðars þáttr* in M is comparable to that of the best classical Sagas of Icelanders. It is characterised by great verbal economy, frequent ellipsis (sometimes sentences are compressed almost to the point of obscurity[2]), and asyndeton. The narrative is swift-moving, straightforward and clear, and the impression of speed is increased by the unusual frequency with which the verb comes at the beginning of the sentence. There is little external description either of people or places (there are remarkably few proper names), and unlike many of the sagas, there is little space devoted to genealogy and scarcely any preamble.[3] But the sparseness of detail in the narrative is in strong contrast to the circumstantial accounts of the conversations, which take up well over half the story, and it is in these that the author shows particular skill in revealing the characters of the speakers with mastery and economy.

[1] See *ÍF* XI, cxiii, cxvi.

[2] e.g. lines 166–8. The sentence is clearer in A and H.

[3] Note the unusually laconic manner in which the otherwise unknown Eyvindr is introduced into the story (line 340): not even his father's name is mentioned.

To a certain extent these stylistic features must represent the individual style of the author (or his school), although some (e.g. the high proportion of conversation, the paucity of proper names) are characteristic of the genre. The simplicity and verbal compression, however, may in large measure be due to the text having been shortened at some time. It is in itself likely that a short text, when it is interpolated into a long saga, will be shortened and adapted to make it fit its new context, apart from any tendency to alter the style in conformity with the style of the work into which it is interpolated. There are some *þættir* that survive in two versions, both as interpolations in Sagas of Kings and as independent stories. In some cases there is reason to believe that the independent versions, although they only survive in later manuscripts, represent the original texts more faithfully than the interpolated ones, which often seem to have been shortened and adapted.[1] Some of the sagas that are characterised by verbal compression comparable to that in *Hreiðars þáttr* also survive (fragmentarily) in more prolix versions that are thought to be closer to the originals.[2] On the other hand, the texts of the sagas thought to have been composed at the beginning of the period of saga-writing are characterised by verbosity and diffuseness.[3] If, as is thought, *Hreiðars þáttr* was also composed at the beginning of this period, the style has evidently been revised to make it conform to the taste for verbal economy that appears to have developed later in the classical

---

[1] e.g. *Sneglu-Halla þáttr*, *Stúfs þáttr*, *Gull-Ásu-Þórðar þáttr* (see ÍF IX, cix ff.; V, xcii f.; XI, cxiv ff.). Cf. Bjarni Aðalbjarnarson, *Om de norske kongers sagaer* (1937), pp. 154–9.

[2] See *Víga-Glúms saga* (ed. G. Turville-Petre, 2nd ed., 1960), pp. xxii–xxxii; ÍF II, lxxxii ff. (*Egils saga*).

[3] e.g. *Heiðarvíga saga* (see ÍF III, cxxxiii, cxxxvii) and *Fóstbrœðra saga* (see ÍF VI, lxx ff.; but cf. now Jónas Kristjánsson, *Eddas and Sagas*, 1988, 279–80).

period. Although it is in some ways a pity not to have the original version of such a work, there is little doubt that such stylistic changes as have been made will on the whole have been for the better.

The construction of *Hreiðars þáttr* is simple and straightforward. The narrative is built round the various conversations between Hreiðarr and the two kings.[1] The story is mostly single-stranded. On the occasions where the author has to tell of two simultaneous events, however, he gets into difficulty, but it is only at these points that the narrative is handled at all clumsily.[2] This is perhaps another indication that the *þáttr* was first composed before the technique of saga-writing had fully developed. The unusual lapse into the first person referring to the narrator (in a place where the author is trying to extricate himself from one of these chronological muddles)[3] is also an indication that the conventions of the classical sagas had not become universal at the time the *þáttr* was written. But apart from this, the *þáttr* is not primitive either in style or construction. Its simplicity and straightforwardness are not the same as are associated with 'oral style', they are the result of conscious literary art (whether of the author or redactor) and there is no reason to think that *Hreiðars þáttr* as it survives is a transcription of an oral story, or that the story itself was ever transmitted except on parchment.

The main point of the story is the development of the character of Hreiðarr. This owes something to the traditional story-hero of the type of the stupid youth who turns out to be a great hero (although it is doubtful whether the author could have known any

---

[1] Compare in this respect the construction of *Auðunar þáttr* (cf. the article referred to above, p. 5, note 2).

[2] lines 416–25, 363 ff., 376. In the later version in A and H these muddles are mostly sorted out.

[3] line 376. The only other case in *Morkinskinna* is in another of the *þættir*, *Frá Eysteini konungi ok Ívari* (*Msk.*, 354 line 6).

stories of this kind in written form), but Hreiðarr is more than this. In his first conversations with his brother he reveals that he knows full well what he wants and how to get it (cf. lines 12, 25, 64)[1] and the perspicacious King Magnús can see that Hreiðarr has his wits about him, even if his behaviour is eccentric (cf. line 145). The extent of Hreiðarr's cleverness is revealed gradually as the story advances, but it is only at the end that the author finally admits that his hero's folly was, at least in part, an act (lines 465–6). Hreiðarr, gifted but inexperienced, wants to experience the whole range of human emotions, especially anger, which his gentle nature has not allowed him to feel; only after he has done this, it is implied, and after his beneficial contact with the personality of King Magnús (cf. note to line 115) does he become a whole man, fully realise his potentialities and fulfil himself. The author has a remarkably articulate understanding of the nature of artistic creativity. Hreiðarr has the first prerequisite of the artist, an eye for detail, as Magnús acknowledges (cf. lines 172, 197 ff.), and it is rare in such an early story to find such a convincing description of an artist's self-discovery and of a poet's gradual attainment of his full powers (cf. lines 368, 441 ff., 464). Gentleness of character, typical perhaps of the intellectual, is also a surprising virtue to be stressed so much in this sort of story. Rather self-conscious, perhaps, is the refusal of the provincial genius to adopt the fine fashions of court, smacking of the inverted snobbery which one fears may have been the author's own. Basically a humorous character-sketch, the portrayal of Hreiðarr is remarkably true to life, and full of individual and realistic details, which are nearly

---

[1] Þórðr's refusal to take his brother abroad is paralleled in *Egils saga* (*ÍF* II, 102–04) and *Áns saga bogsveigis* (*Fornaldar sögur Nordrlanda*, ed. C. C. Rafn, 1829–30, II, 328). The relationships between the pairs of brothers in these three stories are similar in other ways too.

all conveyed dramatically through his words in his conversations with his brother and the two kings. Particularly well constructed is Hreiðarr's first interview with King Magnús, which is a masterpiece of dramatic comedy. Although the story is mainly concerned with Hreiðarr's getting the better of King Haraldr, the author makes quite clear that his more subtle management of King Magnús is the greater achievement. But perhaps the most remarkable thing about the portrayal of Hreiðarr's character is that it is dynamic. His character develops, unlike the static pasteboard figures of so many other medieval stories.

The author has arranged his characters in contrasting pairs: the two kings Magnús and Haraldr, the two brothers Hreiðarr and Þórðr. The contrast between the two last is stressed several times (most clearly at line 98): Þórðr, the obviously successful, clever, handsome, but undersized, Hreiðarr apparently an idiot, ugly, immensely strong, but with latent intellectual gifts, because of which he eventually completely overshadows his conventional and mediocre brother, who is not even mentioned in the second half of the story. Þórðr's character is drawn in less detail than his brother's, but with telling strokes none the less: his concern for appearances and bourgeois outlook are revealed in his words with merciless accuracy (lines 27, 221 ff.). The author relents somewhat, however, by balancing his hopeless pomposity with a touch of kindness: Þórðr loves his brother and is unwilling to reveal his defects to the king, although his honesty compels him to do so (lines 98 ff.).

Hreiðars þáttr survives in another medieval version found in two manuscripts, *Hulda* (AM 66 fol., A) of the fourteenth century, and *Hrokkinskinna* (GkS 1010 fol., H) of the fifteenth century. These two manuscripts contain very similar texts of a later redaction of the same collection of sagas as is found in M. There are numerous differences between the texts of the sagas in this later redaction and that in M. They have been expanded with interpolations from several sources, especially *Heimskringla*, and some *þættir* have been added. The style has also been modified in accordance with the taste of the fourteenth century. Most of the abruptness and verbal economy of the earlier text has been smoothed out, and the impression given is often one of verbosity. The text of *Hreiðars þáttr* in this version is very different from that in M. Most of the archaisms have been replaced,[1] some of the ineptitudes in the narrative and some of the obscurities have been rationalised,[2] and a characteristic trick of the redactor of this version is to replace a single word in the older version by a pair of near-synonyms.[3] The result is the same story told in different words and in a different, less striking, style. But there are scarcely any alterations or additions of substance, except in the matter of place-names.

The later version makes two more definite localisations than the text of M. At the beginning of the story, it specifies the brothers' point of departure from Iceland as Gásar, while M simply says Eyjafjǫrðr (as Gásar was the principal harbour in Eyjafjǫrðr, one would probably have assumed this anyway). At the end, the later version says that the farm where Hreiðarr settled is called Hreiðarsstaðir. This identification was probably made after the *þáttr* was written, and again it was a natural assumption since there was actually a farm of that name in Svarfaðardalr. The redactor clearly preferred more definite localisations to the vagueness of the original. A similar tendency for redactors of early texts to supply proper names lacking in the original versions appears in the textual

[1] But the suffixed pronoun occurs twice (*gerik*), see *Fornmanna sögur*, VI (1831), 201, 208.

[2] e.g. lines 166–8 are clearer in A and H; cf. p. 13, note 2 above.

[3] e.g. line 145 *hugkvæmir*: *ok hǫfðingjadjarfir* adds A; line 161 *viti*: *eðr sjóninni* adds A; line 235 *ágang*: *spotti ok áfangi* A; line 441 *kynligast*: *nokkut stirt ok einrœnligt* A.

history of other *þættir* in Sagas of Kings.[1] A third alteration in the text of *Hreiðars þáttr* in the later redaction is the replacement of Bjǫrgyn (line 34) by Þrándheimr. This is evidently to make the localisation conform with that of the other stories that take place during the period of joint rule by Magnús the Good and Haraldr harðráði, which mostly take place in Þrándheimr.[2]

The texts of the later version may be derived not directly from M but from a closely related sister manuscript. If so, they may in some cases contain readings closer to the original than those of M. But the texts in A and H are chiefly useful because they can help us to reconstruct passages in M that are illegible because of damage to the manuscript (mainly at the bottom corners of each page). This edition follows the text of M (though the spelling has been normalised[3]) supplemented by A in the places where the text of M is illegible. In some cases, however, the texts of the later version depart so far from M that such reconstruction is impossible.

The oldest surviving manuscript of the *þáttr* (M) was written about 1275, but the story is thought to have been first written much earlier than this. The influence of other written texts cannot be demonstrated, and it is believed that the *þáttr* was written in the oldest period of saga-writing, at the end of the twelfth or beginning of the thirteenth century. The evidence for this is chiefly

---

[1] e.g. *Sneglu-Halla þáttr*, see *ÍF* IX, cxi; *Íslendings þáttr sǫgufróða*, see *ÍF* XI, cxiii and 335, note 1.

[2] Cf. *Fornmanna sögur*, VI (1831), 195. This localisation is not in *Morkinskinna*, and the redactor of the *Hulda–Hrokkinskinna* version is probably following *Heimskringla* (see *ÍF* XXVIII, 102). The episode immediately preceding *Hreiðars þáttr* in *Morkinskinna* is localised in the Vík, but this has been transferred to a different part of the saga in the later version. Concern for consistency in localisation seems to have been the reason for much of the rearrangement of episodes in the later redaction.

[3] Cf. p. 37, note 1 below.

linguistic. The language of *Hreiðars þáttr* is more archaic than the main text of the Sagas of Kings in M, although similar archaisms occur in the texts of other *þættir* in the same manuscript. We find in *Hreiðars þáttr* (in M) three cases of the suffixed negative and three of the suffixed pronoun (see glossary, **-a, -k**). Although these forms are common in prose of the twelfth century and in verse of all periods (as part of the artificial language of poetry, the second also often as a metrical convenience), they are rare in thirteenth-century prose except in proverbs, legal formulas, and other stereotyped expressions.[1] There are also the following forms which seem to have fallen out of use by the thirteenth century: *þars* (later *þar er*), *þeygi* (equivalent of *þó eigi*), *vilgis* (intensive adverb), and *er* for the second person singular of *vera*. We also find several words not recorded elsewhere, perhaps because they had fallen out of use by the time the bulk of saga literature came to be written (*kœja, álpun, grópasamliga, sverðskór, ósyknligr*); and some unusual constructions (*mazk vel, ferr undan við fót, sem yfir kykvendum, ætla drepa*—the last is the usual construction in poetry, though it is rare in prose).

The value of early dating on this evidence is however doubtful. It is always difficult to know when individual words and forms became obsolete. Very few of the sagas survive in manuscripts old enough for us to be sure that the texts we have give an accurate picture of the vocabulary of the period when they were first written. *Morkinskinna* is a comparatively old manuscript, and too few manuscripts of the thirteenth century survive for us to be able to be sure what words in it are really archaisms. Some of the unusual words mentioned above have cognates in modern Icelandic,[2] and rather than archaisms, they may simply have been colloquialisms

---

[1] See Einar Ól. Sveinsson, *Dating the Icelandic Sagas* (1958), p. 101.
[2] See glossary s.v. **álpun**; *ÍF* X, 248, note 2.

in Old Icelandic, permissible in the informal *þáttr*, but avoided in sagas (the meanings of some of these words suggest this: *kœja* 'to worry', *álpun* 'tomfoolery', *grópasamliga* 'boastfully' or 'uncouthly'); and the same may apply to the cases of unusual syntax (with *fara undan við fót* compare modern Icelandic *hlaupa við fót*; and cf. the note to line 70). Some of the apparent archaisms may be the result of scribal error (e.g. *þú er(t)*,[1] *ætla (at) drepa*, *ósyknligr*; see notes to lines 419, 102). It may further be noted that all the examples of the suffixed negative and pronoun occur in the speeches of Hreiðarr in the early part of the *þáttr*, and they may be intended by the author to be understood as provincialisms or even vulgarisms (they seem to have fallen out of use in Norway earlier than in Iceland[2]), characterising the rustic speech of the inexperienced peasant at the court of Norway. Dialectal usages and archaisms do not seem to be used for comic effect elsewhere in early Icelandic literature, but there was a high degree of linguistic awareness as early as the twelfth century (as the First Grammatical Treatise testifies), and such usages are by no means impossible with a writer having such a command of language as the author of *Hreiðars þáttr* has. In view of this, the early dating of the *þáttr* cannot be regarded as certain; all that can be said is that it was probably written before the middle of the thirteenth century.

Nothing is known about the author of *Hreiðars þáttr*, and there is little evidence to show where in Iceland it was written. The Icelandic place-names all relate to the north of the country

---

[1] This form also occurs in the Stockholm Homily Book (see *Homiliu-Bók*, Corpus Codicum Islandicorum Medii Aevi VIII (1935), 40b, line 21), but here too it might be an error. Cf. A. Noreen, *Altisländische und altnorwegische Grammatik* (4th ed., 1923), p. 359.

[2] Both forms are common in the Stockholm Homily Book, written about 1200 in Iceland, but neither occurs in the Norwegian Homily Book, written probably only slightly later in Norway.

(Eyjafjǫrðr) and the apparent reference to Víga-Glúmr also suggests northern tradition. But the *þáttr* has little in common with the sagas thought to have been written in the north of Iceland in the early thirteenth century (the oldest Sagas of Kings, *Fóstbrœðra saga*—but cf. p.12, note 3 above), and the phrase *norðr í Svarfaðardal* (line 462), if it derives from the author and not from a later copyist, suggests a place of origin in the south or west of Iceland.

The literary merits of *Hreiðars þáttr* have long been acknowledged, and there are numerous editions and translations. The older version is printed in the editions of *Morkinskinna* (facsimile in Corpus Codicum Islandicorum Medii Aevi, VI (1934), 6r–7v), and with an introduction by Bjǫrn Sigfússon in *ÍF* X (1940). Among the many popular Icelandic editions that in *Ritlist og Myndlist*, II (1948), is most noteworthy, since it has an introduction by Einar Ól. Sveinsson (reprinted in the same author's *Við uppspretturnar* (1956), pp. 164–5). The later version is edited in *Fornmanna sögur*, VI (1831), 200–218; and a new edition of Hulda by Jonna Louis Jensen is eventually to be published in the series Editiones Arnamagnæanæ.

The *Morkinskinna* version is translated rather freely into English with the title 'Hreidar the Halfwit' by Jacqueline Simpson in *The Northmen Talk* (1965), pp. 119–32; with the title 'Hreidar the Fool' by Hermann Pálsson in *Hrafnkel's saga and other Icelandic stories* (Penguin Books 1971), pp. 94–108; and as 'Hreidar's tale' in *The Complete Sagas of Icelanders*, ed. Viðar Hreinsson (1977), I 375–84.

Orms þáttr

Hreiðars þáttr is one of the oldest Icelandic *þættir*, but *Orms þáttr* is one of the latest, and it is a work of a very different kind. It contains a collection of stories about the feats of strength of the Icelandic hero Ormr Stórólfsson, who lived in the tenth century.

The first four chapters tell of those he performed in his youth in Iceland, the remainder are about his adventures abroad, mainly in Norway. The chief episode of this second part concerns his fights with two monsters on an island off the coast of Norway, which he kills to avenge his Danish friend Ásbjörn. This part of the story is similar in style and subject to the Heroic Sagas (*fornaldar sögur*), except that instead of telling of events of the far past, before the settlement of Iceland, it tells of the adventures of a historical tenth-century Icelander.

The stories told about Ormr in Iceland before his travels abroad are much more like those found in Sagas of Icelanders. They take place partly on Ormr's father's farm in the south of Iceland and partly at the Alþingi. It is these stories that will be more to the taste of the modern reader rather than the conventional monster-fights of the second part. Although all the stories in the *þáttr* contain gross exaggerations and absurdities, the first four chapters do give a fairly convincing picture of life on an Icelandic farm (probably valid for the fourteenth century if not for the tenth), with a wealth of technical terms connected with farming, and of the social life at the Icelandic national assembly. Both here and in the last two chapters, where Ormr, famous after his defeat of the monsters, shows off his strength to jarl Eirekr and Einarr þambarskelfir, the author writes with an obvious sense of humour, and reveals that he does not take his invincible hero, or his reputed achievements, too seriously (cf. line 614); indeed on occasion he appears quite sceptical (even about the stories which he himself probably made up, e.g. line 132). He treats the traditional 'strong man' of Icelandic tradition with some irony, portraying him as a man unable to resist a challenge to his brute strength even if he seriously injures himself in carrying it out (lines 170 ff., 614).

Although *Orms þáttr* is obviously almost entirely fiction, most of the characters are historical, or at least have historical names.

The existence of Ormr himself and his family is well attested in *Landnámabók* and several other sources (the name Stórólfshvóll still survives in the south of Iceland), and Ormr's reputation for strength seems to be old.[1] But it is uncertain how much of the tales told of his feats of strength in the *þáttr* is based on tradition and how much is made up by the author. The three stories in chs 1–3, for instance, are clearly modelled on the three stories told of Grettir's boyhood.[2] In both accounts hostility between father and son is the prime motive and there are many verbal correspondences.[3] There is little doubt that *Orms þáttr* is the borrower. The details of the stories in the *þáttr* are different from those in *Grettis saga*, but some of the motives are found in other sagas and some are part of the stock material of folk-tale.[4]

Þórálfr Skólmsson is also a historical character with a traditional

---

[1] He is called Ormr inn sterki in *Ln.*, pp. 106–08 (*Hauksbók*), 218–19 (*Sturlubók*); and in *Njáls saga* (*ÍF* XII, 52), *Egils saga* (*ÍF* II, 59) and *Gríms saga loðinkinna*.

[2] *Grettis saga*, ch. 14. This was first pointed out by R. C. Boer, 'Zur Grettissaga', *Zeitschrift für deutsche Philologie*, XXX (1898), 66–71. The episode in ch. 3 might also be compared with the 'theft' of hay in *Hœnsa-Þóris saga* (*ÍF* III, 13–16). For the legal and social background to such stories see *ÍF* V lxxiv f. and III, xxx f. and p. 16, note 3 and references there.

[3] Compare lines 33–5 with *ÍF* VII, 36/16–20, 42/9 f.; lines 52–3 with *ÍF* VII 38/17–18, 39/10; line 122 with *ÍF* VII, 38/16 f. With the first of these passages cf. also *Áns saga bogsveigis*, in *Fornaldar sögur Nordrlanda* (ed. C. C. Rafn, 1829–30), II, 326–7.

[4] Compare the stories of Ketill hængr's youth (*Fornaldar sögur Nordrlanda* II, 109–13). For some folk-tale parallels see references in F. Panzer, *Studien zur germanischen Sagengeschichte* I (1910), 348–9. Cf. also Jón Árnason, *Íslenskar þjóðsögur og æfintýri* I (1862), 494–5. The motive of the young hero's conflict with his father is also found in *Egils saga* (*ÍF* II, 80 ff.) and *Hervarar saga ok Heiðreks* (ed. G. Turville-Petre and C. Tolkien, 1956, p. 24).

reputation for strength.[1] He is associated with Ormr in *Grettis saga*, where it says:

> It is the opinion of most men that Grettir was the strongest in the land since Ormr Stórólfsson and Þórálfr Skólmsson ceased their feats of strength.[2]

Grettis saga was certainly known to the author of *Orms þáttr*, and it is possible that he invented the episode of ch. 4 on the basis of this passage. There is no other evidence that traditional stories about the two heroes existed. The episode is given a realistic turn by its setting in the booth of the historical Jörundr goði.[3] Melkólfr is not known from other sources. His name (which is of Irish origin) is one that is usually given to a slave in the sagas.

The hostility between Stórólfr and Dufþakr is also mentioned in *Landnámabók*, where the tradition that they both had supernatural powers is also found.[4] But it appears that the author of *Orms þáttr* did not use *Landnámabók*. If he had, he would probably have included the story it tells of the two neighbours, and also have given the names of Ormr's brother and sister and wife which are found there.[5] But the genealogical material in ch. 1 (lines 1–25) is taken, sometimes word for word, but more often somewhat abbreviated, from ch. 23 of *Egils saga*, which is itself following a source independent of *Landnámabók*.[6] The version of *Egils saga*

---

[1] See *Fagrskinna* (ÍF XXIX, 10, 74); *Heimskringla*, ÍF XXVI, 187; *Ln.*, pp. 75, 194. There is part of a *drápa* about him extant by Þórðr Særeksson (eleventh century; *Skj.* B I, 302–03), and verse 13 of *Íslendingadrápa* (by Haukr Valdísarson, probably thirteenth century; *Skj.* B I, 539 ff.) is devoted to him.

[2] ÍF VII, 187.

[3] See ÍF II, 60; XII, 28; *Ln.*, pp. 107 and 218.

[4] See note to line 27.

[5] *Ln.*, pp. 106–09, 218–20.

[6] See ÍF II, xxxii ff.

used by the author of *Orms þáttr* must have been more like the versions in the Wolfenbüttel codex and *Ketilsbók* than the modified redaction found in Möðruvallabók.[1] But another source seems to have been used as well, for neither *Egils saga* nor *Landnámabók* gives the name of Stórólfr's wife (Þórarna, *v.l.* Þórunn), who is said to be the sister of Þorbjörn skólmr, and *Orms þáttr* alone gives the latter the name Þorbjörn—elsewhere he is called either Þorgeirr or simply Skólmr.[2] Nor is the fact that Stórólfr was killed by Dufþakr and avenged by Ormr mentioned in other surviving books. As the source for the latter statement, *Orms þáttr* mentions an otherwise unknown *Íslendingaskrá*. Although it is possible that this work was invented by the author of *Orms þáttr*, there would have been little point in such a fabrication. *Íslendingaskrá* may have been the name of one of the books thought to have been current in the twelfth and thirteenth centuries containing genealogical records similar to those in *Landnamabók*,[3] and it may well be that it was the source of all the facts in *Orms þáttr* mentioned above that are not derived from *Egils saga*.

There is only one of Ormr's feats of strength told in the *þáttr* that is also told of him in an independent source. In verse 15 of Haukr Valdísarson's *Íslendingadrápa*,[4] a poem in which the deeds of famous Icelanders of the saga age are celebrated, we are told that the seaman Ormr challenged twelve of jarl Eirekr's men to single combat and fought them with a beam which he swung at them, forcing the jarl to tell his men to retreat. This is clearly the same story as that told in ch. 10 of *Orms þáttr*, though there are some obvious differences of detail which make it unlikely that

---

[1] See Finnur Jónsson, *Den oldnorske og oldislandske Litteraturs Historie* (2nd ed., 1920–24), II, 757; and cf. *ÍF* II, 57–8, footnotes.

[2] e.g. *Ln.*, pp. 75, 194.

[3] Cf. Jón Jóhannesson, *Gerðir Landnámabókar* (1941), p. 176.

[4] *Skj.* A I, 556 ff., B I, 539 ff.

the author of *Orms þáttr* took his story direct from the poem. He probably derived it independently from oral tradition. *Íslendingadrápa* is only preserved in one fourteenth-century manuscript,[1] and nothing is known of the author besides his name. It is often presumed to be a twelfth-century poem, although it is perhaps more likely that it was inspired by the same interest in Icelandic national history that brought about the great flowering of saga-writing in the thirteenth century. But at any rate it shows that at least one of the stories about Ormr in the *þáttr* is based on a tradition originating not later than the thirteenth century.

In *Orms þáttr* this story is made a sort of re-enactment of the battle of Svöldr, and the motive of one of the defenders of Ormr inn langi fighting with a huge pole seems to have been traditionally associated with this battle, for it is found attached to another Icelandic hero, Þorsteinn uxafótr, in the Greatest Saga of Óláfr Tryggvason,[2] where Þorsteinn is said to have fought in the battle with a ship's boom (*beitiáss*, cf. Ormr's *berlingsáss*) and to have been reproved by the king for fighting in such an ungentlemanly manner. There must be a connection between the two stories, although the exact relationship is not clear. The connection of the story with Þorsteinn need not be older than the fourteenth century, while *Íslendingadrápa* shows that it was told of Ormr in the thirteenth.

There is a separate *þáttr* about Þorsteinn in *Flateyjarbók*, but the story of him fighting on Ormr inn langi with a pole is not in it. But it is interesting to note that there is clearly a literary relationship

---

[1] AM 748 4to, reproduced in facsimile in *Fragments of the Elder and the Younger Edda* (Corpus Codicum Islandicorum Medii Aevi, XVII, 1945).

[2] *Flb.* I, 491; *Óláfs saga Tryggvasonar en mesta* (ed. Ólafur Halldórsson), II (1961), 284. Cf. A. L. Binns, 'The Story of Þorsteinn uxafót', *Saga-Book*, XIV (1953–7), 51–2; also F. Panzer, *Studien zur germanischen Sagengeschichte*, I (1910), 349.

between *Orms þáttr* and *Þorsteins þáttr*, and there are many detailed verbal correspondences.[1] It is difficult to see which is the borrower, and neither story can be dated precisely enough to see which is the older.

Orms þáttr is carefully fitted into the chronology of the historical events of the late tenth and early eleventh centuries in Norway (it is chiefly for this reason, and because Ormr is made a sort of champion of the dead King Óláfr Tryggvason at the court of jarl Eirekr, that the *þáttr* was included in the saga of the king in *Flateyjarbók*), but even so the connection of Ormr with jarl Eirekr and Einarr þambarskelfir can scarcely have any basis in fact. Ketill hængr's settlement in Iceland is thought to have taken place about 890. It is hardly likely that Ormr was born long after say 930. Yet according to *Orms þáttr* he was only thirty at the time of his first voyage to Norway, which is made four years before the coming to power of Óláfr Tryggvason (995). He can hardly have been a contemporary of Þórálfr Skólmsson, who fought with King Hákon Aðalsteinsfóstri at Fitjar in about 960, and also of Einarr þambarskelfir after the accession of jarl Eirekr in the year 1000, though after his other achievements the episode with Einarr's bow is so tame as hardly to seem worth anyone's while to invent.[2]

The author has taken great care to give his story the outward appearance of historicity.[3] Although Ásbjörn prúði and Virfill (*v.l.* Vífill) are fictional characters, they are provided with relatives

---

[1] e.g. compare lines 447–51, 32, 428–30, 308–09, 423–7, 462, 313–16, 491–5 of *Orms þáttr* with *Flb*. I, 254/18–20, 256/17, 257/10–12 and 27–30, 259/4 and 25–36.

[2] Einarr's reputation as a bowman is confirmed from *Heimskringla* (*ÍF* XXVI, 362–3, XXVII, 27). In the margin of F the year 960 is given as the date of Ormr's birth.

[3] He is oddly concerned to account for the preservation of Ásbjörn's verses, see lines 456 ff., 474.

whose names are taken from historical sources. Véseti í Borgundarhólmi is known from *Heimskringla* and *Jómsvíkinga saga*, and (Áslákr) Bifru-Kári from *Landnámabók*, *Þórðar saga hreðu* and *Þorsteins þáttr uxafóts*. Eyvindr snákr and Bergþórr bestill, said to be Asbjörn's cousins (apparently on the mother's side, cf. line 221) appear in the traditional list of the crew of Óláfr's flagship Ormr inn langi, though nothing further is known of them.[1] The name Asbjörn itself may also have been suggested by this list, where it is coupled with a certain Ormr, although there is nothing to connect this pair more closely with the foster-brothers in *Orms þáttr*. Özurr hörzki is not known from other sources, but the name Herröðr for a jarl of Gautland is probably taken from either *Krákumál*[2] or *Ragnars saga loðbrókar*; in both the jarl is probably a fictional character. The conquering of Gautland by two isolated viking adventures at this date, the late tenth century, is obviously not historical.

The episode of the monster fights on Sauðey has many affinities with the Heroic Sagas, particularly with the group of sagas about the family of heroes originating from the island of Hrafnista (Hrafnistumenn). Many Icelanders traced their ancestry to this family,[3] and the sagas about them seem to have been written to celebrate the deeds of the forefathers of some Icelandic families. *Örvar-Odds saga* seems to be the oldest of the group (probably written in the late thirteenth century), and others were written afterwards to complete the chronicle (*Ketils saga hængs* and *Gríms saga loðinkinna* about Oddr's father and grandfather; *Áns saga bogsveigis* about another of Ketill's descendants). Ormr Stórólfs-

---

[1] *ÍF* XXVI, 345.
[2] verse 5, *Skj.* B I, 650.
[3] e.g. Gunnarr of Hlíðarendi, Jón Loptsson, Egill Skalla-Grímsson, Auðr (wife of Gísli Súrsson).

son was also descended from this family, and *Orms þáttr* may have been written to demonstrate that the heroic qualities of the Hrafnistumenn were still present in their Icelandic descendants.

The author of *Orms þáttr* has borrowed many story-motives from *Örvar-Odds saga*. The episode of the sibyl's prophecy to Ásbjörn is imitated from that of the prophecy to Örvar-Oddr: both heroes show hostility to the prophetess and disbelieve her prophecy, and both are told they will die in a certain place (naturally neither can resist going there to test the prophecy). There are several cases of verbal borrowing,[1] and the verses spoken by the prophetesses in the two stories are very similar (such visionary verses are found in the sagas only here and in *Hrólfs saga kraka*, ch. 3). That it is the author of *Orms þáttr* who is the borrower is shown by his use of the words *þessi sveit* (line 193), a detail which he thoughtlessly took over from his model.

Viking expeditions like those related in ch. 6 are commonplaces in the Heroic Sagas, but here again there are verbal echoes of *Örvar-Odds saga*.[2] The relationship between the two foster-brothers has been said to be modelled on that of Örvar-Oddr and Ásmundr,[3] but the identification seems to have been influenced by the chance similarity in the pairs of names; in fact, the relationship of Oddr with Þórðr stafnglámi is much more likely to have been the model for the author of the *þáttr*. Þórðr is killed by the half-monster Ögmundr Eyþjófsbani, on whom Oddr is therefore bound to take vengeance, just as Ásbjörn is killed by Brúsi and

---

[1] Cf. lines 190–92, 196–200 of *Orms þáttr* with *Qrv.* 11/2 ff., 13/8 ff., 15/11 ff. The prophecy episode also has similarities with that in *Vatnsdœla saga* (*ÍF* VIII, 29–30).

[2] Cf. line 269 with *Qrv.* 51/14–15.

[3] See Finnur Jónsson, *Den oldnorske og oldislandske Litteraturs Historie* (2nd ed., 1920–24), II, 757; R. C. Boer, 'Zur Grettissaga', *Zeitschrift für Deutsche Philologie*, XXX (1898), 69 note 1.

avenged by Ormr. The motive of the monster's attack on the guardians of the ship while the leader is away is present in both stories.

Some of the details of Ormr's fight with Brúsi and the cat may have been suggested by episodes in this saga too. The three arrows Ormr shoots at the cat which she catches in her mouth recall the arrow shot by Oddr at a hostile giantess which she sweeps away with her hand.[1]

Örvar-Odds saga survives in two versions. The older, found in two fourteenth-century manuscripts, is believed to have been written in the late thirteenth century. The other version survives in manuscripts of the fifteenth century and later, and contains several episodes not in the older manuscripts. It is not certain when these episodes were written, but it is likely that they were interpolated into the saga in the fourteenth century. One of them, about the dealings of Oddr and his men with the half-monster Ögmundr and his mother (who takes the form of a *finngálkn*, half human, half cat-like animal),[2] contains close verbal correspondences with the Sauðeyjar episode in *Orms þáttr*. One of the more striking of these is where Oddr tears off Ögmundr's beard and all the skin of his face, just as Ormr does to Brúsi.[3] It cannot be told for certain which is the borrower in this case. It is perhaps more likely that the version of *Örvar-Odds saga* used by the author of *Orms þáttr* contained this episode, though it is also possible that the redactor of the later version of the saga used *Orms þáttr* as a source. There

---

[1] *Qrv.* 43–5; cf. also the fight with Álfr bjálki, *Qrv.* 178. For similarities between stories in *Orms þáttr* and *Ketils saga hængs* see p. 22, note 4 above and p. 30 below.

[2] *Qrv.* 126–37 (lower text). The *finngálkn* is described at 127 and 128.

[3] *Qrv.* 136. Compare also lines 252–3, 307–09, 488–91, 462, 517–19 of *Orms þáttr* with *Qrv.* 126/13–14, 128/6 and 28–30, 129/21–4, 133/28–134/2.

is otherwise no reason to think that the interpolated version of the saga is older than *Orms þáttr*.

Many other details in this part of *Orms þáttr* are part of the common stock of story-motives used in many sagas. The friendly female relative of the troll, Menglöð—the name occurs also in two late eddic poems, *Grógaldr* and *Fjölsvinnsmál*, which are not however necessarily older than *Orms þáttr*—is a figure that reappears in many other stories.[1] The breaking of the cat's back,[2] the burning of the dead monsters' bodies (presumably to prevent them walking),[3] and the prayer and miraculous victory of the hero in the extremity of his need[4] are motives found in many places, and in such cases it is unrealistic to speak of sources. The magic gloves given Ormr by Menglöð recall the strength-giving gloves of Þórr, as well as the gloves Agnarsnautar, with the power to heal wounds, in *Gull-Þóris saga*.[5] The name (Ófótan or Ófóti for a giant appears in *Ketils saga hængs* and in *þulur* in *Snorra Edda*. The stone over the mouth of the giant's cave recalls the story of the Cyclops in the Odyssey, Book IX.

---

[1] e.g. Fríðr in *Kjalnesinga saga*. See M. Schlauch, *Romance in Iceland* (1934), pp. 113–15. It has been suggested that the motive of the supernatural black cat, and its hostility both to the hero and its stepdaughter Menglöð, owes something to Celtic tradition. See Einar Ól. Sveinsson, 'Celtic elements in Icelandic tradition', *Béaloideas, Journal of the Folklore of Ireland Society* (1959 for 1957), p. 18. But it is likely that the motive in *Orms þáttr* is derived from *Örvar-Odds saga*.

[2] Cf. *ÍF* VI, 301; XIV, 283; *Flb.* I, 260 (*Þorsteins þáttr*).

[3] Cf. *ÍF* IV, 170; VII, 122; *Qrv.* 130; *Flb.* I, 260.

[4] Cf. *ÍF* VI, 240; VIII, 170; XII, 448, 452; *Flb.* I, 338, *Bárðar saga Snæfellsáss* (ed. G. Vigfússon, 1860), p. 43. See the paper of A. L. Binns quoted above (p. 25, note 2), pp. 54–60.

[5] *Snorra Edda* (ed. Finnur Jónsson, 1931), pp. 29, 105, *Gull-Þóris saga* (ed. Kr. Kålund, 1898), pp. 10, 33; cf. also Konrad Maurer, *Isländische Volkssagen* (1860), p. 314.

The Sauðeyjar episode is a story of the same general type as the Sandhaugar episode in *Grettis saga*, but the dependence of the author of *Orms þáttr* on this saga at this point is not great.[1] Much has been made of the alleged similarity between the names of the scenes of these two stories, but this was based on a misreading of the text of *Orms þáttr*. In both vellum manuscripts the name is clearly Sauðey(jar) not Sandey(jar),[2] and in any case both names are very common in Scandinavia. There is nothing to suggest that the author of *Orms þáttr* had any actual islands in mind (cf. note to line 201). The fact that in a (modern) Faroese version of the story the giant is called Dollur and so presumably lived on Dollsey, an island which has in modern times come to be called Sandøy (this Faroese localisation of the story was probably suggested by another story preserved in *Flateyjarbók*[3]) does not alter the position: the Sandhaugar of *Grettis saga* and the Sauðeyjar of *Orms þáttr* cannot be connected. There is also little similarity between the *trollkona* in

---

[1] It is much exaggerated by R. C. Boer in his article quoted above, p. 22, note 2, and in *Die altenglische Heldendichtung*, I (1912), 175–87.

[2] At every occurrence of the name (although of course they do not distinguish *ð* and *d*). The Skálholt edition (see below, p. 37), which was probably based on a paper manuscript, has *Sandey(jar)*. *Fornmanna sögur* III (1827) prints *Sauðey(jar)* consistently in the text but in a footnote (p. 214) quotes the reading of *Flateyjarbók* at the first occurrence as *Sandey*. *Flb*. I prints *Sandey* on the first occurrence of the name only, elsewhere *Saudey(jar)*, i.e. *Sauðey(jar)*; this is corrected to *Saudey* (i.e. *Sauðey*) in the corrigenda of the edition (III, 698). The error is perpetuated, and has been made the basis of some ill-grounded assumptions, by R. W. Chambers, *Beowulf: An Introduction* (1921, and subsequent editions), pp. 66, 189, note 1, 309, note 8; and N. K. Chadwick, 'The Monsters and Beowulf', *The Anglo-Saxons: Studies . . . presented to Bruce Dickins* (1959), pp. 187–8.

[3] *Flb*. II, 441. The Faroese ballad is *Ormar Tórólvsson*, see p. 37, note 2 below. There is no reason to think that this Faroese localisation is based on any local tradition connected with this island.

Grettis saga and the cat in *Orms þáttr*. The description of Grettir's opponent as a cat (*ketta*) is found only in a modern emendation of a perfectly legible text.[1] The use of the word *fleinn* (line 501) recalls the *heptisax* of *Grettis saga*, which is at first called a *fleinn*,[2] but the word is a generic one for a shafted weapon and the similarity may be accidental. Although the author of *Orms þáttr* knew and used *Grettis saga*, his Sauðeyjar episode is not just a reworking of Grettir's feats at Sandhaugar.[3]

The early scholars of northern antiquities were particularly interested by the poetry in *Orms þáttr*, which was supposed to express the viking hero's indifference to suffering and death. Ásbjörn's Death Song was accordingly edited with a Latin translation by T. Bartholin in *Antiquitates Danicæ* (1689), pp. 158–62. From here it became known to William Herbert, who published an English translation in *Select Icelandic Poetry*, I (1804), 52–5. It must be admitted, however, that the enthusiasm displayed by these early scholars for this poem was largely misplaced. There is little sign of the true heroic spirit in it, although there is a certain amount of elegiac feeling in verse 4, perhaps the only effective verse in the *þáttr*. The main inspiration for these verses was clearly literary, and many of them are no more than feeble imitations of earlier poetry. Verses 1 and 3 are modelled on verses in *Örvar-Odds saga* and *Grettis saga*.[4] The chief model for Ásbjörn's Death Song was *Krákumál*, a twelfth-century poem put into the mouth of the dying Ragnarr loðbrók. The metre of the two poems

---

[1] *Grettis saga* (ed. G. Magnússon and G. Thordarson, 1859), p. 151. The manuscript has *kvinnuna*. R. W. Chambers in his extract from the saga (*op. cit.*, p. 159) prints *k(ett)una*. Cf. also N. K. Chadwick, *loc. cit.*

[2] *ÍF* VII, 215.

[3] Compare also lines 503–04 and 318 ff. of *Orms þáttr* with *ÍF* VII, 120/5–11 and 121/14 ff.

[4] *Qrv.* 15; *ÍF* VII, 203, verse 50.

(irregular *dróttkvætt*) is very similar, particularly in the frequency with which the b-line begins with an unstressed syllable, and the use of a first-line refrain. There are also verbal borrowings.[1]

Ásbjörn's Death Song is also influenced by other autobiographical poems in the sagas. Just as the dying Hjálmarr in *Örvar-Odds saga* sends a poem to his sweetheart, so Ásbjörn sends his as a last greeting to his mother, and there are also verbal borrowings.[2] The list of Ásbjörn's comrades in verses 9 and 10 is imitated from that in Hjálmarr's Death Song.[3] The poem in *Orms þáttr* is delivered under similar circumstances to *Hallmundarkviða* in *Grettis saga*—both are overheard and reported by a woman, both invoke a friend to take vengeance.[4] The first line refrain is borrowed from another verse in *Grettis saga* (verse 14, line 1); that it is secondary in *Orms þáttr* is shown by the fact that it fits the

---

[1] Compare verse 12 with *Krákumál* (*Skj.* B I, 649 ff.) verse 26, and also with the verse of Ragnarr in *Vǫlsunga saga ok Ragnars saga loðbrókar* (ed. M. Olsen, 1906–08), p. 159; and line 404 with *Krákumál* verse 23/3. *Pálmr* is used in kennings for weapons in Old Norse only in *Orms þáttr* line 406 and *Krákumál* verse 15/10. The river-name Ífa is recorded only in *Orms þáttr* line 377 and *Krákumál* verse 4/5 (in *Egils saga* verse 33 it is an editorial guess).

[2] Compare *Orms þáttr* lines 346–53 and 358–9 with *Qrv.* 103/11–12, 104/3–4 and 16; the latter is a common formula, cf. *Hervarar saga* (ed. G. Turville-Petre and C. Tolkien, 1956), 59/1, note. Hjálmarr's Death Song also occurs in *Hervarar saga*, but the poem in *Orms þáttr* is more like the version in *Örvar-Odds saga*.

[3] *Qrv.* 104–05 (not preserved in the oldest manuscripts, but was probably in the original version of the saga, see *Qrv.*, xxviii). The list or *þula* is not in *Hervarar saga*. Such *þulur* are traditional in heroic poetry, cf. *Hálfs saga ok Hálfsrekka*, the Old English *Widsiþ*, the poem on the battle at Brávellir known to Saxo Grammaticus (see Sigurður Nordal, *Litteraturhistorie: Norge og Island* (Nordisk Kultur, VIII: B (1953), p. 89); A. Olrik, 'Bråvallakvadets kæmperække', *Arkiv för Nordisk Filologi*, X (1894), 223–87).

[4] *ÍF* VII, 203–04.

context in only two of the verses in which it is used. Örvar-Oddr's *Ævidrápa* may also have been known to the author of the *þáttr*.[1]

The language of the verses is in general simple and easily comprehensible. There is little to suggest that they are older than the prose, or that they are not by the author of the prose. Both prose and verse use the same sources (*Grettis saga* and *Örvar-Odds saga*). All the verses concern the fictional hero Ásbjörn, and there is no evidence that there were any traditions about him older than *Orms þáttr*. There are some evident disparities between the prose and the verses, e.g. line 368 (see note), and the reference to *Miðjungs traustir mágar* (verse 8) which does not correspond to anything in the prose. But it is doubtful if this is enough to suggest that the verses could not be by the author of the prose. The fact that the companions of Ásbjörn listed in verses 9–10 do not figure in the prose is not significant, for the same applies to the list of heroes in Hjálmarr's Death Song.

The author of *Orms þáttr* has made free and sometimes uncritical use of earlier written stories, and many of the stories he tells of Ormr appear to be reworkings of stories originally attached to other heroes. This suggests that genuine traditions about Ormr were not widespread in his time. But some stories about him must have existed, as *Íslendingadrápa* and *Grettis saga* show, and it is impossible to say definitely what in the *þáttr* is made up by the author and what he has derived from tradition. The formulas such as *þat segja sumir menn, þat er allra manna mál, þat er enn sagt* (lines 90, 132, 440, 614, 179, 57, 307) are literary conventions and do not necessarily imply the use of oral sources, although the words *Sér þessa alls merki enn í dag* (line 83, cf. note) do suggest a local tradition.

Orms þáttr is preserved in three medieval manuscripts. The oldest is *Flateyjarbók* (F),[2] where the *þáttr* is found as part of

[1] Compare lines 350–59, 272–6 with *Qrv*. 198 ff., verses 5, 24, 4.

[2] Cols. 272–8, printed in the editions of *Flateyjarbók* (facsimile in Corpus Codicum Islandicorum Medii Aevi, I, 1930), and in *Fornmanna*

Óláfs saga Tryggvasonar, and this part of the compilation was written *c*. 1387–95. The second is GkS 2845 4to (S),[1] written in the early fifteenth century. Only the beginning of the story (to *ok vendir um heyinu*, line 130) is preserved in the fragmentary AM 567 4to V (B), which was written in the late fifteenth century. In S and B *Orms þáttr* appears as a separate story.

The texts of *Orms þáttr* in S and B are both derived from a lost manuscript closely related to F. It is not certain whether or not this lost manuscript was actually derived from F,[2] but the texts of the *þáttr* in the three manuscripts are very nearly identical. The text of this edition follows F (with the spelling normalised), corrected in cases of obvious scribal error from S.

Orms þáttr must have been written some time before the compilation of *Flateyjarbók*, since the text there is clearly a copy, probably at more than one remove from the author's manuscript. It is likely that the *þáttr* was originally a separate story. Among the sagas known to the author were *Örvar-Odds saga*, believed to have been written in the late thirteenth century, and *Grettis saga*, which in its present form (apparently the form in which the author of *Orms þáttr* knew it) was probably written in the early fourteenth century (though some recent scholars have speculated that it might in fact be as late as the fifteenth century). It is possible that the version of *Örvar-Odds saga* known to the author of *Orms þáttr* was the revised and interpolated one, and this can scarcely have been made long before the middle of the fourteenth century. *Orms þáttr* is therefore likely to have been written in the second or third

---

sögur, III (1827), 204–28, with variants from paper manuscripts; and in several popular Icelandic editions.

[1] Facsimile: *The Saga Manuscript 2845, 4to* (Manuscripta Islandica, ed. Jón Helgason, vol. 2, 1955).

[2] ibid., Jón Helgason's introduction pp. x–xi.

quarter of the fourteenth century. The author may well have lived in the south of Iceland in the neighbourhood of Ormr's home in the district of Rangárvellir, where, if anywhere, traditions about the hero are likely to have been preserved.

In editing a text of the middle of the fourteenth century there is little point in archaising the spelling in accordance with the system usually used for thirteenth-century texts. In this edition of *Orms þáttr*, therefore, a spelling more in keeping with the conventions of the fourteenth century is used. No attempt is made to indicate in the spelling all the changes in pronunciation that must have taken place in Icelandic by the time the *þáttr* was written, but in accordance with common usage in fourteenth-century manuscripts the following spellings have been adopted: the sounds usually represented by the symbols 'ǫ' and 'ø' had fallen together and are not distinguished; the modern symbol 'ö' is used for both (F generally uses 'ô' or 'o'). Similarly the sounds usually represented by 'œ' and 'æ' had also fallen together and are not distinguished; 'æ' is used for both. The diphthongisation of short vowels before 'ng' is reflected in the spellings '-eing-' and '-aung-' for older '-eng-' and '-ǫng-', '-øng-'. After 'v', 'ó' is written instead of 'á' (thus 'vón', 'hvórr' for 'ván', 'hvárr'). In low-stressed words 'y' and 'i' are not distinguished (thus 'firir', 'þikkja' for 'fyrir', 'þykkja'). The consonant groups 'rl' and 'll' (after 'a') are not distinguished (thus 'kall', 'jall' for 'karl', 'jarl'); and 'rst' is not distinguished from 'st' (thus 'fyst' for 'fyrst'). The spelling 'ft' replaces 'pt' ('oft', 'loft' for 'opt', 'lopt'). In the endings of verbs in the middle voice '-st' and '-zt' replace '-sk' and '-zk'.

There are some spellings that are usual in F that have not been adopted in this edition because they seem to have been severely restricted both geographically and chronologically. Such are the spelling '-æi-' for '-ei-' (a habit apparently influenced by Norwegian spelling), and 'orb' for 'orf' (lines 61, 63), which never attained a very wide currency. But such forms as 'báði' (= 'bæði'), 'ei' (negative adverb), the analogical 'vorðinn' (= 'orðinn', pp. of 'verða'), and the ending '-i' for the first person singular of the past tense of weak verbs (older '-a'), which are much commoner, have been retained in the places in which they occur in F.[1]

As with all forms of normalisation of manuscript spellings, some compromises are necessary. F does not distinguish 'd' and 'ð', but in this edition the two symbols have been used in the positions considered appropriate for the fourteenth century. F is inconsistent in the use of double consonants, and does not use the accent; in both these matters ordinary usage has been followed. Nevertheless it will be seen that the presentation of the text in this edition represents a move towards less alteration of the manuscript, and is an attempt to avoid minimising the differences between two texts separated by at least a century both in date of composition and in the dates of the manuscripts in which they survive.

The story of Ormr has enjoyed great popularity, not only in Iceland, where besides the three surviving medieval manuscripts, it was copied into at least twenty-six later ones, and printed in the editio princeps of *Óláfs saga Tryggvasonar* (Skálholt, 1689; apparently from a paper manuscript), but also in other countries. A poem was made about Ormr (either in Iceland or, perhaps, the Faroes) from which are derived two Faroese and two Swedish ballads.[2]

---

[1] The spellings used for the forms of *nakkvarr* (in both texts) were chosen in the light of the investigation by Hreinn Benediktsson, 'Óákv. forn. nokkur, nokkuð', *Íslenzk Tunga*, III (1961–2), 7–38.

[2] *Ormar Tórólvsson* and *Brúsajökils kvæði*, in Færöiske Kvæder (ed. V. U. Hammershaimb), II (1855), 74–92 (reprinted with other versions in *Føroya kvæði: Corpus carminum Færoensium*, I, 3 (ed. N. Djurhuus, 1963), 498–533); *Essbjörn Prude och Ormen Stark* and *Ulf den Starke* in *Svenska fornsånger*, I (ed. A. I. Arwidsson, 1834), 87–106. The relationship of the four poems to each other and to *Orms þáttr* is discussed by R. C. Boer, *Die altenglische Heldendichtung*, I (1912), 187–99.

The story has changed considerably during the oral transmission of these ballads, which were not written down until the late eighteenth and early nineteenth centuries. Only the central episode of the adventure with the monsters is preserved in them, but it is very probable that ultimately these poems are derived from a written version of *Orms þáttr*. There is no reason to think that this was very different from the surviving one, though in their present form the ballads contain a considerable admixture of conventional story-motives from other sources.

For modern scholars the *þáttr* has chiefly been interesting because in Ormr and Ásbjörn's fights with the monsters there was thought to be a close parallel to the monster fights in the Old English poem *Beowulf*. The similarity between the two stories was first noted briefly by J. H. E. Schück in 1886,[1] and simultaneously, but independently and in much greater detail, by S. Bugge.[2] Bugge pointed out a large number of alleged correspondences between the two stories, which he thought proved that they were closely related, and was of the opinion that a version of the *Beowulf* story was carried from England to Iceland and there became attached to Ormr (and Grettir). Many of Bugge's parallels are fanciful, and some of the motives, like the hero's youthful laziness and great strength, are common features of many stories. There is no close resemblance between Grendel and the cat of the *þáttr*. Even less convincing is the attempt to identify Ásbjörn and Ormr with Æschere and Yrmenlaf.

Bugge's views have been much criticised by later scholars, who have not been willing to admit any such close relationship between the two stories. Especially critical was R. C. Boer, who stressed the dependence of *Orms þáttr* on earlier written stories, and

---

[1] *Svensk Litteraturhistoria*, I (1886–90), 62.

[2] 'Studien über das Beowulfepos', *Beiträge zur Geschichte der Deutschen Sprache und Literatur*, XII (1887), 58–68 and 360–65.

maintained that because of this it could not be considered an independent analogue of the *Beowulf* story.[1]

In spite of this, however, F. Panzer treated not only *Orms þáttr* but also the Faroese and Swedish ballads based on the same story as independent versions of the 'Bear's Son' story.[2] Panzer's way of approaching these questions has not been followed by most later *Beowulf* scholars, and his method was sharply criticised by Boer in his book on *Beowulf* of 1912,[3] where he again stressed the literary borrowings in *Orms þáttr*, and tried to prove that the ballads were dependent on it. In 1921 R. W. Chambers reviewed the question in his monumental study of *Beowulf*[4] and concluded that, even though *Orms þáttr* depended in some degree on *Grettis saga*, it was still possible that it preserved some elements from an earlier version of the fight with the monsters independently of the saga, though he stressed that these elements were not very striking. Boer was again critical even of this moderate opinion.[5]

Fr. Klaeber, in his first edition of *Beowulf*,[6] was willing to admit 'a genetic relation of some kind' between *Beowulf* and *Orms þáttr*, but was more hesitant in his third edition.[7] One of the most recent writers to touch on the subject was A. L. Binns in an article primarily concerned with *Þorsteins þáttr uxafóts*.[8] He discussed

---

[1] 'Zur Grettissaga', *Zeitschrift für Deutsche Philologie*, XXX (1898), 65–71.

[2] *Studien zur germanischen Sagengeschichte*, I (1910), 344–63.

[3] *Die altenglische Heldendichtung*, I (1912), 175–99.

[4] *Beowulf: An Introduction* (1921), pp. 53–4, 65–7.

[5] 'Beowulf', *English Studies*, V (1923), 109. Chambers's reply: 'Beowulf's fight with Grendel, and its Scandinavian parallels', *English Studies*, XI (1929), 82–4.

[6] *Beowulf and the Fight at Finnsburg* (1922), p. xiv.

[7] 1936, p. xvi, note 2.

[8] 'The Story of Þorsteinn uxafót', *Saga-Book,* XIV (1953–7), 36–60, esp. 54–60.

the motive of the prayer of the hero and his miraculous defeat of the monster and showed that this motive was not really a parallel to anything in *Beowulf*, but that the stories which contain it, far from being survivals of a very old Scandinavian folk-tale, ought rather to be considered as 'treatments of a highly propagandist Christian tale, more or less associated with King Óláf (Tryggvason) and his introduction of Christianity to the North'.

There is no doubt that the Sauðeyjar episode in *Orms þáttr* contains many similarities to the account in *Beowulf* of the fights of the hero with Grendel and Grendel's mother, and there is at least one motive in *Orms þáttr* which is parallelled in *Beowulf* but which cannot be derived from *Grettis saga*: this is the relationship of the two monsters as mother and son. *Orms þáttr*, however, seems to have derived this motive from *Örvar-Odds* saga (Ögmundr and his *finngálkn* mother), where it is found in a story that has little further resemblance to the *Beowulf* episodes. Most of the similarities between *Orms þáttr* and *Beowulf* are of this general nature, and must be considered part of the common stock of narrative material current in stories from the whole of Europe, rather than as elements confined to one particular type of story. *Orms þáttr* and *Beowulf* cannot be considered as versions of essentially the same story; they are two stories which happen to share certain narrative elements. *Orms þáttr* cannot be used in any attempt to reconstruct a hypothetical prototype story which may be assumed to lie behind both *Beowulf* and its Scandinavian analogues. The final judgement of Chambers seems best: 'The resemblance between the *Orm*-story and *Beowulf* seems to me too vague to help us very much.'[1]

---

[1] *Beowulf: An Introduction* (2nd ed., 1932), p. 453.

HREIÐARS ÞÁTTR

[Frá Hreiðari]

Þórðr hét maðr. Hann var Þorgrímsson, Hreiðars sonar, þess er Glúmr vá. Þórðr var lítill maðr vexti ok vænn. Hann átti sér bróður er Hreiðarr hét. Hann var ljótr maðr ok varla sjálfbjargi fyrir vits sǫkum. Hann var manna frávastr ok vel at afli búinn ok hógværr í skapi, ok var hann heima jafnan, en Þórðr var í fǫrum ok var hirðmaðr Magnúss konungs ok mazk vel.

Ok eitt sinni, er Þórðr bjó skip sitt í Eyjafirði, þá kom Hreiðarr þar, bróðir hans, ok er Þórðr sá hann, spurði hann hví hann væri þar kominn. Hreiðarr segir,

'Eigi nema ørendit væri.'

'Hvat viltu þá?' segir Þórðr.

'Ek vil fara útan,' segir Hreiðarr.

Þórðr mælti, 'Ekki þykki mér þér fallin fǫrin. Vil ek heldr þat til leggja við þik at þú hafir fǫðurarf okkarn, ok er þat hálfu meira fé en þat er ek hefi í fǫrum.'

Hreiðarr svarar, 'Þá er lítit vit mitt,' segir hann, 'ef ek tek þenna fjárskakka, til þess at gefa mik svá upp sjálfan ok láta þína umsjá, ok mun þá hverr maðr draga af mér fé okkat, alls ek kann engi forræði þau er nýt eru. Ok era þér þá betra hlut í at eiga, ef ek ber á mǫnnum, eða gerik aðra óvísu þeim er um fé mitt sitja at lokka af mér, en eptir þat sé ek barðr eða meiddr fyrir mínar tilgerðir. Enda er þat sannast í, at þér mun torsótt at halda mér eptir er ek vil fara.'

'Vera kann þat,' segir Þórðr, 'en get ekki þá um ferð

þína fyrir ǫðrum mǫnnum.'

Því hét hann. Ok þegar er þeir brœðr eru skilðir, þá
segir Hreiðarr hverjum er heyra vill, at hann ætlar útan
at fara með bróður sínum, ok firna allir Þórð um, ef hann
flytr útan afglapa.

Ok er þeir eru búnir, sigla þeir í haf, ok verða vel reiðfara, koma við Bjǫrgyn, ok þegar spyrr Þórðr eptir konungi,
ok var honum sagt at Magnús konungr var í bœnum, ok
hafði skǫmmu áðr komit, ok vildi eigi láta kœja sik samdœgris, þóttisk þurfa hvíldar er hann var nýkominn. Brátt
litu menn Hreiðar, at hann var afbragð annarra manna.
Hann var mikill ok ljótr, ómállatr við þá er hann hitti.

Ok snemma um moruninn, áðr menn væri vaknaðir,
stendr Hreiðarr upp ok kallar,

'Vaki þú, bróðir. Fátt veit sá er søfr. Ek veit tíðendi, ok
heyrðak áðan læti kynlig.'

'Hverju var líkast?' spyrr Þórðr.

'Sem yfir kykvendum,' segir Hreiðarr, 'ok þaut við
mjǫk, en aldri veit ek hvat látum var.'

'Lát eigi svá undarliga,' segir Þórðr. 'Þat mun verit
hafa hornblástr.'

'Hvat skal þat tákna?' spyrr Hreiðarr.

Þórðr svarar, 'Blásit er jafnan til móts eða til skip-
dráttar.'

'Hvat táknar mótit?' spyrr Hreiðarr.

'Þar eru dœmð vandamál jafnan,' segir Þórðr, 'ok slíkt
talat sem konungr þykkisk þurfa at fyrir alþýðu sé upp
borit.'

'Hvárt mun konungr nú á mótinu?' spyrr Hreiðarr.

'Þat ætla ek víst,' svarar Þórðr.

'Þangat verð ek þá at fara,' segir Hreiðarr, 'því at ek
vilda þar koma fyrst, er [ek sæa sem flesta menn] í senn.'
  'Þá skýtr í tvau horn með okkr,' segir Þórðr. 'Mér 60
þœtti því betr er þú kœmir þar síðr er fjǫlmennt væri, ok
vil ek h[vergi fara.'
  'Ekki tjáir sl]íkt at mæla,' segir Hreiðarr, 'fara skulu vit
báðir. Muna þér betra þykkja at ek fara einn, en ekki fær
þú mik lattan [þessarrar farar].' 65
  Hleypr Hreiðarr á brott. En Þórðr sér nú at fara mun
verða, ok ferr hann nú eptir er Hreiðarr ferr hart undan,
ok er mjǫk langt milli þeira. Ok er Hreiðarr sér at Þórðr
fór seint, þá mælti hann,
  'Þat er þó satt at illt er lítill at vera þá er aflit nær ekki. 70
En þó mætti vera fráleikrinn, en lítit ætla ek þik af honum
hafa hlotit. Ok væria þér verri vænleikr minni, ok kœmisk
þú með ǫðrum mǫnnum.'
  Þórðr svaraði, 'Eigi veit ek mér verr fara óknáleik minn
en þér afl þitt.' 75
  'Handkrœkjumsk þá, bróðir,' segir Hreiðarr.
  Ok nú gera þeir svá, fara um hríð. Ok er svá, at Þórði
tekr at dofna hǫndin, ok lætr hann laust, þykkir eigi verða
vinveitt at þeir haldisk á við álpun Hreiðars. Hreiðarr ferr
nú undan svá við fót, ok nemr stað síðan á hæð nakkvarri, 80
ok er allstarsýnn, sér þaðan fjǫlmennit þangat sem mótit
var. Ok er Þórðr kømr eptir, mælti hann,
  'Fǫrum nú báðir saman, bróðir.'
  Ok Hreiðarr gerir svá.
  Ok er þeir koma á þingit, kenna margir menn Þórð ok 85
fagna honum vel, ok verðr konungr áheyrsli. Ok þegar
gengr Þórðr fyrir konung ok kveðr hann vel, ok tekr

konungr blíðliga kveðju hans. Þegar skilði með þeim
brœðrum er þeir kvámu til þingsins, ok verðr Hreiðarr
90 skauttogaðr mjǫk ok fœrðr í reikuð. Hann er málugr ok
hlær mjǫk, ok þykkir mǫnnum ekki at minna gaman at
eiga við hann. Ok verðr honum nú fǫrin ógreið.

Konungr spyrr Þórð tíðenda, ok síðan spyrr hann hvat
þeira manna væri í fǫr með honum er hann vildi at til
95 hirðvistar fœri með honum.

'Þar er bróðir minn í fǫr,' segir Þórðr.

'Sá maðr mun vel vera,' segir konungr, 'ef þér er líkr.'

Þórðr segir, 'Ekki er hann mér glíkr.'

Konungr mælti, 'Þó má enn vel vera. Eða hvat er
100 ólíkast með ykkr?'

Þórðr mælti, 'Hann er mikill maðr vexti, hann er ljótr
ok heldr ósyknligr, sterkr at afli ok lundhœgr maðr.'

Konungr mælti, 'Þó má honum vel vera farit at mǫrgu.'

Þórðr segir, 'Ekki var hann kallaðr vizkumaðr á unga
105 aldri.'

'At því fer ek meir,' segir konungr, 'sem nú er. Eða
hvárt má hann sjálfr annask sik?'

'Ekki dála er þat,' segir Þórðr.

Konungr mælti, 'Hví fluttir þú hann útan?'

110 'Herra,' segir Þórðr, 'hann á allt hálft við mik, en hefir
øngar nytjar fjárins, ok engi afskipti sér veitt um pen-
ninga, beizk þessa eins hlutar, at fara útan með mér, ok
þótti mér ósannligt at eigi réði hann einum hlut, þars
hann lætr mik mǫrgum ráða. Þótti mér ok glíkligt at hann
115 mundi gæfu af yðr hljóta, ef hann kœmi á yðarn fund.'

'Sjá vilda ek hann,' segir konungr.

'Svá skal ok,' segir Þórðr, 'en brottu er hann nú rjáðr

nokkvor.'

Konungr sendi nú eptir honum. Ok er Hreiðarr heyrði sagt at konungr vildi hitta hann, þá gengr hann uppstert mjǫk, ok nær á hvat sem fyrir var, ok var hann því óvanr at konungr hefði beizk fundar hans. Hann var á þá leið búinn at hann var í ǫkulbrókum ok hafði feld grán yfir sér. Ok er hann kømr fyrir konung, þá fellr hann á kné fyrir konung ok kveðr hann vel. Konungr svaraði honum hlæjandi, ok mælti,

'Ef þú átt við mik ørendi, þá mæl þú skjótt slíkt er þú vill. Aðrir eigu enn nauðsyn at tala við mik síðan.'

Hreiðarr segir, 'Mitt ørendi þykki mér skyldast. Ek vilda sjá þik, konungr.'

'Þykki þér nú vel, þá,' segir konungr, 'er þú sér mik?'

'Vel víst,' segir Hreiðarr, 'en eigi þykkjumk ek enn til gǫrla sjá þik.'

'Hvernug skulu vit nú þá?' segir konungr. 'Vildir þú at ek stœða upp?'

Hreiðarr svarar, 'Þat vilda ek,' segir hann.

Konungr mælti, er hann var upp staðinn, 'Nú muntu þykkjask gerla sjá mik mega?'

'Eigi enn til gǫrla,' segir Hreiðarr, 'ok er nú þó nær hófi.'

'Viltu þá,' segir konungr, 'at ek leggja af mér skikkjuna?'

'Þat vilda ek víst,' segir Hreiðarr.

Konungr mælti, 'Vit skulum þar þó nokkvot innask til áðr um þat málit. Þér eruð hugkvæmir margir, Íslendingar, ok veit ek eigi nema þú virðir þetta til ginningar: nú vil ek þat undan skilja.'

Hreiðarr segir, 'Engi er til þess færr, konungr, at ginna þik eða ljúga at þér.'

150 Konungr leggr nú af sér skikkjuna, ok mælti, 'Hyggðu nú at mér svá vandliga sem þik tíðir.'

'Svá skal vera,' segir Hreiðarr. Hann gengr í hring um konunginn ok mælti opt it sama fyrir munni sér, 'Allvel, allvel,' segir hann.

155 Konungr mælti, 'Hefir þú nú sét mik sem þú vilt?'

'At vísu,' segir hann.

Konungr spurði, 'Hversu lízk þér nú á mik þá?'

Hreiðarr svarar, 'Ekki hefir Þórðr, bróðir minn, ofsǫgum frá þér sagt, þat er vel er.'

160 Konungr mælti, 'Máttu nokkvot at finna um þat er þú sér nú, ok þat er eigi sé í alþýðu viti?'

'Ekki vil ek at finna,' segir hann, 'ok ekki má ek þegar, því at þannug mundi hverr sik kjósa sem þú ert, þó at sjálfr mætti ráða.'

165 'Mikinn tekr þú af,' segir konungr.

Hreiðarr svarar, 'Háttung er ǫðrum á, þá,' segir hann, 'at lofgjarnliga sé við mælt, ef þú átt þetta eigi at sǫnnu sem mér lízk á þik ok ek sagða áðan.'

Konungr mælti, 'Finn til nokkvot, þó at smátt sé.'

170 'Þat helzt þá, herra,' segir hann, 'at auga þitt annat er litlu því ofar en annat.'

'Þat hefir einn maðr fyrr fundit,' segir konungr, 'en sá er Haraldr konungr, frændi minn. Nú skal jafnmæli með okkr,' segir konungr. 'Skaltu nú standa upp ok leggja af 175 þér skikkju, ok vil ek sjá þik.'

Hreiðarr fleygir af sér feldinum, ok hefir saurgar krummur—maðrinn hentr mjǫk ok ljótr—en þvegnar heldr latliga. Konungr hyggr at honum vandliga. Ok þá mælti Hreiðarr,

'Herra,' segir hann, 'hvat þykkisk þú nú mega at mér 180 finna?'

Konungr segir, 'Þat ætla ek at eigi fœðisk ljótari maðr upp en þú ert.'

'Slíkt verðr mælt,' segir Hreiðarr. 'Er nokkvot þá,' segir hann, 'at til fríðenda sé um mik, at því sem þú leggr ætlun 185 á?'

Konungr mælti, 'Þat sagði Þórðr, bróðir þinn, at þú værir lundhœgr maðr.'

'Þat er satt ok,' sagði Hreiðarr, 'ok þykki mér þat illt, er svá er.' 190

'Þú munt reiðask þó,' sagði konungr.

'Mæl heill, herra,' segir Hreiðarr, 'eða hvé langt mun til þess?'

'Eigi veit ek þat gǫrla,' segir konungr. 'Helzt á þessum vetri, at því er ek get til.' 195

Hreiðarr mælti, 'Seg heill sǫgu.'

Konungr mælti, 'Ertu nokkvot hagr?'

Hreiðarr segir, 'Aldrigi hefi ek reynt, má ek því eigi vita.'

'Til þess þœtti þó ekki ólíkligt,' segir konungr. 200

'Seg heill sǫgu,' kvað Hreiðarr. 'Svá mun vera jafnt, þegar er þú segir þat. En vetrvistar þœttumk ek þurfa.'

Konungr sagði, 'Heimil er mín umsjá. En betr þykki mér þér þar vistin felld vera er heldr er fátt manna.'

Hreiðarr svaraði, 'Svá er þat ok,' segir hann. 'En eigi 205 mun svá mannfátt vera at eigi komi þat þó upp er mælt verðr, allra helzt þat er hlœgi þykkir í, en ek maðr ekki

orðvarr, ok jafnan berr mér mart á góma. Nú kann vera at
þeir reiði orð mín fyrir aðra menn, ok spotti mik ok drepi
þat at ferligu er ek hefi at gamni eða mælik. Nú sýnisk
mér hitt vitrligra at vera heldr hjá þeim er um mik hyggr,
sem Þórðr er, bróðir minn, þótt þar sé heldr fjǫlmenni, en
hinnug, þótt menn sé fáir ok sé þar engi til umbóta.'

Konungr mælti, 'Ráð þú þá, ok farið báðir brœðr til
hirðarinnar ef ykkr líkar þat betr.'

Þegar hljóp Hreiðarr á brott er hann heyrði þessi orð
konungs, ok segir hverjum manni er á vill hlýða at hans
fǫr hefir allgóð orðit á konungs fund, segir ok einkum
Þórði bróður sínum at konungr hefir leyft honum at fara
til hirðvistar. Þá mælti Þórðr,

'Bú þik þá sœmiliga at klæðum eða vápnum, því at þat
eitt samir, ok skortir okkr ekki til þess, ok skipask margir
menn vel við góðan búning, enda er vandara at búa sik í
konungs herbergi en annars staðar, ok verðr síðr at
hlœgi gǫrr af hirðmǫnnum.'

Hreiðarr svarar, 'Eigi getr þú allnær at ek muna
skrúðklæðin á mik láta koma.'

Þórðr mælti, 'Skerum vaðmál þá til.'

Hreiðarr svarar, 'Nær er þat,' segir hann.

Svá er nú gǫrt við ráð Þórðar, ok lætr Hreiðarr eptir
leiðask. Hefir hann nú vaðmálsklæði, ok fágar sik ok
þykkir nú þegar allr annarr maðr, sýnisk nú maðr ljótr
ok grettir vaskliga.

Svá er þó mót á manninum, er þeir Þórðr eru með
hirðinni, at Hreiðarr verðr í fyrstu fyrir miklum ágang af
hirðmǫnnum, ok breyttu þeir marga vega orðum við
hann, ok fundu at hann var ómállatr, kom við sem

mátti. Ok hendu þeir mikit gaman at því at eiga við hann, ok var hann jafnan hlæjandi við því er þeir mæltu, ok lagði hvern þeira fyrir, svá var hann leikmikill, bæði um mælgina ok allra helzt [í aflraunum]. En fyrir því at hann var rammr at afli, ok er þeir finna at hann gefsk ekki at grandi, þá þvarr þat allt af þeim hirðmǫnnum, [. . .] hirðinni.

Í þetta mund váru þeir báðir konungar yfir landi, Magnús konungr ok Haraldr konungr. En þá hǫfðu sakar gǫrzk [. . .] at hirðmaðr Magnúss konungs hafði vegit hirðmann Haralds konungs, ok var lagðr til sáttarfundr, at konungar skyldu [sjálfir finnask] ok skipa málinu. Ok er Hreiðarr heyrir þetta, at Magnús konungr skal fara til móts við Harald konung, þá ferr hann á fund Magnúss konungs ok mælti,

'Sá hlutr er,' segir hann, 'er ek vilda þik biðja.'

'Hverr er sá?' sagði konungr.

Hreiðarr mælti, 'At fara til sáttarfundar. Em ek ekki víðfǫrull, en mér er mikil forvitni á at sjá tvá konunga senn í einum stað.'

Konungr svarar, 'Satt segir þú, at þú ert ekki víðfǫrull. En þeygi mun ek leyfa þér þessa fǫrna, því at ekki er þér fellt at ganga í greipr mǫnnum Haralds konungs, ok beri svá til at þér verði at því ólið eða ǫðrum. Ok em ek um þat hræddr, at þá sœki þik heim reiðin, er þú langar til, en mér þœtti bezt at við bærisk.'

Hreiðarr svarar, 'Nú mæltir þú gott orð. Þá skal at vísu fara, ef ek veit þess vánir at ek reiðumk.'

Konungr segir, 'Muntu fara ef ek leyfi eigi?'

Hreiðarr svarar, 'Eigi þá síðr.'

'Ætlar þú at þér muni þvílíkt við mik at eiga sem við Þórð, bróður þinn? Því at þar hefir þú jafnan þitt mál.'

270 Hreiðarr segir, 'Því ǫllu betra mun mér við yðr at eiga sem þú ert vitrari en hann.'

Konungr sér nú at hann mun fara þó at hann banni, eða hann fari eigi í hans fǫruneyti, ok þykkir eigi þat bezt ef hann kømr annars staðar til fǫruneytis, ok þykkir þá í 275 reiðingum vera hversu honum eirir ef hann vælir einn um, ok leyfir honum nú heldr at fara með sér, ok er Hreiðari fenginn hestr til reiðar.

Ok þegar er þeir váru á ferð komnir, þá reið hann mjǫk ok ætlaði sér varla hóf um, ok þraut hestinn undir honum. 280 Ok er konungr verðr þess varr, mælti hann,

'Nú gefr vel til. Fylgi nú Hreiðari heim, ok fari hann eigi.'

Hann segir, 'Eigi heptir þetta ferðina mína, þótt hestrinn sé þrotinn. Kømr mér til lítils fráleikrinn ef ek fæ 285 eigi fylgt yðr.'

Fara þeir nú, ok lǫgðu margir fram hjá honum hesta sína, ok þótti gaman at reyna fráleik hans, svá grópasamliga sem hann sjálfr tók á. En svá gafsk at hann þreytti hvern hest er frammi var lagðr, ok lézk eigi verðr at koma 290 til fundarins ef hann gæti eigi fylgt þeim, ok fyrir þetta sátu nú margir af sínum hestum.

Ok er þeir koma þar er konungar skulu finnask, þá mælti Magnús konungr við Hreiðar,

'Ver þú mér nú fylgjusamr, ok ver á aðra hǫnd mér ok 295 skilsk ekki frá mér. En miðlung segir mér hugr um hversu ferr þá er menn Haralds konungs koma ok sjá þik.'

Hreiðarr kvað svá vera skyldu sem konungr mælti—

'ok þykki mér því betr er ek geng yðr nær'.
  Nú finnask konungar, ok ganga þeir á tal ok rœða mál
sín. En menn Haralds konungs gátu líta hvar Hreiðarr 300
gekk, ok hǫfðu heyrt getit hans, ok þótti þeim um it
vænsta. Ok er konungar tǫluðu, þá gengr Hreiðarr í flokk
Haralds manna, ok hǫfðu þeir hann til skógar er skammt
var þaðan, skauttoguðu hann mjǫk, ok hrundu honum
stundum. En þar lék á ýmsu: stundum fauk hann fyrir 305
sem vindli, en stundum var hann fastr fyrir sem veggr, ok
hrutu þeir frá honum. Nú dregsk þó svá leikrinn, at þeir
gera honum nakkvat harðleikit, létu ganga honum øxar-
skǫpt ok skálpana, ok námu naddar af sverðskónum í
hǫfði honum, ok skeindisk hann af. Ok svá lét hann 310
sem honum þœtti it mesta gaman at ok hló við jafnan. Ok
er svá hafði fram farit um hríð, þá tók leikrinn ekki at
batna af þeira hendi. Þá mælti Hreiðarr,
  'Nú hǫfum vér átt góðan leik um stund, ok er nú ráð at
hætta, því at nú tekr mér at leiðask. Fǫrum nú til konungs 315
yðvars, ok vil ek sjá hann.'
  'Þat skal verða aldri,' sǫgðu þeir, 'svá fjándligr sem þú
ert, at þú skylir sjá konung várn, ok skulu vér fœra þik til
heljar.'
  Honum finnsk þá fátt um, ok þykkisk sjá at þat mun 320
fram fara. Ok er nú þar komit, at honum renn í skap ok
reiðisk hann, fær hǫndum þann mann er mest sótti at
honum ok verst lék við hann, ok vegr á lopt ok fœrði niðr
at hǫfðinu, svá at heilinn var úti, ok er sá dauðr. Nú
þykkir þeim hann trautt mennskr maðr at afli, ok stukku 325
þeir nú í víginu, fara ok segja Haraldi konungi at drepinn
var hirðmaðr hans. Konungr svarar,

'Drepið þann þá er þat hefir unnit.'

'Eigi er þat enn hœgra,' segja þeir, 'hann er nú í brottu.'

330 Þat er nú frá Hreiðari at segja at hann hittir Magnús konung. Konungr mælti,

'Veiztu nú hvernug þat er at reiðask?'

'Já,' segir hann, 'nú veit ek.'

'Hvernug þótti þér?' segir konungr. 'Hitt fann ek, at
335 þér var forvitni á.'

Hreiðarr svarar, 'Illt þótti mér,' segir hann. 'Þess var ek fúsastr at drepa þá alla.'

Konungr mælti, 'Þat kom mér jafnt í hug,' segir konungr, 'at þú mundir illa reiðr verða. Nú vil ek senda
340 þik á Upplǫnd til Eyvindar, lends manns míns, at hann haldi þik fyrir Haraldi konungi, því at ek treystumk eigi at þín verði gætt ef þú ert með hirðinni, því at vér finnumk, en Haraldr frændi er brǫgðóttr, ok er vant við at sjá. Kom þá aptr til mín er ek sendi eptir þér.'

345 Nú ferr Hreiðarr í brott unz hann kømr á Upplǫnd, ok tekr Eyvindr við honum eptir orðsending konungs. Konungar hǫfðu sáttir orðit á þat mál er áðr var milli þeira, ok var því sætt, en hér verða þeir eigi á sáttir. Þykkir Magnúsi konungi þessir menn hafa sjálfir fyrir-
350 gǫrt sér ok valdit ǫllum sǫkum, ok þykkir hirðmaðr fallit hafa óheilagr, en Haraldr konungr beiðir bóta fyrir hirð-mann sinn, ok skilðusk nú með øngri sætt.

Eigi liðu langar stundir áðr Haraldr konungr spyrr hvar Hreiðarr er niðr kominn, gørir síðan ferð sína ok kømr á
355 Upplǫnd til Eyvindar, hefir með sér sex tigu manna. Hann kømr þar um morgun snimma, ok ætlaði at koma á óvart. En þat var þó eigi, því at Eyvindr þóttisk vita

fyrir at hann mundi koma ok var hann á øngri stundu vanbúinn við. Hafði hann stefnt liði at sér af launungu, ok var þat í skógum þeim er nálægir váru bœnum. Skyldi 360 Eyvindr gefa þeim mark ef Haraldr konungr kœmi ok þœttisk hann liðs þurfa.

Þat er sagt, einhverju sinni áðr Haraldr konungr kœmi, at Hreiðarr beiddisk at Eyvindr skyldi fá honum silfr ok nokkvot gull. 365

'Ertu hagr?' segir hann.

Hreiðarr svarar, 'Þat sagði Magnús konungr mér. En eigi má ek annat til vita, því at ek hefi aldri við leitat. En því mundi hann þat segja at hann mundi vita, ok því trúi ek er hann sagði.' 370

Eyvindr mælti, 'Þú er undarligr maðr,' segir hann. 'Nú mun ek fá þér efnin. Skaltu fá mér silfrit ef ónýtt verðr smíðat, en njót sjálfr elligar.'

Hreiðarr er byrgðr í einu húsi, ok er hann þar at smíðinni. Ok áðr en gǫrt verði þat er Hreiðarr smíðaði, 375 þá kømr Haraldr konungr. Ok er nú sem ek gat áðr, at Eyvindr er at øngu óbúinn, ok gerir hann konungi veizlu góða. Ok nú er þeir sitja í drykkju, þá fréttir konungr eptir ef Hreiðarr sé þar—'ok muntu hafa vináttu af mér í móti ef þú selr oss manninn'. 380

Eyvindr svarar, 'Eigi er hann hér nú,' segir hann.

'Ek veit,' segir konungr, 'at hann er, ok þarftu eigi dylja.'

Eyvindr mælti, 'Enn þótt þat sé, þá geri ek eigi þann mun ykkar Magnúss konungs at ek selja þann mann í 385 hendr þér er hann vill skýla láta,'—gekk út síðan ór stofunni. Ok er hann kømr út, þá brýzk Hreiðarr á hurðina ok kallar at hann vill á brott.

'Þegi þú,' segir Eyvindr, 'Haraldr konungr er hér
390 kominn ok vill drepa þik.'

Hreiðarr brýzk út eigi at síðr, ok lézk hitta vildu konung.
Eyvindr sér þá at hann mun brjóta upp hurðina, gengr til
ok lýkr upp ok mælti,

'Gramir munu taka þik,' segir hann, 'er þú gengr til
395 banans.'

Hreiðarr gengr inn í stofuna ok fyrir konung ok kveðr
hann ok mælti,

'Herra, tak af mér reiðina, því at ek em þér vel felldr
fyrir margs sakir at gera þat er þú vill gera láta, þó at
400 eigi sé allrífligt, í mannraunum eða því er við berr, ok mun
ek þess ólatr er þú vilt mik til hafa sendan. Hér er nú
gripr er ek vil gefa þér,'—setr á borðit fyrir hann, en þat
var svín, gǫrt af silfri ok gyllt. Þá mælti konungr, er hann
leit á svínit,

405 'Þú ert hagr svá at trautt hefi ek sét jafnvel smíðat með
því móti sem er.'

Nú ferr þat með manna hǫndum. Segir konungr at
hann mun taka sættir af honum,—'ok er gott at senda þik
til stórvirkja; þú ert maðr sterkr ok ófælinn at því er ek
410 hygg'.

Nú kømr svínit aptr fyrir konung. Tekr hann þá upp
ok hyggr at smíðinni enn vandligar, ok sér þá at spenar eru
á ok þat var gyltr; fleygir þegar í brott, ok sér at til háðs
var gǫrt, ok mælti,

415 'Hafi þik allan troll. Standi menn upp ok drepi hann.'

En Hreiðarr tekr svínit ok gengr út, ok ferr þegar á
brott þaðan, [ok] kom á fund Magnúss konungs ok segir

honum hvat í hefir gǫrzk. En í ǫðru lagi standa menn upp
ok út eptir honum ok ætla drepa hann. Ok er [þeir koma]
út, þá er Eyvindr þar fyrir ok hefir fjǫlmenni mikit, svá
at ekki máttu þeir eptir Hreiðari halda, ok skilja þeir
Eyvindr [ok Haraldr konungr] við svá búit, ok líkar
konungi illa.

Ok er þeir hittask, Magnús konungr ok Hreiðarr, fréttir konungr eptir hvernug farit hefir, en Hreiðarr segir
frá [it sanna ok sýndi konungi] svínit. Magnús konungr
mælti, þá er hann hugði at svíninu,

'Geysihagliga er þetta smíðat. En hefnt hefir Haraldr
konungr frændi várr mjǫk minni háðungar en í þessu er,
ok eigi ertu allráæðislítill, ok þó með ǫllu hugkvæmr.'

Hreiðarr var nú þar nakkvara stund með Magnúsi
konungi. Ok eitthvert sinn kømr hann at máli við konung
ok mælti,

'Þat vilda ek, konungr, at þú veittir mér þat er ek mun
biðja þik.'

'Hvat er þat?' spyrr konungr.

'Þat, herra,' segir Hreiðarr, 'at þér hlýddið kvæði er ek
hefi ort um yðr.'

'Hví skal eigi þat?' segir konungr.

Nú kveðr Hreiðarr kvæðit, ok er þat allundarligt, fyrst
kynligast, en því betra er síðar er. Ok er lokit er kvæði,
mælti konungr,

'Þetta kvæði sýnisk mér undarligt, ok þó gott at nestlokum. En kvæðit mun vera með þeim hætti sem ævi þín:
hon hefir fyrst verit með kynligu móti ok einrœnligu, en
hon mun þó vera því betr er meir líðr á. Hér eptir skal ek
ok velja kvæðislaunin. Hér er hólmr einn fyrir Nóregi sá

er ek vil þér gefa. Hann er með góðum grǫsum, ok er þat gott land þó at eigi sé mikit.'

450 Hreiðarr mælti, 'Þar skal ek samtengja með Nóreg ok Ísland.'

Konungr mælti, 'Eigi veit ek hversu þat ferr. Hitt veit ek, at margir menn munu búnir at kaupa at þér hólminn ok gefa þér fé fyrir, en ráðligra ætla ek vera at ek leysa til
455 mín, at eigi verði at bitbeini þér eða þeim er kaupa vilja. Er nú ok ekki vel felld vist þín vilgis lengi hér í Nóregi, því at ek þykkjumk sjá hvern Haraldr konungr vill þinn hlut, ef hann á at ráða, sem hann mun ráða ef þú ert lengi í Nóregi.'

460 Nú gaf Magnús konungr honum silfr fyrir hólminn, ok vill nú eigi þar hætta honum, ok fór Hreiðarr út til Íslands, ok bjó norðr í Svarfaðardal, ok gerisk mikill maðr fyrir sér. Ok ferr hans ráð mjǫk eptir getu Magnúss konungs, at þess betr er, er meir líðr fram hans ævi, ok
465 hefir hann gǫrt sér at mestum hluta þau kynjalæti er hann sló á sik inn fyrra hlut ævinnar. Bjó hann til elli í Svarfaðardal, ok eru margir menn frá honum komnir. Ok lýkr hér þessi rœðu.

ORMS ÞÁTTR

Hér er þáttr Orms Stórólfssonar

Hængr hét maðr, son Ketils Naumdælajalls, en móðir Ketils jalls hét Hrafnhildr, dóttir Ketils hængs ór Hrafnistu. Hængr var göfugr maðr. Hann varð í missætti við Harald konung Dofrafóstra af drápi Hildiríðarsona, ok því stökk hann ór landi. Hængr sigldi vestr í haf at leita Íslands. Þeir urðu við land varir, ok vóru firir sunnan at komnir, sigldu upp í árós einn mikinn ok lögðu við hit eystra land. Sú á heitir nú Þjórsá. Þeir könnuðu víða landit.

Hængr var hinn fysta vetr firir útan Rangá, en um vórit nam hann land milli Þjórsár ok Markarfljóts, allt í milli fjalls ok fjöru, ok bjó at Hofi við Rangá hina eystri. Ingunn hét kona hans. Hon fæddi son um vórit, er Hrafn hét. Hængr gaf land skipverjum sínum en seldi sumum, ok eru þeir landnámamenn kallaðir.

Herjúlfr hét annarr son Hængs. Hans son var Sumarliði. Helgi hét hinn þriði. Vestarr hét hinn fjórði. Hrafn Hængsson var fystr lögsögumaðr á Íslandi. Hann bjó at Hofi eftir föður sinn. Þorlaug var dóttir hans, er átti Jörundr goði. Hinn fimmta son átti Hængr, er Stórólfr hét. Hann er kallaðr mestr sona hans, en Hrafn göfgastr. Stórólfr átti Þórörnu, systur Þorbjarnar skólms, þess er var faðir Þórálfs. Stórólfr bjó at Hvóli, er síðan var kallaðr Stórólfshvóll.

Stórólfr var allra manna sterkastr, ok þat var allra manna mál at hann væri eigi einhamr. Hann var fróðr

maðr ok margvíss, var hann af því kallaðr fjölkunnigr.
Hann átti son við Þórörnu konu sinni er Ormr er nefndr.
Hann var snemmendis báði mikill ok sterkr, ok vel at
íþróttum búinn, því at þá er hann var sjau vetra sam-
vægði hann hinum sterkustum mönnum um afl ok allar
íþróttir. Ekki hafði hann ástríki mikit af föður sínum,
enda var hann honum ódæll ok vildi ekki vinna, en móðir
hans unni honum mikit. Ekki lagðist Ormr í eldaskála.

Óx hann nú upp þangat til er hann var tólf vetra gamall.
Stórólfr var iðjumaðr mikill ok verks ígjarn. Þat var einn
dag um sumarit at Stórólfr lét færa hey saman, ok geingu
fernir eykir. Stórólfr hlóð heyi, en handfátt varð upp at
bera, en honum þótti heldr regnligt gerast. Kallaði hann
þá á Orm, son sinn, ok bað hann til hjálpa ok leggja upp
heyit. Ormr gerði ok svó, en er í tók at draga skúrirnar,
gerðist Stórólfr mikilvirkr á heyinu, ok eggjaði Orm fast
at hann skyldi duga ok neyta aflsins, ok sagði hann bæði
slyttinn ok linaflaðan, ok meir gefinn vöxtr en afl eðr harka.
Ormr reiddist nú, ok bar upp fúlguna alla á lítilli stundu,
ok í því kom at eykrinn. Greip Ormr þá upp hlassit ok
hestinn með öllum akfærunum ok kastaði upp á heyit, ok
svó snart, at Stórólfr kall fell út af heyinu ok ofan í geilina.
Varð þat svó þungt fall at brotnaði í honum þrjú rifin.
Stórólfr mælti þá,

'Illt er at eggja ofstopamennina, ok er þat auðsét at
þú munt ófirirleitinn verða.'

Mikil aflraun þótti þetta öllum mönnum af jafnungum
manni sýnd.

(2) *Ormr Stórólfsson fór til sláttar*

Þat er enn sagt, einnhvern dag, at Stórólfr kom at máli
við Orm, son sinn, ok bað hann fara á eingjar ok slá—'því
at húskörlum geingr lítt í sumar'.

'Hvar er ljár sá er ek skal slá með?' sagði Ormr.
Stórólfr fekk honum þá orf ok nýjan ljá, ok var hvórtveggja
mjök stórkostligt. Ormr vatt ljáinn í sundr milli
handa sér en steig í sundr orfit, ok kvað sér hvórki skyldu.
Snýr Ormr þá í brottu, ok fær sér tvó fjórðunga járns, ok
ferr til smiðju ok gerir sér ljá. Síðan tók hann sér einn ás
ór viðarbulungi, ok gerði sér mátuliga hátt ok færði í tvó
hæla stóra, ok lét þar í koma ljáinn þann nýja, ok vafði
síðan með járni, gekk síðan ofan á eingjar.

Þar var svó háttat landslegi at þar var þýft mjök en báði
loðit ok grasgott. Ormr tekr til at slá ok slær þann dag
allan til kvelds. Stórólfr sendi griðkonur sínar at raka
ljána eftir Ormi, en er þær kvómu á eingjarnar, sá þær at
Ormr hafði haft múgaslátt. Tóku þær þá til ok ætluðu at
hvirfla heyit, en þat gekk þeim eigi svó greitt sem þær
ætluðu, því at þær gátu aungan múga hrært, hvórki með
hrífu né höndum, fóru heim síðan ok sögðu bónda. Fór
hann þá ok reið á eingjar um kveldit. Sá hann þá at Ormr
hafði slegit af þúfur allar ok fært þær saman í múga. Hann
bað hann þá upp gefa ok ónýta eigi meira. Ormr gerði þá
ok svó, ok var þá ljár hans máðr upp í smiðreim. Þá hafði
Ormr slegit átta stakka völl, ok þær einar eingjar eru
sléttar af Stórólfshvóli, ok er kallaðr ákvæðisteigr milli
hverra múga. Sér þessa alls merki enn í dag.

(3) *Ormr bar heyit*

85 Dufþakr er maðr nefndr. Hann bjó á þeim bæ er heitir í Holti, ok er síðan kallat í Dufþaksholti. Dufþakr var mikill ok mjök trylldr, svó at hann var eigi einhamr. Þeir Stórólfr eldu laungum grátt silfr, en stundum vóru með þeim blíðskapir, en þó átti með þeim illan enda at síðustu,
90 því at þat segja sumir menn, at Dufþakr yrði Stórólfi at bana.

Nú líðr áfram þar til at Ormr er átján vetra gamall. Þá kom vetr mikill svó at gerði jarðbönn, en Stórólfr hafði fénaðar mart, at tók þá at draga fast at heyjum hans er á
95 leið, svó at hann þóttist sjá firir at hann mundi fella fénað sinn ef aungra bragða væri í leitat, því at hey kunni hvergi at fá í byggðinni, útan Dufþakr hafði hey með afgaungum, ok vildi við aungan af standa. Þá var heldr fátt með þeim Stórólfi.

100 Stórólfr sendi þá Orm, son sinn, til móts við Dufþak at fá af honum nokkut af heyi, því at þá gerðist tímum mjök fram komit, en fénaðr dreginn mjök. Ormr fór þá til móts við Dufþak, ok falaði af honum hey, en hann kvazt ekki til sölu hafa, en er Ormr herti fast at, þá sagði Dufþakr at
105 hann skyldi hafa byrði sína ef hann vildi—'ok má ykkr þó at gagni koma ef svó mikit leggr hverr til í byggðinni'.

'Þetta er lítit tillát, en þó skal ek hafa, eðr hvar skal ek af taka?'

'Úti í garði,' segir Dufþakr, 'standa tveir heykleggjar,
110 annarr fjögurra faðma en annarr tveggja, ok vel tveggja faðma þykkt, ok því nærri hátt, ok þikkir vón at sigit muni. Þar skaltu hafa af hinu minna.'

'Ek mun fara heim fyst,' segir Ormr, 'ok sækja mér
bendi.'

Ok svó gerði hann, sagði nú föður sínum.

'Þetta er gaungumannliga til látit,' segir Stórólfr, 'enda
skal hann hér ekki verð firir hafa, ok þikkir mér þó ráð
at ek sæki heldr byrðina, því at ek mun heldr borit fá en
þú.'

'Eigi skal þat vera,' sagði Ormr, 'því at svó mikit var
gefit sem ek bæra.'

'Hertu þik þá, mannskræfan,' segir Stórólfr.

Snýr Ormr þá í brottu ok til gervibúrs, ok tekr reip á
tíu hesta, ok leysir af hagldir, kastar þá saman báði at
leingd ok digrð, svó at hann gerir ór eitt, geingr síðan yfir
í Holt ok at heygarðinum ok brýtr á hlið, geingr inn í
garðinn ok at hinum meira heykleggjanum, ok ryðr af ofan
torfi, ok því sem vest var orðit. Síðan styðr hann á höndum ok losar til heyit niðri við jörðina, dregr síðan undir
reipin, ok bregðr í hagldirnar ok vendir um heyinu. Færist
hann þá undir í fatla ok vegr upp á herðar sér, en þat
segja sumir menn at hann hafi haft hinn minna kleggja í
firir. Gekk hann með þetta heim til Stórólfshvóls. Var
bóndi úti ok sá. Fannst honum mikit um, ok lét á sannast
at hann mundi eigi sjálfr svó miklu orkat hafa. Var þá inn
borit í hlöðu, ok var hon þá full. Dugði þetta hey svó vel
fénaði Stórólfs bónda at hann felldi ekki um vórit. Var
síðan betr í frændsemi þeirra feðga þaðan af en áðr, því at
Stórólfr sá hvert afbragð Ormr var annarra manna.

En er Dufþakr kall kom út um daginn, ok sá vegsummerki, at í burtu vóru hey hans bæði, en þat eina eftir er
vettugi var nýtt, ok þó eigi vel at unnit—sá hann ok hvar

Ormr gekk ór garði ok bar heykleggjana báða —, þótti honum mikil furða í, hversu stóra byrði Ormr gat borit.
145 En um vórit fór Dufþakr til Hvóls ok heimti heyverð at Stórólfi ok fekk ekki. Þótti honum heyit eigi minna vert en sex kúgilda. Leiddi af þessu langan óþokka með þeim Stórólfi ok mikinn fjándskap, sem síðar mun sagt verða.

(4) *Ormr ok Þórálfr reyndu knáleik sinn*

150 En er Ormr var tvítögr at aldri reið hann til alþingis sem oftar. Þá var þingit fjölmennt. Þórálfr Skólmsson var kominn á þingit norðan frá Myrká ór Hörgárdal, frændi Orms. Með honum var sá maðr er Melkólfr hét. Hann hafði sex kalla afl. Þeir vóru allir í búð með Jörundi goða,
155 mági Orms.

Jörundi goða vóru gefnir aurskór einir. Þeir vóru svó stórir ok járnmiklir at þeir stóðu hálft pund saumlausir. Þeir fóru um búðina til sýnis, en er skórnir kómu til Þórálfs, tók hann skóna fjóra ok lét saman, ok helt á nok-
160 kura stund, rétti síðan at Ormi, ok vóru þá allir réttir sem kerti. Ormr tók við ok beygði í einu alla skóna fjóra sem áðr höfðu verit, ok þótti þetta mikil aflraun hvórtveggja.

En um daginn er þeir geingu út, stóð hituketill hjá heituhúsinu sá er tók tvær tunnur. Hann fylldu þeir upp
165 af sandi. Eftir þat gekk at Melkólfr, ok fleytti honum með annarri hendi. Þórálfr gekk þá at ok lyfti honum upp með tveim fingrum. Síðast gekk at Ormr, ok krækti undir hödduna hinum minnsta fingri ok fleytti honum jafnhátt ökla, ok brá hendinni undir kápuna. Þórálfr mælti:

'Sýn mér nú fingrinn.' 170
'Eigi vil ek þat,' segir Ormr.
'Kost átta ek at meiða mik, ef ek vildi,' segir Þórálfr, 'ok vilda ek eigi.'
Mönnum þótti sem í sundr hefði geingit hold ok sinar niðr at beini. 175
Síðan riðu menn heim af þingi, ok sat Ormr um kyrrt. Mikils þótti mönnum vert um aflraunir Orms, þær sem hann hafði gert ok gerði síðan, því meiri sem hann var þá ellri, ok því er þat allra manna mál, vina hans ok óvina, at hann hafi sterkastr maðr verit á öllu Íslandi, bæði at 180 fornu ok nýju, sá er einhamr hefir verit.

(5) *Af Ásbirni prúða*

Virfill hét maðr. Hann átti at ráða firir einu þorpi í Danmörk þar er á Vendilskaga heitir. Þeir vóru brœðr ok Véseti í Borgundarhólmi. Virfill var kvóngaðr maðr, ok 185 átti einn son við konu sinni er Ásbjörn er nefndr. Hann var snemma mikill ok vænn ok vel at íþróttum búinn. Hann var hverjum manni kurteisari; af því var hann kallaðr Ásbjörn prúði.

Þat var þá tízka í þær mundir at konur þær fóru yfir 190 land er völvur vóru kallaðar, ok sögðu mönnum firir örlög sín, árferð, ok aðra hluti þá er menn vildu vísir verða. Þessi sveit kom til Virfils bónda. Var völvunni þar vel fagnat, því at þar var veizla hin bezta.

En er menn vóru komnir í sæti um kveldit, var völvan 195 frétt at forspám sínum, en hon sagði at Virfill mundi þar

til elli búa ok þikkja nýtr bóndi—'en þeim unga manni er
þar sitr hjá þér, bóndi, er gott at heyra sín forlög, því at
hann mun fara víða, ok þikkja þar mestr maðr sem þá er
200 hann helzt, ok vinna mart til framaverka, ok verða ellidauðr ef hann kemr eigi á Norðmæri í Nóregi eðr norðr
þaðan í þat land'.

'Þat ætla ek,' sagði Ásbjörn, 'at ek sé eigi þar feigari en
hér.'
205 'Muntu eigi ráða því, hvat er þú ætlar,' segir völvan,
ok varð henni þá ljóð á munni:

        (1) 'Þó at þú látir
           yfir lögu breiða
           byrhest renna,
210   ok berist víða,
           nær mun þat leggja
           at norðr firir Mæri
           þú bana hljótir:
           bezt mun at þegja.'

215 Síðan var völvan þar svó leingi sem ætlat var, ok leyst í
burt með góðum gjöfum.

Ásbjörn óx nú upp, en þegar at aldr færðist yfir hann,
þá hafði hann sik í förum til ýmissa landa, ok kynndi sér
svó siðu annarra manna, ok var mikils metinn af öllum
220 höfðingjum. Móðir hans var ættuð norðan ór Nóregi, af
Hörðalandi ok Norðmæri, komin af ætt Bifru-Kára. Sat
Ásbjörn þar laungum hjá móðurfrændum sínum, mikils
metinn sakir íþrótta sinna ok atgervi.

(6) Ormr ok Ásbjörn unnu Gautland

Nú er þar til at taka er fyrr var frá horfit, at Ormr Stórólfsson sat á Íslandi. Ok er hann var kominn á þrítögsaldr,
tók hann sér fari með þeim manni er Özurr hörzki hét, er
skip átti uppi standanda í Þjórsá, ok fór útan með honum.
Özurr átti garð á Hörðalandi, ok sat Ormr hjá honum um
vetr. Þá var Ásbjörn prúði á Hörðalandi, ok bar oft saman
fundi þeirra Orms, ok fell vel á með þeim ok gerðist þar
skjótt vinátta. Reyndu þeir margar íþróttir ok vóru á allar
jafnir, þær sem eigi reyndi afl með, en miklu var Ormr
sterkari. Svó kom at þeir sórust í fóstbræðralag at fornum
sið, at hvórr skyldi annars hefna, sá er leingr lifði, ef hinn
yrði vópndauðr.

En um vórit talaði Ásbjörn við Orm, at hann vildi fara
norðr á Mæri at hitta Eyvind snák ok Bergþór bestil,
frændr sína.

'Er mér ok forvitni á,' segir hann, 'at vita hvórt þegar
dettr líf ór mér er ek kem þar, sem sagði völvan arma.'

Ormr lézt þeirrar farar búinn—'en eigi þikki mér þú
þar mega um keppa, því at gnógu mart vita þess háttar
menn sem hon er'.

Síðan fóru þeir á tveim skipum norðr á Mæri, ok tók
Eyvindr ok Bergþórr allvel við Ásbirni, frænda sínum, því
at þeir vóru systkinasynir. Þetta var á ofanverðum dögum
Hákonar Hlaðajalls.

Þar spurði Ásbjörn at eyjar tvær lágu norðr firir landi,
ok hét hvórtveggi Sauðey, ok réði firir inni ýtri eyjunni
jötunn sá er Brúsi héti, hann væri mikit troll ok mannæta,
ok ætluðu menn at hann mundi aldri af mennskum mönn-

um unninn verða, hversu margr væri. En móðir hans var
þó verri viðreignar, en þat var kolsvört ketta ok svó mikil
255 sem þau blótnaut at stærst verða. Eingi gæði höfðu menn
af landi ór hvórigri eyjunni firir þessum meinvættum.

Gerðist Ásbjörn fúss at fara til eyjanna, en Ormr aflatti
ok kvað fátt verra en við fjándr slíka at eiga, ok því varð
ekki af ferðinni. Heldu þeir um sumarit suðr í Danmörk,
260 ok sátu hjá Virfli um vetrinn, en at vetri liðnum ok vóri
komnu heldu þeir í hernað með fimm skip ok fóru víða
um eyjar ok útsker ok höfðu sigr ok gagn hvar er þeir
kvómu. Urðu þá eigi aðrir menn frægri í víkingu heldr en
þeir.

265 En um sumarit er á leið, lögðu þeir til Gautlands ok
herjuðu þar. Þá réð þar firir sá jall, er Herröðr hét. Þar
áttu þeir marga bardaga, ok feingu vald yfir landinu, ok
sátu þar vetr hinn þriðja.

Þar vóru drykkjur stórar um vetrinn ok gleði mikil. Þat
270 var einn dag um vetrinn er þeir Ásbjörn ok Ormr sátu ok
drukku, þá kvað Ásbjörn vísu þessa:

> (2) 'Sagði mér á seiði,
> saung um þat laungum,
> at ek á feigum fæti
> 275 færik norðr á Mæri.
> Vætki vissi völva:
> vera mun ek enn með mönnum
> glaðr í Gautaveldi.
> Gramir eigi spá hennar.'

280 Um vórit fóru þeir Ormr ok Ásbjörn, ok undu þar eigi
leingr, ok fóru um sumarit norðr í Danmörk ok svó til

Nóregs, ok vóru þar vetr hinn fjórða með Özuri hörzka.
En um vórit töluðust þeir með, fóstbræðr. Vildi Ásbjörn í hernað, en Ormr út til Íslands, ok því skildu þeir ok þó með kærleikum ok vináttu. Fór Ormr til Íslands 285 með Özuri hörzka, urðu vel reiðfara, kómu skipi sínu í Leiruvóg firir neðan heiði. Þá frétti Ormr þau tíðendi at Stórólfr kall, faðir hans, hafði dáit í viðskiftum þeirra Dufþaks. Var hann fám mönnum harmdauði. Fór Ormr þá heim á Stórólfshvól ok setti þar bú saman, ok bjó þar 290 leingi, eftir þat er hann hafði hefnt Stórólfs, föður síns, eftir því sem segir í Íslendingaskrá.

(7) *Dráp Ásbjarnar*

Litlu síðar en þeir Ormr ok Ásbjörn höfðu skilit, fýstist Ásbjörn norðr í Sauðeyjar. Fór hann við fjóra menn ok 295 tuttugu á skipi, heldr norðr firir Mæri, ok leggr seint dags at Sauðey hinni ytri, ganga á land ok reisa tjald, eru þar um náttina ok verða við ekki varir.

Um morgininn árla ríss Ásbjörn upp, klæðir sik, ok tekr vópn sín ok geingr upp á land, en biðr menn sína bíða sín. 300 En er nokkut svó var liðit frá því er Ásbjörn hafði í brott geingit, verða þeir við þat varir at ketta ógurlig var komin í tjaldsdyrrnar. Hon var kolsvört at lit ok heldr grimmlig, því at eldar þóttu brenna ór nösum hennar ok munni; eigi var hon ok vel eyg. Þeim brá mjök við þessa sýn, ok 305 urðu óttafullir. Kettan hleypr þá innar at þeim ok grípr hvern at öðrum, ok svó er sagt at suma gleyfti hon, en suma rifi hon til dauðs með klóm ok tönnum. Tuttugu

menn drap hon þar á lítilli stundu, en þrír kvómust út ok
undan ok á skip, ok heldu þegar undan landi.

En Ásbjörn geingr þar til er hann kemr at hellinum
Brúsa, ok snarar þegar inn í. Honum var nokkut dimmt
firir augum, en skuggamikit var í hellinum. Hann verðr
eigi fyrr varr við en hann er þrifinn á loft ok færðr niðr
svó hart at Ásbirni þótti furða í. Verðr hann þess þá varr
at þar er kominn Brúsi jötunn, ok sýndist heldr mikilligr.
Brúsi mælti þá,

'Þó lagðir þú mikit kapp á at sækja hingat. Skaltu nú
ok eyrendi hafa, því at þú skalt hér lífit láta með svó miklum harmkvölum at þat skal aðra letja at sækja mik heim
með ófriði.'

Fletti hann þá Ásbjörn klæðum, því at svó var þeirra
mikill aflamunr at jötunninn varð einn at ráða þeirra í
milli. Bálk mikinn sá Ásbjörn standa um þveran hellinn,
ok stórt gat á miðjum bálkinum. Járnsúla stór stóð nokkut
svó firir framan bálkinn. .

'Nú skal prófa þat,' segir Brúsi, 'hvórt þú ert nokkut
harðari en aðrir menn.'

'Lítit mun þat at reyna,' segir Ásbjörn, 'en ógæfusamliga hefir mér tekizt at ek skyldi aungri vörn firir mik
koma, ok er þat líkast at feigð kalli at mér,'—ok kvað vísu
þessa:

(3) 'Sinni má eingi
íþrótt treysta:
aldri er hann svó sterkr
né stórr í huga;
svó bregzt hverjum
á banadægri

ORMS ÞÁTTR

>   hjarta ok megin
>   sem heill bilar.' 340

Síðan opnaði Brúsi kvið á Ásbirni, ok náði þarmaenda hans ok knýtti um járnsúluna, ok leiddi Ásbjörn þar í hring um, en Ásbjörn gekk einart, ok röktust svó á enda allir hans þarmar. Ásbjörn kvað þá vísur þessar jafnframmi: 345

>   (4) 'Segist þat minni móður,
>   mun hon ei syni kemba
>   svarðar láð í sumri,
>   svanhvít í Danmörku.
>   Hafði ek henni heitit 350
>   at ek heim koma munda:
>   nú mun segg á síðu
>   sverðs egg dregin verða.
>
>   (5) Annat var, þá er inni
>   ölkátir vér sátum 355
>   ok á fleyskipi fórum
>   fjörð af Hörðalandi.
>   Drukkum mjöð ok mæltum
>   mart orð saman forðum:
>   nú er ek einn í aungvar 360
>   jötna þraungvar geinginn.
>
>   (6) Annat var, þá er inni
>   allstórir saman fóru.
>   Stóð þar upp í stafni
>   Stórólfs burr inn frækni, 365

þá er langskipum lagði
lundr at Eyrasundi:
nú mun ek, tældr í tryggðum,
trolla byggðir kanna.

(7) Annat var, þá er inni
Ormr at Hildar stormi
gekk enn gráðgum blakki
Geitis sylg at veita.
Rekk at rómu dökkri
raunmargan gaf vargi
seggr ok sárt nam höggva
svinnr at Ífuminni.

(8) Annat var, þá er inni
ek veitta ferð sveittri
högg með hvassri tuggu
Herjans, suðr í skerjum
Elfar. Oft nam kólfi
Ormr hagliga at forma,
mest þá er Miðjungs traustir
mágar eftir lágu.

(9) Annat var, þá er inni
allir saman várum,
Gautr ok Geiri,
Glúmr ok Starri,
Sámr ok Sæmingr,
synir Oddvarar,
Haukr ok Háma,
Hrókr ok Tóki.

(10) Annat var, þá er inni
    oft á sæ fórum,   395
    Hrani ok Högni,
    Hjálmr ok Stefnir,
    Grani ok Gunnarr,
    Grímr ok Sörkvir,
    Tumi ok Torfi,   400
    Teitr ok Geitir.

(11) Annat var, þá er inni
    alllítt vér spörðumst
    at samtogi sverða.
    Sjaldan ek latta   405
    at brynpálmar brýndir
    biti hvassliga seggi.
    Þó var Ormr at ímun
    æ oddviti þeirra.

(12) Mundi Ormr   410
    ófrýnn vera
    ef hann á kvöl þessa
    kynni at líta,
    ok grimmliga
    gjalda þussi   415
    vórar viðfarar
    víst, ef hann næði.'

Síðan lét Ásbjörn líf sitt með mikilli hreysti ok dreingskap.

(8) Ormr hittir Menglöðu í Sauðey

Þat er at segja at þeir þrír menn er undan kómust sóttu knáliga róðr ok léttu eigi fyrr en þeir kómu at landi, sögðu þau tíðendi er gerzt höfðu í þeirra förum, kvóðust ætla Ásbjörn dauðan, en kunnu ekki frá at segja hversu at hafði borizt um hans líflát. Kvómu þeir sér í skip með kaupmönnum ok fluttust svó suðr til Danmerkr. Spurðust nú þessi tíðendi víða ok þóttu mikil.

Þá var orðit höfðingjaskifti í Nóregi, Hákon jall dauðr, en Óláfr Tryggvason í land kominn ok bauð öllum rétta trú.

Ormr Stórólfsson spurði út til Íslands um farar ok líflát Ásbjarnar, er mönnum þótti sem vera mundi. Þótti honum þat allmikill skaði, ok undi eigi leingdar á Íslandi, ok tók sér fari í Reyðarfirði ok fór þar útan. Þeir kómu norðarliga við Nóreg, ok sat hann um vetrinn í Þrándheimi. Þá hafði Óláfr ráðit þrjá vetr Nóregi.

Um vórit bjóst Ormr at fara til Sauðeyja. Þeir vóru því nær margir á skipi sem þeir Ásbjörn höfðu verit. Þeir lögðu at hinni minni Sauðey síð um kveldit, ok tjölduðu á landi ok lágu þar um náttina. Þat segja menn at Ormr væri prímsigndr í Danmörku, en hafi kristnazt á Íslandi.

En er Ormr var sofnaðr, sá hann at kona gekk inn í tjaldit, mikil ok errilig, vel búin ok væn at yfirlitum. Hon gekk innar at þar er Ormr lá ok nam þar staðar. Ormr þóttist heilsa henni ok spyrja hana at nafni, en hon kvezt Menglöð heita, dóttir Ófótans norðan ór Ófótansfirði— 'en vit erum systkin ok Brúsi at föður, en ek átti mennska móður, en móðir hans er sú in kolsvarta ketta er þar er

í hellinum hjá honum. En þó at vit sém skyld, þá erum
vit þó ekki lyndislík. Ræðr hann firir eyjunni ýtri, ok er
hon sýnu betri. Veitir hann mér þungar búsifjar, svó at
ek hygg at ek muna í brottu stökkva. Veit ek ok hvert
eyrendi þitt er: þú ætlar at hefna Ásbjarnar, fóstbróður
þíns, ok er þat vórkunn, því at þú átt eftir hraustan mann
at mæla. Mun þér ok forvitni á at vita hversu honum var í
hel komit, en þar munu ekki margir kunna frá at segja
útan Brúsi ok ek.'

Hóf hon þá upp alla sögu ok sagði frá lífláti Ásbjarnar,
ok svó kvað hon allar þær vísur er hann hafði kveðit—
'en eigi þikkjumst ek þar sjá firir mun um, hvórt meira
má trollskapr Brúsa ok móður hans eðr hamingja þín,
en aungvan mann óttast hann útan þik einn, ok viðrbúnað hefir hann veittan, ef þú kynnir at koma. Hann
hefir fært þat bjarg í hellisdyrrnar at ekki má í hellinn
komast meðan þat stendr þar, en þó at þú sér sterkr, þá
hefir þú hvórki afl við Brúsa né bjarginu í brott at koma.
Nú eru hér glófar at ek vil gefa þér, ok fylgir sú náttúra at
þeim verðr aldri aflafátt sem þá hefir á höndum. Yrði þat
svó, at þú ynnir Brúsa, þá vilda ek at þú gæfir Sauðey í
vald mér, en ek mun heldr vera þér í sinni, því at mér
erþú vel í þokka, þó at vit megim eigi njótast sakir trúar
þinnar.'

Síðan hvarf konan, en Ormr vaknaði, ok vóru þar
glófarnir, en hann mundi allar vísurnar. Stóð Ormr þá
upp ok vakti menn sína, ok helt út til eyjarinnar, gekk á
land ok bað menn sína bíða á skipi til annars dags í þær
mundir, en halda á burt ef hann kæmi þá eigi.

(9) *Dráp Brúsa*

Nú geingr Ormr þar til er hann kemr at hellinum. Sér
480 hann nú bjargit þat stóra, ok leizt ómáttuligt nokkurum
manni þat í brott at færa. Þó dregr hann á sik glófana
Menglaðarnauta, tekr síðan á bjarginu ok færir þat burt
ór dyrunum, ok þikkist Ormr þá aflraun mesta sýnt hafa.

Hann gekk þá inn í hellinn, ok lagði málajárn í dyrrnar,
485 en er hann var inn kominn, sá hann hvar kettan hljóp með
gapanda ginit. Ormr hafði boga ok örvamæli. Lagði hann
þá ör á streing ok skaut at kettunni þremr örum, en hon
hendi allar með hvóftunum ok beit í sundr. Hefir hon sik
þá at Ormi ok rekr klærnar framan í fangit svó at Ormr
490 kiknar við, en klærnar geingu í gegnum klæðin svó at í
beini stóð. Hon ætlar þá at bíta í andlit Ormi. Finnr hann
þá at honum mun eigi veita, heitr þá á sjálfan guð ok hinn
heilaga Petrum postula at ganga til Róms ef hann ynni
kettuna ok Brúsa son hennar. Síðan fann Ormr at minnk-
495 aðist afl kettunnar. Tekr hann þá annarri hendi um
kverkr henni, en annarri um hrygg, ok geingr hana á bak,
ok brýtr í sundr í henni hrygginn, ok geingr svó af henni
dauðri.

Ormr sá þá hvar bálkr stórr var um þveran hellinn.
500 Hann geingr þá innar at, en er hann kemr þar, sér hann
at fleinn mikill kemr útar í gegnum bálkinn. Hann var
báði digr ok langr. Ormr grípr þá í móti fleininum ok
leggr af út. Brúsi kippir þá at sér fleininum, ok var hann
fastr, svó at hvergi gekk. Þat undraðist Brúsi, ok gægðist
505 upp yfir bálkinn, en er Ormr sér þat, þrífr hann í skeggit
á Brúsa báðum höndum, en Brúsi bregzt við í öðrum stað.

Sviftast þeir þá fast um bálkinn. Ormr hafði vafit skegginu um hönd sér, ok rykkir til svó fast at hann rífr af Brúsa allan skeggstaðinn, hökuna, kjaftana báða, vangafillurnar upp allt at eyrum. Gekk hér með holdit niðr at beini. Brúsi lét þá síga brýnnar ok grettist heldr greppliga.

Ormr stökkr þá innar yfir bálkinn. Grípast þeir þá til ok glíma leingi. Mæddi Brúsa þá fast blóðrás. Tekr hann þá heldr at ganga firir. Gefr Ormr þá á, ok rekr Brúsa at bálkinum, ok brýtr hann þar um á bak aftr.

'Snemma sagði mér þat hugr,' sagði Brúsi, 'at ek munda af þér nokkut erfitt fá, þegar ek heyrða þín getit, enda er þat nú fram komit. Muntu nú vinna skjótt um ok höggva höfuð af mér, en þat var satt at mjök pínda ek Ásbjörn prúða þá er ek rakta ór honum alla þarmana, ok gaf hann sik ekki við fyrr en hann dó.'

'Illa gerðir þú þat,' segir Ormr, 'at pína hann svó mjök, jafnröskvan mann. Skaltu ok hafa þess nokkurar menjar.'

Hann brá þá saxi, ok reist blóðörn á baki honum, ok skar öll rifin frá hryggnum, ok dró þar út lungun. Lét Brúsi svó líf sitt með litlum dreingskap.

Síðan bar Ormr eld at ok brenndi upp til ösku báði Brúsa ok kettuna. Ok er hann hafði þetta starfat, fór hann burt ór hellinum með kistur tvær fullar af gulli ok silfri, en þat sem meira var fémætt gaf hann í vald Mengladar, ok svó eyna. Skildu þau með mikilli vináttu. Kom Ormr til manna sinna í nefndan tíma, heldu síðan til meginlands. Sat Ormr í Þrándheimi vetr annan.

(10) *Frá Ormi ok Eireki*

At sumri bjóst Ormr til Rómferðar, ok tókst sú ferð vel, kom sunnan til Danmerkr um haustit eftir Svöldrarorrostu, ok spurði þar þau tíðendi er þar höfðu vorðit. Fór
540 hann þá til Nóregs á fund Eireks jalls, ok hitti hann á Hlöðum, gekk firir jall ok kvaddi hann. Jall tók honum vel ok spurði hann at nafni. Hann lézt Ormr heita. Jall mælti,

'Ertu Ormr sterki?'

545 'Kalla megi þér svó, herra, ef þér vilið, en þat er eyrendi mitt at ek vildi vera gestr yðvarr í vetr.'

Jall kvað honum þat til reiðu, ok skipaði honum á hinn æðra bekk útarliga. Ormr var fáskiftinn um vetrinn ok óhlutdeilinn.

550 Þat var einn tíma at talat var til Svöldrarorrostu, ok hversu kappar Óláfs konungs höfðu dreingiliga vörn sýnt, ok hversu seint at Ormrinn hafði unninn vorðit, eðr hversu harða atsókn Eirekr jall hafði veitt, at hann fekk unnit þat skip er eingi ætlaði at á þíðum sjó mundi unnit
555 verða. Ormr svarar,

'Seinna mundi Ormrinn langi unninn hafa vorðit ef ek hefða þar verit með öðrum köppum konungs.'

Nú var sagt jalli at Ormr hefði mikit um talat at Ormrinn langi mundi eigi unninn orðit hafa ef hann hefði
560 þar verit. Jall lætr þá kalla Orm firir sik, ok spyrr hvórt hann hefði þat talat at Ormrinn mundi eigi unninn hafa vorðit ef hann hefði þar verit.

'Eigi er þat, herra,' sagði Ormr. 'Hitt sagða ek, at seinna mundi unninn hafa vorðit Ormrinn ef ek hefða þar verit.'

Jall svarar: 'Lítinn mun mundi þat segja um einn mann, svó mörgum ok miklum köppum sem þar var saman skipat, en þó skal gera tilraun nokkura. Þú skalt vera einn á skipi, ok skulu sækja at þér fimmtán skeiðr, ok er þat þó lítit af þeim skipafjölda er var við Svöldr.'

'Þér munuð ráða, herra,' sagði Ormr, 'en ekki mun ek fyrr upp gefast en ek er yfirkominn.'

Ormr gekk þá út ok tók einn berlingsás digran, þrettán álna langan. Síðan fór hann á skip ok lét frá landi. Síðan vóru menn til feingnir á fimmtán skeiðum, ok sóttu at Ormi, en svó er sagt at á lítilli stundu hafði Ormr slegit í kaf sjau skeiðr, lamit ok brotit. Þá kallaði jall ok bað þá hætta þessum leik. Var ok svó gert. Varð þá borgit flestum öllum mönnum.

Síðan bað jall sex tigu manna sækja at Ormi úti á víðum velli, ok svó var gert. Ormr hafði ekki vópna nema ásinn, ok veifði honum um sik sem hreytispeldi, svó at eingi þorði nærri at koma, því at þeir sá vísan bana, hverr sem firir yrði. Bað jall þá hætta þessum leik ok svó var gert. Jall mælti,

'Eigi ætla ek at þat væri oftalat, Ormr, þótt seinna ynnist Ormrinn langi ef þú hefðir á verit, því at hann mundi aldri unninn hafa orðit ef þú hefðir þar til varnar verit.'

Síðan gerðist Ormr hirðmaðr Eireks jalls, ok var með honum í miklum kærleikum sakir atgervi sinnar.

(11) *Ormr kom til Einars á Gimsar*

Þat var einn tíma at Ormr fór á kynni, þar sem hann hafði fyrr verit, í Þrándheimi. Hann kom um leið á Gims-
595 ar, ok var Einarr heima. Þat var í þann tíma sem Einarr var at kirkju. Bogi hans var úti firir kirkjudyrum. Ormr gekk at ok tók upp, ok lagði ör á streing ok dró firir odd, ok lét svó örina standa í boganum, ok lagði síðan niðr aftr ok gekk í brottu.

600 En er Einarr kom út, sá hann hversu bogi hans var til háttaðr, ok undraðist mjök, ok spurði eftir hverr með boga hans mundi farit hafa, en þess varð hann leingi ekki víss fyrr en Ormr sjálfr sagði honum. Einarr kvezt þat ok vita at þat mundi ekki skræfa verit hafa er boga
605 hans hafði firir odd dregit.

Eirekr jall fór at veizlum austr um Víkina. Þá var Ormr með jalli. En er þeir kvómu þar sem Ormrinn langi hafði verit upp högginn, lá þar siglutrét. Jall bað menn prófa hversu margir þyrfti undir at ganga áðr en axlat
610 yrði. Skipaði hann Ormi undir mitt trét. Sex tigir manna tóku trét. Síðan bað jall sinn mann tínast undan hvórum enda, ok svó var gert, þar til at Ormr stóð einn undir trénu. Þá gekk hann með þat þrjú fet, ok lagði niðr síðan. Segja menn at Ormr muni valla samr orðit hafa síðan ok
615 áðr.

Var hann með jalli nokkura vetr, fór síðan út til Íslands, ok settist í bú at Stórólfshvóli, ok þótti æ hinn mesti maðr, ok varð ellidauðr ok helt vel trú sína.

TEXTUAL NOTES

Hreiðars þáttr

For the text of M the facsimile edition has been used. The readings of A and H are quoted from proofs of the edition of Hulda still to be published kindly provided by the Arnamagnæan Institute, see p. 20 above.

1 *The heading is illegible in M, but probably read* Frá Hreiðari (*the word* þáttr *is not used in headings in M*); Af Hreiðari ok Þórði *A*, Capitulum. Hreiðars þáttr *H*.   17 hálfu: *M omits the* l.   59–65 *The words in brackets are illegible in M and are supplied from A.*   76 Handkrœkjumsk: *M omits the* m.   82 kømr: *M omits the* m.   104 Ekki *written twice in M*.   113 einum: *M omits the* m.   122 at: *M omits the* t.   147 skilja: *M omits the* i.   152 gengr: *M omits the* r.   176 fleygir: *written* fleyg^r (*i.e.* fleygar) *in M*.   221 klæðum: *M omits the* m.   233 grettir vaskliga: *emendation*; greit vaxligr *M*, karlmannligr *A and H*.   241, 249 *The words in brackets are illegible in M and are supplied from A.*   243, 247 *The text of M is damaged, and the texts of A and H do not correspond closely enough for the missing words to be supplied from them. There is room for three or four words in both places. The two words before* hirðinni *may be* nú með, *and the sentence perhaps ended* ok Hreiðari ferr vel nú með hirðinni. *In the edition in* Væringjar: leskaflar fyrir unglinga úr íslenzkum bókmenntum I, ed. Höðver Sigurðsson (1950), *the lacuna is filled* Dvalðisk hann nú með. *The missing words in line 247 may have been* um þetta mál.   257 einum: *M omits the* i.   276 með: mér *M*.   278 þá: þó *M*.   336 hann *omitted in M*.   362 þœttisk: þóttisk *M*.   368 hefi *omitted in M*.   417 *The first* ok *illegible in M*.   419–426 *The words in brackets are illegible in M and are supplied with the help of A.*

Orms þáttr

The readings of both manuscripts are taken from the facsimile editions, see pp. 34–5 above.

24 Stórólfr: *so* S; Þórólfr *F*.   36 þangat til: *so* S; þann veg *F*.   60 sagði Ormr: *so* S; er Ormr sagði *F*.   63 í sundr *written twice in F*.   70 tekr: *so* S; tek *F*.   74 hvirfla: *so* S; *F omits the* f.   84 heyit: *F omits the* h.   86 Dufþaksholti: *so* S; *F omits the* i.   96 leitat: *so* S; *F omits the* e.   135 hafa: *so* S; *F omits*.   136 í: *so* S; *F omits*.   136 Dugði: *so* S; *F omits the* ð.   152 ór: *so* S; ok *F*.   153, 165 Melkólfr: *so* S; Mækólfr *F* (*probably an error, since this spelling is not found elsewhere in Old Norse; the name is from the Irish* Maelcoluim).   185 var: *so* S; *F omits the* r.   245 norðr: *so* S; *F omits the second* r.   247 á ofanverðum dögum: á dögum *S*, ofanverðum dögum *F*.   260 Virfli: Virlvi *F*.   307 at (2): *so* S; *F omits*.   322 þeirra: afla *adds F* (*dittography*).   354 er: *so* S; ek *F*. *Where the line is repeated in verses* 6 *to* 11 *the word is abbreviated* e. *in F, but written* er *each time in S*.   396 ok *written twice in F*.   406 brynpálmar: *emendation*; brunpálmar *F and S*.   421 er (2): *so* S; *F omits*.   439 hinni: *so* S; *F omits*.   466 afl: *so* S; *F omits the* l.   482 bjarginu: *so* S; bjargina *F*.   490 klærnar: *F omits the first* r.   547 kvað *written twice in F*.   552 seint: *so* S; synt *F*.   563 sagði Ormr: *so* S; *F omits*.   583 þorði: *F adds* j (*i.e.* í *or* jall).   608 siglutrét: *so* S ('-treid'); siglutré *F*.

GENERAL NOTES

Hreiðars þáttr

1/3 The reference to Glúmr is omitted in A and H. The use of the name alone, without patronymic, implies that it is the well-known Víga-Glúmr Eyjólfsson, the hero of *Víga-Glúms saga*, who is meant, though the author also fails to give the name of the father of the otherwise unknown Eyvindr (line 340). Chronologically it is possible for the grandfather of Hreiðarr and Þórðr, who are apparently in the prime of life at the beginning of Haraldr harðráði's reign (1046), to have been a younger contemporary of Víga-Glúmr (*c*. 930 to 1003), but Víga-Glúmr's killing of a man called Hreiðarr is not mentioned in *Víga-Glúms saga* or any other source.

1/9 A and H specify that the brothers sailed from Gásar, which was the principal harbour in Eyjafjǫrðr.

1/16 Under Icelandic law a man's property was divided equally between his sons after his death, irrespective of which was the eldest, or else was held by them as common property. Cf. *Grágás*, I (ed. V. Finsen, 1852), 220.

1/34 According to A and H the brothers landed in Þrándheimr, not Bjǫrgyn.

1/36 *Kæja* (spelt *køia* in M) is not recorded elsewhere, and the etymology is doubtful: it is not certain whether the vowel should be *æ* or *œ*, but the spelling in M (which usually distinguishes the two sounds) implies *œ*.

1/50 Ships were generally beached during the winter and launched again in the spring. A trumpet was used to summon all available hands to drag the ships up the beach when they arrived at Norwegian harbours in the autumn, and penalties were imposed on those who failed to respond to this summons without good reason, see *Norges gamle Love indtil 1387*, II (ed. R. Keyser and P. A. Munch, 1848), 45, 208, 250–01. *Skip(s)dráttr* is mentioned also in *Grágás* (ed. V. Finsen, 1852), I, 13, and II, 69–70, but conditions in Iceland would make the use of a trumpet inappropriate there, and other methods of summoning help were used.

Björn Sigfússon (*ÍF* X, 248) assumes that Hreiðarr asks the meaning of 'assembly' because he is familiar with ship-launchings in Iceland, but not with public meetings; but it is perhaps more likely that his ignorance is only pretended, and that he knows perfectly well what the fanfare is for: his devious questions are only a prelude to his insistence on attending the assembly.

1/65 Instead of *þessarar*, the form *þessar* would be more in keeping with the language of the text in *Morkinskinna*.

1/70 The usual present tense of *ná* in Old Icelandic is *náir*, and *nær* is usually considered a late form. But the two forms reflect a variation in Primitive Germanic in the stem of weak verbs of the *hafa* type between -æi̯- and -i̯-, and so both forms must have been current in Old Icelandic, though the usual literary form is *náir*. There is therefore no reason to interpret *nær* here as an adverb ('then one's strength is almost nothing', cf. the punctuation in *ÍF* X, 249) since it gives better sense as a verb ('when one's strength is inadequate').

1/71 Compare the proverb *Margur er knár, þó hann sé smár* 'many a little fellow is tough' (Guðmundur Ólafsson, *Thesaurus adagiorum* (ed. G. Kallstenius, 1930), no. 2285).

1/80 *við fót*: S. Blöndal, *Islandsk-Dansk Ordbog* (1920–24), glosses *hlaupa við fót* as 'halvt løbe'.

1/102 *ósyknligr* is an otherwise unknown word and may be the result of scribal error. It would appear to be compounded from *sykn* 'free of legal charges', a legal term applied to a man released from outlawry. *Ósyknligr* would presumably mean 'unlikely to become *sykn*, irredeemable'. This would be a very odd usage, and the description accords ill with the insistence elsewhere in the story that Hreiðarr is a mild person (it is only King Magnús who realises that one day he will lose his temper). Moreover in this context a word referring to physical appearance would be more suitable, and it may be that the original reading was *ósýniligr* ('unsightly'). A and H have *seinheppiligr* ('slow to achieve success, backward'). Compare the description of the similar character Grímr Eyjúlfsson in *Gull-Þóris saga* (*Þorskfirðinga saga*, *ÍF* XIII, 197).

1/115 *Gæfa* was conceived as a sort of power emanating from a person predisposing their undertakings to success. Thus a *gæfumaðr* is someone for whom everything always turns out right (like Auðunn in *Auðunar þáttr*). *Konungs gæfa* (or *gipta*) was a power emanating from a king which could extend its influence over people in his service or those who came into contact with him. In *Hreiðars þáttr* the implication is that by contact with the king Hreiðarr will be cured of his mental retardment and become a *gæfumaðr*, much as the touch of a king's hand was believed to be able to cure certain physical illnesses.

1/117 *Rjáðr* is usually found in the phrase *rjáðr ok rekinn* ('persecuted'), and here presumably means 'chased off' (passive). An intransitive meaning would, however, be more natural in the context ('dashed away, rushed off like a fool'). Cf. *ÍF* VII, 231: *Hann kvazk niðr hafa lagt at rjá* 'he said he had given up horseplay'; and the reading of A later in *Hreiðars þáttr* (line 315): *því at mér tekr at leiðask þessi rjá* 'because I am getting tired of this horseplay'.

1/121 *nær á hvat sem fyrir var* is to be taken with *gengr*: 'he almost tripped over whatever was in front of him'. Cf. the reading of A: *bar hann sik upp mjǫk ok sásk lítt fyrir ok gekk nær (á) hvat sem fyrir var*.

1/123 Ankle-length breeches in Old Icelandic are always associated with the clothing of very young men or idiots, and were considered unseemly or ridiculous for grown men. They seem to have been the traditional attire of the unpromising hero in his youth, to be discarded when he finally attained his full heroic stature, see H. Falk, *Altwestnordische Kleiderkunde* (1919), p. 119. Note the readings of A (*leistabrókum*: 'breeches with footpieces') and H (*leistalausum brókum*: 'breeches without foot-pieces').

1/131 *Þykki þér nú vel*: perhaps 'are you favourably impressed?' rather than 'are you content?'

1/165 *Mikinn tekr þú af*: 'You speak strongly, you exaggerate, you are overdoing it.' *Mikinn* is the acc. sg. m. of the adjective *mikill*, apparently used as an adverb on the analogy of adverbs in *-an* like *gjarnan*, *jafnan*, which appear to have been apprehended as acc. sg. m. of the adjectives *gjarn*, *jafn*. Cf. *gengu skipin mikinn* (*Flb.* II, 16).

1/167 *at lofgjarnliga sé við mælt*: either 'that they (i.e. other people) have been the victims of flattery' or 'that they have been guilty of speaking flatteringly of you'. In either case, it is clear that the sentence is intended as an elaborate compliment. A reads: *Háttung er flestum ǫðrum at oflofaðir sé ef lofsamliga er við mælt.*

1/170 This feature of the king's appearance is not mentioned elsewhere, although according to Snorri Sturluson (*Heimskringla, ÍF* XXVIII, 198–9) Haraldr harðráði had a similar defect, in that one of his eyebrows was set higher than the other.

1/173 Haraldr harðráði (the son of Sigurðr sýr) and King Magnús's father St Óláfr (the son of Haraldr grenski) were half-brothers: their mother was Ásta Guðbrandsdóttir.

1/214 This probably does not mean that Hreiðarr was being made a *hirðmaðr*, but only that he was to be allowed to stay with the *hirðmenn* as a temporary guest. New members of the *hirð* had to be accepted by the rest of the *hirðmenn*, and membership was a higher honour than would have been accorded Hreiðarr at this stage (cf. *ÍF* V, 288).

1/230 *við ráð Þórðar*: perhaps 'under Þórðr's supervision' rather than 'according to Þórðr's advice'.

1/233 *grettir vaskliga*: the text of M here seems meaningless, and the original reading may be irrecoverable (the reading of A and H is probably the guess of an intelligent scribe). The first word may have been some part of the verb *gretta*, although it may have been a noun; *greppr vaskligr* ('a fine-looking fellow') would fit the context well, and the comparative rarity of the word might account for the corruption. But it is perhaps possible to keep the reading of the manuscript (see p. 79 above) and take *greit(t)* as a neuter adjective used adverbially in an intensive sense (see **greiðr** in glossary) and *vaxligr* as an adjective related to *vaxa*. The phrase might then be rendered 'right doughty', or 'really grown up'. See *Kleine Erzählungen aus Landnámabók und Morkinskinna*, ed. W. H. Vogt (1935), p. 51, and *Væringjar* I, ed. Hlöðver Sigurðsson (1950), pp. 85 and 92.

1/237 *kom við sem mátti*: 'happen what might, whatever happened'. It is also possible to read this as an independent clause introducing the next sentence (with a full stop after *ómállatr*), 'It went as it would', 'Things went as might be expected', or 'He responded as best he could', or 'as much as he could'.

1/245 According to all the Scandinavian accounts Magnús the Good and Haraldr harðráði were joint rulers over Norway from the time of Haraldr's return to Scandinavia from the East in 1046 until Magnús's death the same year (though according to *Morkinskinna* they ruled together for two years) and so evidently the author intends us to think of these events as taking place during that year. Haraldr continued to reign alone until his death at Stamford Bridge in 1066.

1/260 ff. This passage has by earlier editors been punctuated with a full stop after *konungs* and a comma after *ǫðrum ok*, thus making the clause *ok beri . . . ǫðrum ok* conditional, qualifying *em ek um þat hræddr*. The present arrangement seems better, taking *ok beri . . . ǫðrum* to indicate the possible result of the preceding clause. M has a punctuation mark after *ǫðrum*.

1/281 *fylgi* has usually been emended to *fylgið* (imperative plural) but the third person singular (or plural) optative ('let someone take') is not impossible.

1/289 *verðr*: on the nominative where one might expect the accusative, see A. Heusler, *Altisländisches Elementarbuch* (4th ed., 1950), § 446, pp. 141–2; *A New Introduction to Old Norse* II (2004), 3.9.4. Cf. 2/242, 2/542 below.

1/322 *fær*: the manuscript contraction *f* with superscript curl is normalised *ferr* (to *fara*) in *ÍF* X, 256, but it could equally well stand for *fær*. The idiom *fara hǫndum* usually means 'to feel, touch', and *fá hǫndum* 'grasp with the hands' is more suitable to the context here.

1/329 The use of the comparative is odd, since there is no second element to the comparison and it is not easy to see what should be supplied (A and H completely rephrase the sentence). Cf. *ÍF* VII, 259: *Eigi er þat it hœgra* 'that is not the easier thing (for them to be doing)', i.e. of the two possible activities suggested. *Enn, en* (which is in fact the spelling of the manuscript here) or *in* with a comparative in a negative sentence is common in verse and appears to be idiomatic and pleonastic; e.g. *Þrymskviða* verse 25. See Finnur Jónsson, *Lexicon Poeticum* (1931), s.v. 1 **enn** 4. The meaning here may be ironical: 'that is not made easier by the fact that he has now got away'. Cf. A. Heusler, *op. cit.*, §§ 162 and 392, pp. 51 and 119.

1/340 *Lendr maðr* ('landed man') was a high-ranking man holding land in fief from the king in return for various services (especially military service). The term corresponds in meaning to the medieval Scottish rank of 'thane'.

1/351 *Heilagr* ('sacred') as a legal term means 'under the protection of the law', *óheilagr* 'outside the protection of the law, not entitled to compensation for injury or death'. A person who started a fight could in so doing make himself an outlaw in Norse law, and a man who killed his assailant in self-defence was not liable to pay compensation. See *Norges gamle Love indtil 1387*, I (ed. R. Keyser and P. A. Munch, 1846), 68; *Grágás* I (ed. V. Finsen, 1852), 145. Compare the phrase *stefna e-m til óhelgi* ('to summons s-one on a charge warranting outlawry') used when depriving a man of his legal rights after he has been killed so that one is not liable to pay compensation for him. See e.g. *ÍF* XII, 161; *Víga-Glúms saga* (ed. G. Turville-Petre, 2nd ed., 1960), 16.

1/412 f. King Haraldr's father, Sigurðr Hálfdanarson, had been nicknamed Sýr ('Sow'), and Hreiðarr's gift of a silver sow is an insulting reminder to the king of this fact, and touches on a sore point with him. The origin of the nickname, which is also sometimes applied to the goddess Freyja, is somewhat obscure: the author of *Hreiðars þáttr* evidently understood it to mean 'sow', and it is translated *scrofa* in *Historia Norvegiæ*. But the nickname often declines differently from the common noun, having gen. *sýrs*, *sýrar* or *súrar* instead of *sýr*, dat. and acc. *sýr* instead of *sú* (this last peculiarity is shared by *kýr* when used as a nickname), see A. Noreen, *Altisländische und altnorwegische Grammatik* (4th ed., 1923), p. 286; A. M. Sturtevant, 'Old Norse Phonological Notes', *Journal of English and Germanic Philology* XLII (1943), 539–40. Because of this, other origins have been proposed for it ('Syrian', *Sivǫr, *Sigvǫr), see J. de Vries, *Altnordisches Etymologisches Wörterbuch* (1961), p. 574. But since sows were probably sacred to Freyja, as boars were to Freyr, it is likely that when applied to her the nickname meant 'the sow-goddess'. Applied to the farmer-king Sigurðr it may have been intended to imply that he was mean, and he certainly has that reputation in literary sources (see *Saga Óláfs konungs hins helga* (ed. O. A. Johnsen and Jón Helgason, 1941), pp. 737, 741, 762; cf. *ÍF* XXVII, 41), but this may have been due to the misunderstanding of the nickname by saga-writers: it perhaps originally meant 'worshipper or devotee of the sow-goddess'. As a farmer, Sigurðr is particularly likely to have concerned himself with a fertility god or goddess.

1/419 With *ætla* the infinitive with *at* is generally found in prose, and the plain infinitive here is probably to be explained as an archaism, since this construction is also found in poetry.

1/434 The following conversation is remarkably similar to that between Stúfr and King Haraldr in *Stúfs þáttr* (*ÍF* V, 286 ff.).

1/462 In A and H the name of Hreiðarr's home is specified as Hreiðarsstaðir (*þar sem síðan heitir á Hreiðarsstǫðum* A). This is probably the addition of a redactor who knew there was a farm of that name in Svarfaðardalr and assumed that it had been named after this Hreiðarr. Although this is not impossible, it is rather more likely that the farm was named after another Hreiðarr (the name is comparatively common), and that it was only associated with the probably fictional hero of this story after the *þáttr* had been written. Hreiðarsstaðir is otherwise first mentioned in a document of 1473, see *Diplomatarium Islandicum* V (1899–1902), 718.

1/467 Nothing is known of Hreiðarr's descendants, any more than of his forbears, those who are mentioned being mere names. The statement here is conventional, and its vagueness strengthens the impression given elsewhere that Hreiðarr and his brother are fictional characters.

Orms þáttr

2/2 f. The genealogy given here has been subject to some confusion, perhaps partly scribal, partly due to the author, and partly to his source. From other sources (particularly *Landnámabók* and *Ketils saga hængs*) it can be seen that it ought to read: *Ketill hængr hét maðr, son Þorkels Naumdælajalls, en móðir Ketils hét Hrafnhildr, dóttir Ketils hængs ór Hrafnistu.*

2/2–3 Hængr was at first a nickname ('the hooked one'?), and later came to be used also as a personal name. It is a contraction of *hœingr*, related to *hór* 'hook'; a male salmon is called *hængr* from the shape of its mouth. A legendary account of the origin of the nickname is given in *Ketils saga hængs*, ch. 1.

2/5 Haraldr hárfagri Hálfdanarson (Dofrafóstri), king of Norway *c.* 885–931, was the first king of Norway to extend his rule over the whole country, and opposition to him on the part of petty landowners is the traditional reason given in many of the sagas for the emigration of many of the Norwegian settlers of Iceland. The legend of his being fostered by the troll Dofri is related most fully in *Flb.* I, 565–6, though it is referred to in many other sagas, mostly late ones; there is no evidence that it is older than the late thirteenth century. See Finnur Jónsson, 'Sagnet om Harald hårfagre som "Dovrefostre"', *Arkiv för Nordisk Filologi* XV (1899), 262–7.

The sons of Hildiríðr (so called because of the early death of their father Björgólfr, and also perhaps because they were illegitimate) were Hárekr and Hrærekr, both favourites of King Haraldr. The story of how Hængr killed them to avenge the death of his friend Þórólfr Kveld-Úlfsson on the king, and so had to flee the country, is told in *Egils saga*, ch. 23, which is the author's main source for this passage.

2/11 *firir útan Rangá*, sc. *hina ýtri* (cf. *ÍF* II, 58).

2/19 The lawspeaker was a sort of president of the Icelandic parliament under the Commonwealth, and his main duty was the recitation of the code of laws at the annual assembly (*Alþingi*). In fact Úlfljótr, who is said to have drawn up the code of laws for the first session of the Alþingi when it was founded, is likely to have been the first lawspeaker (see *Íslendingabók*, ch. 3). Hrafn became lawspeaker in 930.

2/21 *Goði* was the title of the holders of the *goðorð* in ancient Iceland. These were primarily secular chieftains, though their office included priestly functions in heathen times (the word *goði* is related to *goð* '(heathen) god'). The office was usually hereditary, although it could also be sold, given away, and even lent or divided. The power of these chieftains was not territorial, but extended only over those men who voluntarily allied themselves with them, although naturally a *goði*'s followers would mostly come from his own district.

2/22 Cf. *Egils saga* (*ÍF* II, 60): *Hrafn var gǫfgastr sona Hængs*. By his alteration of his source the author of *Orms þáttr* shows that he wants to accentuate the importance of the father of his hero.

2/27 There are several stories of shape-shifters in Old Icelandic, and it is told in *Ln*. (pp. 109, 220, 237) how Stórólfr and his neighbour Dufþakr (see below lines 85 ff.) fought together one night in the forms of a bear and a bull respectively. The bear won, but both men were injured and were confined to bed afterwards. See P. E. K. Kålund, *Bidrag til en historisk-topografisk Beskrivelse af Island*, I (1877), 230–31.

2/48 *Akfæri* means the harness and gear used to fasten a load on a horse, but the term can also include a cart or sledge and the accompanying tackle. The context here does not make it clear whether carts were being used or not.

2/58 *Eing* means uncultivated grassland in its natural state, usually some distance from the farm, as opposed to the *tún*, the cultivated levelled hayfields round the farm buildings.

2/64 *Fjórðungr* ('quarter') was a unit of weight, equal to 20 *merkr* or one-eighth of a *vætt*, i.e. about 4.3 k. or 10 lb. avoirdupois.

2/82 *Ákvæðisteigr* is a day's mowing for one man, the amount of meadow reckoned to be a full day's work for one man to mow. As a measure, it was probably the same as *dagslátta*, i.e. about three-quarters of an acre.

2/83 The author was probably writing in the middle of the fourteenth century. The place where Ormr is supposed to have done his mowing is now known as Ormsvöllur, though there is nothing to distinguish it from the surrounding countryside today. See P. E. K. Kålund, *Bidrag til en historisk-topografisk Beskrivelse af Island*, I (1877), 230–31.

2/85–6 Place-names in several languages are formed in this way with prepositions, e.g. Noke (Old English *æt þæm acum*), Rye (*æt þære iege*), Istanbul (from the Greek for 'in the city').

2/88 *Elda grátt silfr* means literally 'to smelt drossy silver', or perhaps 'to smelt silver so that it becomes grey (through oversmelting)', i.e. to behave so that one's relationship with another person turns out badly, to be on bad terms. See Halldór Halldórsson, *Íslenzk orðtök* (1954), pp. 318–19,

2/94 *at* (1): 'So that'. The word is omitted in S, and earlier editors have emended it to *ok*, but this is perhaps not strictly necessary. It seems to be a case of mixture of constructions: 'S. had so many cattle that . . .', 'S. had many cattle, so that . . .'.

2/110 The larger stack would be about 24 foot long, 12 high, and 12 wide. Dufþakr says it had probably sunk (*sigit*), that is become compressed by its own weight so that its weight in relation to its size would be much greater than that of a newly made stack. The amount of hay carried by Ormr in this stack alone would have weighed at least twelve tons (the normal weight of hay is reckoned to be 100 kilos per cubic metre at minimum)!

2/111 *þykkt . . . hatt . . . sigit* are neuter adjectives agreeing with an implied *hey* (*kleggi* is masculine). Similarly in line 112 *hinu minna* (sc. *heyi*).

2/133 The author's tendency to ironic understatement gives the impression here that the distance between the two farms is quite short. In fact (as his original readers would have known) Dufþaksholt is about three kilometres from Stórólfshvóll.

2/147 In the fourteenth century a *kúgildi* was reckoned equal in value to one *hundrað*, i.e. 120 ells of homespun 2 ells wide (worth $3^1/3$ ounces of silver).

2/148 The author, however, omits to tell us any more of these quarrels, beyond again mentioning that Dufþakr killed Stórólfr (below, line 288).

2/156 *Aurskór* appears also in *Búalög* (*Sögurit* XIII: 1, 1915), p. 9: *fimm álnar kemr á at gera sláttuljái eðr aurskó eðr annat slíkt búsmíði*. See also p. 25 of the same work. The first element is apparently *aurr* 'mud', though it is possible that the word was originally a scribal corruption of *járnskór*.

2/163 The custom of brewing ale in large quantities for the use of those present at the Alþingi is well described in *Ǫlkofra þáttr* (*ÍF* XI, 83 ff.).

2/189 *Prúðr* means 'fine, stately; gentle, courteous (cf. *háttprúðr*, *siðprúðr*); gallant, brave (cf. *hugprúðr*)'. As a nickname *prúði* could in this case be translated 'the gallant', but it probably usually implied chiefly finery in dress, see *ÍF* V, 225, XIV, 70; *Saga Óláfs konungs hins helga* (ed. O. A. Johnsen and Jón Helgason, 1941), p. 810.

2/190 Besides the episode in *Örvar-Odds saga* on which this is clearly modelled, this custom is well documented in other sagas, e.g. *Eiríks saga rauða* (*ÍF* IV, 206–09), *Vatnsdæla saga* (*ÍF* VIII, 29–30), *Víga-Glúms saga* (ed. G. Turville-Petre, 2nd ed., 1960, p. 21).

2/193 *Þessi sveit* implies that the prophetess had some attendants with her, like the one in *Örvar-Odds saga* who was accompanied by fifteen boys and fifteen girls (the plural *völvur* at line 191 is clearly used in a generic sense, and in the following episode there is no question of there being more than one prophetess at Virfill's house). Since they are not mentioned again, however, it seems that the author has taken this detail from his source automatically, without fully assimilating it.

2/201 *á Norðmæri* (*norðr á Mæri* S): the author does not seem to distinguish between *á Norðmæri* (here, cf. also line 221) and *norðr á Mæri* (lines 238, 245; cf. *norðr firir Mæri*, lines 212, 296). In fact there were two districts, Nordmærr and Sunnmærr (now Nordmøre and Sunnmøre), separated by Raumsdalr. The geography of the islands where Ásbjörn died is (perhaps intentionally) vague, though some of the confusion could be scribal.

2/222 *þar* i.e. in Hörðaland, see lines 230, 238. He did not yet venture to Nordmærr.

2/234 The ceremony is described in *Gísla saga* and *Fóstbræðra saga* (*ÍF* VI, 22–3, 125).

2/248 The jarls of Hlaðir (now Lade, near Trondheim in northern Norway) were a powerful family in the tenth and eleventh centuries. Hákon (inn ríki) Hlaðajarl was ruler of Norway from *c.* 974 to 995, though like the other members of his family he never assumed the title of king. After Ásbjörn and Ormr's first visit to Mærr they were engaged on viking voyages for two years, and in the third Ásbjörn made his fatal expedition to Sauðey, and this is said to have been about the same time as Hákon's death (see line 428). The visit to Eyvindr and Bergþórr must therefore be thought of as having taken place in 992.

2/255 On sacred oxen see the article 'Blotnaut' by C. N. Gould in *Studies in honour of Hermann Collitz* (1930), pp. 141–54. *Blótnaut* can mean either '(*a*) a bovine animal destined for sacrifice, or (*b*) one which is the object of worship' (p. 143, n. 15). Animals chosen for the former purpose were usually selected for their massive size, and the latter kind were thought to be imbued with size and strength by virtue of the act of worshipping them (note the use of the verb *verða* here). Cf. *Vǫlsunga saga ok Ragnars saga loðbrókar* (ed. M. Olsen, 1906–08), p. 133. Oxen were particularly associated with the worship of Freyr.

2/268 *vetr hinn þriðja* i.e. since Ormr first came to Norway (cf. *vetr hinn fjórða* line 282).

2/272 *Seiðr* means 'magic, magic rites', particularly those performed to find out the future, but can also refer to the chant or incantation forming part of those rites, and to the song in which the prophecy is expressed; and perhaps to the platform or structure on which prophetesses performed their rites (cf. *ÍF* V, 106). *Á seiði* here could therefore mean 'in her song of prophecy' or 'during her magic rites' or 'as she sat on her seat of prophecy'. *Seiðr* was a particularly disreputable form of magic, generally only practised by women, and considered dishonourable for men to indulge in. For details of the rites involved, besides the episodes referred to above (note to line 190) see *ÍF* V, 99, 105–06, and the full treatment of Dag Strombäck, *Sejd* (1935).

2/273 The line as it stands in F is a syllable short. S inserts *ok* before *saung*, and this gives an acceptable line (an unstressed syllable at the beginning of the b-line is not uncommon in verses of this date, and such lines are also found at 347, 351, 379, 409, and frequently in *Krákumál*, one of the author's models), though 5-syllable lines are also found elsewhere in the verses in this text (lines 403, 405). E. A. Kock (*NN* 2620; *Den Norsk-Isländska Skaldediktningen* II (1949), 197) makes this line more regular by changing *laungum* to *fyr laungu*, but this is hardly justifiable since it alters the sense.

2/277 A similar line appears in a verse in *Landnámabók*, *ÍF* I, 361, verse 29/8.

2/292 *Íslendingaskrá*: see Introduction, p. 27.

2/305 *eigi var hon ok vel eyg*: litotes. This detail is somewhat reminiscent of the description of Grendel in *Beowulf* 726 f.: *him of eagum stod | ligge gelicost | leoht unfæger*. See S. Bugge, 'Studien über das Beowulfepos', *Beiträge zur Geschichte der Deutschen Sprache und Literatur* XII (1887), 59–60.

2/309 There is some discrepancy in the numbers. The cat killed twenty men, and three got away, while earlier (line 295) we were told that Ásbjörn went to the island with twenty-four men. Some seventeenth-century manuscripts alter this first number to twenty-three, but it is probable that lines 295–6 originally read vid *fjórða mann ok tuttuganda*, the usual way of saying that there were twenty-four men including their leader; a copyist may have misread the ordinal as cardinal numbers. The motive of the three men who escaped and sailed away without waiting for their leader has only a slight resemblance to that of the 'faithless companions' in versions of the 'Bear's Son' story (cf. *Beowulf* (ed. Fr. Klaeber, 3rd ed., 1936), pp. xiii–xiv).

2/340 *sem heill bilar*: 'when his good luck deserts him'. But *heill* seems to be used sometimes in a personified sense, implying the notion of 'guardian spirit': 'when his guardian spirit deserts him'. Cf. *Hálfs saga ok Hálfsrekka* (ed. A. Le Roy Andrews, 1909), p. 114:

> Yðr munu dauðar
> dísir allar,
> heill kveðk horfna
> frá Hálfsrekkum.

The concept of *heill* is closely allied to that of *hamingja* (line 461) and *gæfa* (*Hreiðars þáttr*, line 115).

2/341 This method of execution seems to have been quite widespread in the Middle Ages, especially in eastern Europe. In Icelandic sources it is also described in two accounts of the Battle of Clontarf (*Brjánsbardagi*) which was fought in Ireland in 1014 (the execution of the viking Bróðir), see *Njáls saga* (*ÍF* XII, 453) and *Þorsteins saga Síðu-Hallssonar* (*ÍF* XI, 302). The historicity of these accounts is doubtful. According to Saxo Grammaticus (*Gesta Danorum*, ed. A. Holder (1886), p. 403), the same method of execution was used on some vikings who raided Denmark and were captured at Jómsborg during the reign of Erik the Good (1095–1103). Another account is found in Helmold's *Cronica Slavorum*, book I, ch. 52 (ed. J. M. Lappenberg, rev. B. Schmeidler (1909), p. 103), relating to the treatment of Christians by rioting heathen slaves in Wagria and Polabia in the early twelfth century. This form of execution was prescribed in various parts of Germany and eastern Europe in the late Middle Ages as a punishment for damaging trees, see Jacob Grimm, *Deutsche Rechtsalterthümer* (4th ed., 1899), II, 39–40, 269–70. The ferocity of the punishment is probably to be explained by assuming that it had earlier been a punishment for damaging sacred trees (tree-worship is well attested as part of the religion of the ancient Germanic races), and was perhaps understood as the symbolic restitution of the bark of the tree by the offender. In still earlier times the practice, rather than being a punishment, may have been a form of sacrifice to a tree-god. In Christian times the chief fascination of evisceration must have been simply its cruelty, and it has apparently retained this fascination into modern times. According to a tract called *Popish Cruelty, display'd by Facts* (London 1745), p. 10, it was used by 'the Irish Popish Rebels' upon a Scottish protestant in 1641. The author of *Orms þáttr* probably knew of the practice from *Njáls saga* or *Þorsteins saga*.

2/349 *svanhvít* may be an adjective, but it could also be the name of Ásbjörn's mother. Cf. E. H. Lind, *Norsk-isländska Dopnamn* (1905–15), col. 984.

2/354 See textual note. With this line (and the following one) cf. Sigvatr's *Austrfararvísur* 9/1, 'Kátr var ek opt, þá er úti'. E. A. Kock (*NN* 2495 A) suggested taking *inni* as first person sg. pres. tense of the verb *inna* 'to speak of, relate', since the adverb ('inside') is unsuitable to the context in five of the seven verses in which the refrain occurs. But since this line is borrowed word for word from a verse in *Grettis saga* (*ÍF* VII, 52), where *inni* is certainly the adverb, it must be assumed that the reading of S is correct, and that the author of the verses chose the refrain because it expressed his general meaning adequately although it was not entirely appropriate for every verse in which he used it. For similar criticism of a refrain in *Vǫluspá*, see the edition of Sigurður Nordal (1952), pp. 3–8.

2/360 f. Note the rhyme *aungvar—þraungvar*; similarly in the next verse. It is impossible to say whether these two words represent *aungr* a. and *þraung* f. (noun) or *aungvar* f. pl. (noun) and *þraungr* a. The meaning is the same in either case.

2/363 *fóru*: S has *fórum*, which would accord better with the similar lines at 355–6, 387, etc.

2/367 Cf. *leggfjǫturs . . . | lundr í Eyrar sundi*, *Skj.* A I, 308, and *Heimskringla*, *ÍF* XXVII, 289 (Hárekr Eyvindarson, 1027).

In the verse in *Orms þáttr*, *lundr* ('tree') is a half-kenning for 'man'. Kennings for 'man' using *lundr* as the basic word (e.g. *auðar lundr*, *seima lundr*, *hjǫrs lundr* 'tree of riches, tree of the sword') became so common in scaldic verse that eventually *lundr* came to be used on its own as a poetical term for 'man'. The same half-kenning is found in the first verse in *Hrólfs saga kraka* (ed. D. Slay, 1960), p. 8 (*lofðungs lundar*). Half-kennings are quite common in scaldic verses, especially late ones, and are particularly frequent in the verses in *Víglundar saga*, *Gísla saga* and *Kormaks saga*, when they have not been emended out of existence by editors. Certainly in late verses like these in *Orms þáttr* there is no justification for trying to complete such kennings by emendation (Finnur Jónsson in *Skj.* B II, 365 emends line 366 to *hjörs langskipum lagði*; cf. *NN* 184 and R. Meissner, *Die Kenningar der Skalden* (1921), pp. 78 ff.).

2/368 *tældr í tryggðum* hardly accords with the context of the poem since Ásbjörn has not been betrayed by Brúsi.

2/373 Geitir is a giant-name, and 'horse of the giant' is a kenning for wolf. To give drink to the greedy wolf is to shed blood, to fight.

Traditionally the wolf was the mount of giantesses, but in such a late poem this variation is nothing unexpected. It may have arisen from imitation of kennings using a neuter word like *troll*, e.g. *trolls fákr* 'the horse of the troll(-wife)' (*ÍF* XXVIII, 178).

2/374 There is no necessity for Finnur Jónsson's and E. A. Kock's alteration of *rekk* to *rökk* 'it grew dark' (*Skj*. B II, 366; E. A. Kock, *Den Norsk-Isländska Skaldediktningen* II (1949), 198). The second half of the verse reads in prose word-order: *Svinnr seggr gaf raunmargan rekk vargi at dökkri rómu, ok nam höggva sárt at Ífuminni*: 'the wise (keen) warrior (Ormr) gave many a man to the wolf (i.e. killed them) in the dark battle, and did strike hard at the mouth of the Ífa'.

2/377 The river Ífa is not identifiable, although it is presumably supposed to be in Gautland if this verse is referring to the expedition of ch. 6. The author probably took the name from *Krákumál* verse 4 (*lǫgðum upp í Ívu*), cf. p. 33, note 1 in the Introduction above. In *Vafþrúðnismál* verse 16 a river-name *Ífing* occurs.

2/380 *tuggu herjans* is obviously a kenning for 'sword', though the literal meaning is obscure. *Tugga* means 'something bitten, a mouthful', and *úlfs tugga* 'the mouthful of the wolf' is an accepted kenning for 'sword', referring to the story of how a sword was wedged in the mouth of the wolf Fenrir, see *Edda Snorra Sturlusonar* (ed. Finnur Jónsson, 1931), p. 37. Herjan is a name of Óðinn, but it may here be intended as a synonym of *úlfr* ('the ravager', cf. *herja* 'to harry'), or it may be a scribal corruption of a word meaning 'wolf'. R. Meissner, in *Die Kenningar der Skalden* (1921), p.150, suggests *hergarmr* 'dog of battle'. Cf. *NN* 2495.

2/381–2 *skerjum Elfar* must refer to Elfarsker, though for two halves of a compound to be placed in different half-verses is unparalleled in scaldic verse. Although the apparently intransitive use of *forma* here is very unusual, E. A. Kock's suggestion (*NN* 2495) that *elfar* should be taken as the object of this verb ('create rivers' i.e. of blood) is hardly acceptable, since the compound Elfarsker is so common (it occurs several times in *Örvar-Odds saga*, one of the author's sources for these verses), and the words *suðr í skerjum* would be meaningless on their own. The departure from normal metrical usage is not really surprising in a poem of this date;

there is also no grammatical break between the two halves of verse 11. Cf. also Einarr Skúlason's *Geisli*, verse 17 lines 1–2: *á Stikla | víðlendr stǫðum* ('. . . at Stiklastaðir', *Skj.* A I 462). See K. Reichardt, 'A Contribution to the Interpretation of Skaldic Poetry: Tmesis', *Old Norse Literature and Mythology, A Symposium*, ed. E. C. Polomé (1969), pp. 200–226.

2/384 Miðjungr is among the names of giants listed in manuscripts of Snorri's *Edda*, but the meaning of *Miðjungs traustir mágar* here is obscure. It may be intended as a kenning for 'warriors', or, if Miðjungr is a personal name, it may refer to a story about Ormr that the author of the *þáttr* has omitted to tell us. It is also possible that *Miðjungs* is a scribal error for *miðlungs* ('middlingly trustworthy' i.e. 'untrustworthy'), but the reference would still be obscure. It is further conceivable that 'Miðjungr' refers to Þórálfr.

2/410 Although a line with only three syllables is perhaps an acceptable licence in a poem of this date, it is probable that the author intended *Ormr* to be pronounced with two syllables (*Ormur*). The development of a epenthetic vowel *u* between a consonant and final *-r* took place in Icelandic about the end of the thirteenth century.

2/428 AD 995. Óláfr Tryggvason was the first king of Norway to attempt to Christianise the country methodically, and he was also instrumental in bringing about the acceptance of the new religion in Iceland.

2/434 It is odd that Ormr should be made to sail from Reyðarfjörðr, which is on the east coast of Iceland, rather than from somewhere in the south or west near his home.

2/441 *Prímsigning* (Latin *prima signatio*) was a sort of preliminary baptism, where the sign of the cross was made over a person. After submitting to this ceremony men were allowed to associate with both Christians and heathens, being neither completely committed to Christianity nor completely divorced from heathendom. The author probably imagined Ormr to have been baptised during the mission of Þangbrandr to Iceland in 997, when several of the leading men of the country were converted (see *Íslendingabók*, ch. 7).

2/461 *Hamingja* is often conceived as a personal entity (cf. *heill* line 340 and *gæfa*, *Hreiðars þáttr*, line 115). Víga-Glúmr's *hamingja* comes to him from his maternal grandfather on the latter's death and takes the form of a gigantic woman in a dream, and is thus a sort of guardian spirit watching over the fortunes of a family, see *Víga-Glúms saga* (ed. G. Turville-Petre, 2nd ed., 1960), p. xi. In Ormr's case it is probably intended to be understood as the spiritual power invested in him by baptism, even a guardian angel, which is set against the supernatural powers of darkness that are on Brúsi's side (*trollskapr*).

2/469 *Sauðey* sc. *hina ýtri*, since she already possessed the lesser Sauðey.

2/471 Ormr cannot marry Menglöð because she is not a Christian, and she cannot become Christian because of her nature, being half a troll. Compare the story of the cairndweller Brynjarr in *Þorsteins þáttr uxafóts* (*Flb*. I, 255), who, although by his nature unable to receive the benefits of baptism, yet thinks it may do him some good if his name is given in baptism to another person.

2/475 I.e. to the other island, Sauðey hin ýtri, where Brúsi lived. Part of the reason for Ormr's success on his expedition (besides the advantage of his Christianity) was that he chose to go to Menglöð's island first.

2/484 It is not apparent what the significance of this action is. The decorations or patterning on the sword (implied in the prefix *mála-*, cf. *Víga-Glúms saga* (ed. G. Turville-Petre, 2nd ed., 1960), note to 14/33) perhaps included runes with magical power, or the sword may have had a cross-shaped hilt (in the Faroese ballad *Brúsajökils kvæði*, which is derived from *Orms þáttr*, verse 64, the hero cuts a cross in the door of the cave); so the laying down of the sword in the entrance may be an act of magic to prevent the escape of the trolls or to prevent more coming in and attacking Ormr from the rear. In one version of *Heiðreks saga*, Svafrlami uses a *málajárn* to prevent two dwarfs from escaping (the verb used is *vígja*). See *The Saga of King Heiðrek the Wise*, ed. C. Tolkien (1960), p. 68. Alternatively Ormr may simply leave his sword behind to leave his hands free, or because he knows that such weapons will be useless against trolls (as they are against Grendel, *Beowulf*, lines 801 ff.).

2/518 *þegar ek heyrða þín getit*: presumably referring to Ásbjörn's mention of Ormr in verse 12, with its threat of vengeance. Compare the reaction of King Ella when the dying Ragnarr loðbrók revealed in a similar verse that vengeance could be expected to be taken on his slayer, see *Vǫlsunga saga ok Ragnars saga loðbrókar* (ed. M. Olsen, 1906–08), p. 159.

2/526 This method of execution seems to have been particularly associated with vengeance for the slaying of a father. Examples are Torf-Einarr's vengeance for his father Rǫgnvaldr on Halfdan háleggr (*ÍF* XXXIV, 13), the vengeance for the death of Ragnarr loðbrók by his sons on King Ella (*Ragnars saga*, ed. cit., p. 168; also related by Saxo Grammaticus, *Gesta Danorum* (ed. A. Holder, 1886), p. 315), and Sigurðr the dragonslayer's vengeance for his father Sigmundr on Lyngvi (*Reginsmál* verse 26). In later stories, like *Sigurðar saga þǫgla*, in *Late Medieval Icelandic Romances* II (ed. Agnete Loth, 1963), 127, where the phrase is *rísta uglu*, and refers to an act of torture, not an execution, the practice seems to be described simply for its sadistic appeal. In *Orms þáttr* it is Ormr's answer to Brúsi's method of killing Ásbjörn, and the author seems to have had a particular interest in strange methods of taking life. In origin the practice is almost certainly a form of sacrifice to an eagle-god, probably Óðinn (who assumes the form of an eagle in the story told in *Edda Snorra Sturlusonar* (ed. Finnur Jónsson, 1931), p. 85; cf. also the eagle that hovers over Valhǫll, *Grímnismál*, verse 10). In *Orkneyinga saga* Torf-Einarr is said to give Hálfdan to Óðinn *til sigrs sér* ('in order to bring himself victory'). On another interpretation of the origin of the phrase *rísta blóðǫrn* see Roberta Frank, 'The blood-eagle again', *Saga-Book* XXII, 287–9; 'The blood-eagle once more. B. Ornithology and the interpretation of skaldic verse', *Saga-Book* XXIII, 81–3.

2/540 Eirekr was the son of Hákon inn ríki (cf. line 248). Together with King Óláfr of Sweden and King Sveinn of Denmark, he was one of the chief opponents of Óláfr Tryggvason at his last battle (Svöldr, AD 1000). After the latter's death the kingdom of Norway was divided between the three victors, though the actual government was left chiefly to Eirekr and his brother jarl Sveinn. Eirekr was the more dynamic of the two and was the virtual ruler of Norway until about 1013 when he went to England to support King Knútr. During this time most of Óláfr Tryggvason's work in Christianising Norway was undone, although both Eirekr and his brother were nominally Christians (see *ÍF* XXVI, 370–72). In the following episodes of the *þáttr* Ormr is clearly being set up as a champion of the dead Óláfr Tryggvason among the enemies who succeeded him.

2/548 The two benches in a Norse hall were along the longer walls, and the 'higher' bench was the one facing the sun, i.e. on the north wall (cf. *Msk.*, p. 289). The king's (or jarl's) high seat was in the middle of the hall halfway along this higher bench, and the seats closest to the high seat were the most honourable, while those nearer to the ends of the tables were lower in rank (Óláfr kyrri, 1067–93, is said to have been the first Norwegian king to introduce the custom of having the high seat at the gable end of the hall, on a cross-bench, *Msk.*, p. 290). Ormr was given a seat on the higher bench, but *útarliga*, that is down towards the end of the hall near the door, a position of rather low rank. This is probably the reason for his quietness and aloofness (lines 548–9).

2/552 The gallant defence of Ormrinn langi ('the Long Serpent'), King Óláfr's flagship in his last battle, against overwhelming odds, is described, among other places, in *Heimskringla* (*ÍF* XXVI, 357 ff.).

2/554 Cf. Oddr Snorrason's *Saga Óláfs Tryggvasonar* (ed. Finnur Jónsson, 1932), p. 231: *Þessi orrosta* (i.e. at Svǫldr) *hefir verit frægst á Norðrlǫndum, fyrst af vǫrn drengiligri, er Ormrinn var variðr, ok því næst af atsókninni ok sigrinum, er þat skip var hroðit er engi maðr ætlaði at unnit myndi verða á vatni fljótanda.*

2/569 *Skeið* is often used synonymously with *dreki* or *langskip*, but usually refers only to large warships with sixty or more oars, as opposed to the smaller *snekkja*. See H. Falk, 'Altnordisches Seewesen', *Wörter und Sachen* IV (1912), 104–05.

2/573 *Berlingsáss* is not recorded elsewhere in Icelandic, though there are several cognate words in other languages which all mean some kind of beam or pole, see Carl J. S. Marstrander, *Bidrag til det norske Sprogs Historie i Irland* (1915), 21–2, 132; *OED*, s.v. *barling*. It was probably some part of a ship's equipment, perhaps the same as *beitiáss*, 'tacking boom', the boom on the lower edge of a sail. Cf. Introduction, p. 25 above.

2/574 The length of an ell has varied considerably at different times and in different places, but in Iceland in the Middle Ages it seems to have been about 48 cm. This would make Ormr's club about 20 foot long.

2/582 *Hreytispeld(i)* is not recorded elsewhere and the meaning is unknown. 'Top' (the child's toy) would fit the context, but is difficult to justify by the etymology. *Speld(i)* is a small flat piece of wood, *hreyta* means 'to scatter'. The compound might mean something like a chip of wood such as flies from an axe, or perhaps a piece of wood used as a shovel or spatula. It could even refer to an equivalent of the English 'tipcat'. *Sem hreytispeldi* therefore may mean 'like a small piece of wood, as if it were a mere splinter'. But Helgi Guðmundsson has suggested that *hreytispeldi* might mean 'bull-roarer' (cf. *hrjóta*, 'roar'), i.e. 'a flat slip of wood a few inches long . . . fastened by one end to a thong for whirling it round, when it gives an intermittent whirring or roaring noise' (*OED*). This would fit the context perfectly. See Helgi Guðmundsson, 'Hreytispeldi', *Gripla* III (1979), 224–6.

2/594 *Í Þrándheimi* goes with *þar* (locative), not *verit*. Þrándheimr nearly always means the district (now Trøndelag) rather than the town (now Trondheim) which in the Middle Ages (until the fifteenth century) was called Niðaróss (an attempt was recently made to revive this name) or Kaupangr. Gimsar is in the Þrándheimr district, and so the meaning must be 'to the place where he had been before, (which was) in Þrándheimr'. The events of the previous episode were also localised in Þrándheimr (at Hlaðir, see line 541). Of course it is difficult to say how clear an idea the author of *Orms þáttr* had of the geography of Norway.

2/606 The rulers of Norway used to travel round the landowners in succession (*fara at veizlum*), and these were obliged to provide for the king or jarl and his retinue for a certain length of time each. This was a form of taxation which formed a substantial part of the royal revenue. Cf. *ÍF* XXVII, 100.

2/608 According to *Flb*. I, 520, Eirekr gained possession of the ship after the battle of Svölðr, and when he had sailed it back to the Vík he had it broken up ('but some men say that he had it burnt') because it had a list and would no longer steer properly. In its time Ormrinn langi was reputed to have been the biggest ship ever built in Norway (see *Flb*. I, 433).

GLOSSARY

Ö, ǫ, and ø are treated as a single letter, and so are æ and œ.

Words that appear in both texts are glossed under the spelling used in *Hreiðars þáttr*. When such words are spelt very differently in *Orms þáttr* a cross reference is included under the later spelling. Words that appear in only one of the texts are glossed under the spelling used for that text. When words glossed under their spelling in *Orms þáttr* may be difficult to identify, the usual normalised thirteenth-century spelling is added in brackets.

Words, phrases, and meanings that appear only in the verses are preceded by †.

All words in the texts are glossed except common pronouns, but only select references are given. 1 before a line-number refers to *Hreiðars þáttr*, 2 to *Orms þáttr*.

The following abbreviations are used:

a.	adjective	*n.*	neuter
abs(ol).	absolute(ly)	*neg.*	negative
acc.	accusative	*nom.*	nominative
adv.	adverb(ial)	*num.*	numeral
art.	article	*ord.*	ordinal
aux.	auxiliary	*o-self*	oneself
comp.	comparative	*p.*	past
conj.	conjunction	*pers.*	person
dat.	dative	*pl.*	plural
def.	definite	*poss.*	possessive
e-m	einhverjum	*pp.*	past participle
e-n	einhvern	*prep.*	preposition(al)
e-s	einhvers	*pres. (p.)*	present (participle)
e-t	eitthvert	*pret.-pres.*	preterite-present
e-u	einhverju	*pron.*	pronoun
f.	feminine	*rel.*	relative
gen.	genitive	*sg.*	singular
imp.	imperative	*s-one*	someone
impers.	impersonal	*s-thing*	something
indecl.	indeclinable	*subj.*	subjunctive
inf.	infinitive	*subst.*	substantive
interrog.	interrogative	*sup.*	superlative
irreg.	irregular	*sv.*	strong verb
m.	masculine	*vb.*	verb
md.	middle voice	*wv.*	weak verb

-a *neg. suffix used with verbs*: *era* is not 1/21, *muna* will not 1/64, *væria* would not be 1/72.

á (1) *prep*. (1) w. acc. (motion) to, in, on, at; into 1/121; onto 1/227, 2/310. (2) w. dat. (rest) at, in, on 1/80, in place-names 2/184 (cf. **í**). (3) as adv. in this (matter) 1/166; on it, on board 2/587; *spenar eru* ~ there are teats on it 1/413.

á (2) *f*. river.

á (3) 1/110, 458 see **eiga**.

áðan *adv*. a little while ago 1/43; just now, just 1/168.

áðr *adv*. before; first 1/145; previously 1/347; ~ (*en*) as conj. (often followed by subj.) before 1/40, 375, 2/609.

af *prep*. (with dat.) from 2/357; of (partitive) 1/71; away from; off 1/141, 291; by 1/225, 2/54, 252; because of 2/5; on the part of 1/243 (see **þverra**); ~ *því* for this reason 2/28, as adv. from 2/108; *þaðan* ~ see **þaðan**.

afbragð *n*. paragon, superior; ~ *annarra manna* an outstandingly fine person, a most unusual person (ironic) 1/38; *hvert* ~ *Ormr var annarra manna* what an exceptional person O. was 2/139.

afgangr *m*. excess, surplus; *með afgaungum* to spare 2/97.

afglapi *m*. idiot 1/32.

afl *n*. strength; *at afli* in strength 1/6; *hafa* ~ *við e-m* to have the strength for s-one, to be a match for s-one 2/466.

aflafátt *a. n.* wanting in strength, in the phrase *e-m verðr aflafátt* one is not strong enough 2/468.

aflamunr *m*. difference in strength, *svó var þeirra mikill* ~ so great was the difference between them in strength 2/323.

afletja (-latta) *wv*. to dissuade, speak against, be against s-thing 2/257.

aflraun *f*. trial of strength, a game involving strength 1/241; a feat of strength, 2/54, 162, 483.

áfram *adv*. forward, onward.

afskipti *n. pl*. dealings (with s-thing); *veita sér engi* ~ *um* not to concern o-self with, have nothing to do with 1/111.

aftr see **aptr**.

ágangr *m*. aggression, annoyance, teasing, horseplay 1/235.

áheyrsli *a. indecl*., *verða* ~ to get to hear (of s-thing) 1/86.

akfæri *n. pl*. driving-tackle 2/48, see note.

ákvæðisteigr *m*. 2/82, see note.

aldr (*gen*. **aldrs**) *m*. age; *á unga aldri* as a boy, when he was young 1/105; *tvítögr at aldri* twenty years old 2/150; maturity, manhood: *þegar at* ~ *færðist yfir hann* as soon as he came of age 2/217.

aldri *adv*. never 2/335; intensive neg. (without reference to time) not at all (cf. **hvergi**) 1/46.

aldrigi *adv.* never.
alin (*pl.* **álnar**) *f.* ell 2/574.
all- *intensive prefix* very.
alláræðislítill *a.* of very small courage; *eigi ~* by no means lacking in pluck 1/430.
allgóðr *a.* very good, very successful 1/218.
†**alllítt** *adv.* very little, i.e. not at all 2/403.
allmikill *a.* very great 2/433.
allnær *adv.* very close 1/226.
allr *a.* all, every; *allir* everyone 1/31, 2/429, †we all 2/387; complete 1/232 (see **annarr**); whole 2/180, 458, 509; *þann dag allan* the whole of that day 2/71; *hafi þik allan troll* may the trolls carry you off entire (i.e. altogether) 1/415; *n. as subst. allt* everything; *þessa alls* of all this, of all these events 2/83; *með ǫllu* in everything, in every way 1/430; *því ǫllu betra sem* all the better in that 1/270; *with sup. allra helzt* most of all, especially 1/241; *n. as adv. allt* completely entirely, altogether; *upp allt at* right up to 2/510; *allt í milli fjalls ok fjöru* right from the mountains to the shore 2/12.
allrífligr *a.* very profitable, likely to be rewarding (particularly used of journeys); *þó at eigi sé allrífligt* though the mission may not be a very rewarding one 1/400.
alls *conj.* since.

allstarsýnn *a.* with fixed gaze: *vera ~* to stand staring 1/81.
†**allstórr** *a.* very big; *pl. as subst. allstórir* the mighty ones 2/363.
allundarligr *a.* very strange 1/440.
allvel *adv.* very well; very good, very nice 1/154; *taka ~ við e-m* give s-one a hearty welcome 2/246.
álpun *f.* foolery, clumsy way of walking; *við ~ Hreiðars* with H. rushing about like that 1/79 (not recorded elsewhere; cf. modern Icelandic *álpa(st)* to walk clumsily, fool around).
alþingi *n.* the Icelandic annual general assembly.
alþýða *f.* the people, the general public; *ok þat er eigi sé í alþýðu viti* and which is not publicly known, obvious to all 1/161.
andlit *n.* face; *bíta í ~ e-m* bite s-one in the face 2/491.
annarr *pron. and ord. num.* (1) another, other 1/28; any other 1/23; *annars staðar* elsewhere; *í öðrum stað* see **staðr**; *allr annarr maðr* a completely new man 1/232; *aðrir* others, other people 1/128; *annat* anything else, otherwise, any different 1/368; †*annat var* it was different, things were different 2/354. (2) the second 2/17; *vetr annan* for a second winter 2/535; *til annars dags* until the next day 2/476. (3) one (of

two): *á aðra hǫnd mér* on one side of me, at my side 1/294; *með annarri hendi* with one hand 2/166; *annarr . . . annarr* the one . . . the other: *auga þitt annat . . . annat* one of your eyes . . . the other 1/170; *annarri hendi . . . en annarri* with one hand . . . and with the other 2/495; *hvórr skyldi annars hefna* the one should avenge the other 2/235; *hverr at öðrum* one after the other 2/307.

annask (að) *wv.* to take care of; ~ *sik* to look after o-self 1/107.

aptr, aftr *adv.* back, backwards 2/516; again 2/598.

árferð *f.* season, harvest; *segja mönnum firir* ~ tell men what the harvest would be like 2/192.

árla *adv.* early.

armr *a.* poor, wretched (as a term of contempt) 2/241.

áróss *m.* river mouth, estuary 2/8.

aska *f.* ash, ashes 2/529.

áss *m.* a beam of wood, pole 2/65.

ástríki *n.* affection, love 2/33.

at (1) *conj.* that 1/250; in order that 1/249; so that 1/455, 2/94 (see note); inasmuch as 2/553; *þat bjarg . . .* ~ such a rock . . . that, i.e. a rock of such a size that 2/464; *þar til . . .* ~ at the point of the story . . . where 2/225; pleonastic *hversu seint* ~ how slowly 2/552; as rel. particle (= **er**) 1/185, 2/255, 467 (1).

at (2) *particle with inf.* to, in order to; ~ *fara* (permission) to go 1/255.

at (3) *prep.* (with dat) at, in, to; up to 2/126, 127; towards 2/487; engaged in 1/374; †in (battle) 2/371, 374, 408; ~ *hǫfðinu* head first 1/324; according to 2/234; ~ *því sem (er)* according to what 1/185, 195; ~ *því er ek hygg* in my opinion 1/409; ~ *því* because of this, as a result of this 1/261; as adv. in it, in this 1/311; *ekki* ~ *minna gaman* no less fun for that, even more fun because of that 1/91.

atgervi *f.* accomplishments 2/223.

átján *num.* eighteen.

atsókn *f.* attack, offensive 2/553.

átt, átti 1/4, 314 see **eiga**.

átta *num.* eight.

auðsénn *a.* obvious, clear 2/52.

auga *n.* eye 1/170.

aung- see **engi**.

†aungvar (ǫngvar) *f. pl.* straits; ~ *þraungvar* narrow straits 2/360 (see note).

aurskór *m.* horseshoe; ~ *einir* a set of (four) horseshoes 2/156, see note.

austr *adv.* in the east.

axla (að) *wv.* to shoulder, raise and put on the shoulder 2/609.

báði see **bæði** and **báðir**.

báðir (*f.* **báðar**, *n.* **bæði, báði**) *pron. pl.* both.

bak *n.* back; *á* ~ backwards; *ganga e-n á* ~, *brjóta e-n á* ~

aftr (*um e-t*) bend s-one over backwards (over s-thing) 2/496, 516; *á baki honum* on his back 2/526.

bálkr *m.* partition, interior wall; screen 2/324 (apparently about shoulder high, cf. line 505).

†**banadægr** *n.* death-day 2/338.

bani *m.* death 2/213, 583; *ganga til banans* to go to one's death 1/395; cause of death, slayer; *verða e-m at bana* to kill s-one 2/91.

banna (**að**) *wv.* to forbid; *absol.*: *þó at hann banni* even if he forbid it 1/272.

bardagi *m.* battle 2/267.

batna (**að**) *wv.* to improve, get better; *tók ekki at ~* began to get worse (rougher) 1/313.

beiða (**dd**) *wv.* to ask (*e-s* for s-thing), demand 1/351; md. *beiðask e-s* to ask for s-thing for o-self 1/112.

bein *n.* bone.

bekkr *m.* bench.

bendi *n.* rope, a piece of rope used as a harness for carrying a bundle of hay 2/114.

bera (**bar**) *sv.* to carry 2/84; bring; *svó mikit . . . sem ek bæra* as much as I could carry 2/121; *var þá inn borit* then it (the hay) was carried in 1/136; *~ upp* to pass up 2/40, bring forward, make public 1/55; *~ eld at* make a fire, light a fire 2/529; impers. there is brought, there comes (involuntarily) 1/208; *bar saman fundi* (acc. pl.) *þeirra* they happened to meet 2/230; *~ til* to happen; *ok beri sva til at* for then it might happen that 1/260; *~ við* to happen; *í . . . því er við berr* involving whatever may happen, whatever it involves 1/400. Md. †betake o-self, travel 2/210; *berask við* to pass by, be prevented, be avoided 1/263; *berask at* to happen; *hversu at hafði borizt um e-t* how s-thing had come about 2/425.

berja (**barða**) *wv.* to hit, beat 1/24; *~* **á mǫnnum** assault people 1/22.

berlingsáss *m.* pole, spar, boom 2/573, see note.

bestill *m.* a nickname, apparently derived from *bast* n. bast, bark 2/238.

betr *adv. comp.* better; *þess ~ er, er meir líðr fram hans ævi* it gets better the older he gets 1/464; *því ~ er* 1/61, see **síðr**.

betri *a. comp.* better 1/441, 2/451; n. as adv. *era þér þá betra* it will not then be better (easier) for you 1/22.

beygja (**gð**) *wv.* to bend (transitive) 2/161.

bezt *adv. sup.* best; *en mér þætti ~ at* but which it seems to me best should 1/263; †*~ mun at þegja* it will be best to be silent 2/214.

beztr *a. sup.* best 1/273; finest;

veizla hin bezta a very fine feast a special celebration 2/194.
bíða (beið) *sv.* to wait, wait for (with gen.).
biðja (bað) *sv.* to ask (*e-n e-s* s-one for s-thing); *with inf.* to ask s-one to do s-thing, tell s-one to do s-thing 2/41, 79; to order 2/577, 580.
†**bila (að)** *wv.* to give way, fail 2/340.
bíta (beit) *sv.* to bite 2/491; †to pierce, cut 2/407.
bitbeinn *n.* bone of contention (*e-m* for s-one); ~ *þér eða þeim er* a bone of contention between you and those who 1/455.
bjarg *n.* rock, boulder 2/464.
bjarga (barg) *sv.* to save (with dat.). Impers. *varð þá borgit flestum öllum mönnum* nearly all the men were rescued 2/578.
bjó see **búa**.
bjóða (bauð) *sv.* to offer, proclaim, preach: *bauð öllum rétta trú* preached the true faith to all 2/429.
†**blakkr** *m.* poetical word for (a dun-coloured) horse 2/372.
blása (blés) *sv.* to blow (a trumpet): *blásit er* a trumpet (a fanfare) is blown 1/50.
blíðliga *adv.* joyfully, in a friendly way, pleasantly 1/88.
blíðskapr *m.* friendship; often in pl. *vóru með þeim blíðskapr* there were friendly relations between them 2/89.

blóðrás *f.* flowing of blood, loss of blood 2/514.
blóðörn *m.* blood-eagle (the shape of an eagle cut on s-one's back with a sword) 2/526 (see note).
blótnaut *n.* a sacrificial or holy ox 2/255 (see note).
bogi *m.* bow.
bóndi *m.* farmer; yeoman, freeholder 2/197; master of the house; (in direct address) master, sir 2/198; (in apposition to a name) *Stórólfr* ~ farmer S. 2/137; *Virfill* ~ master V. 2/193.
borð *n.* table.
borgit *pp.* of **bjarga**.
bót (*pl.* **bœtr**) *f.* remedy; in pl. compensation (for the death of a slain man) 1/351.
brá see **bregða**.
bráðr *a.* quick; n. as adv. *brátt* soon 1/37.
bragða see **brögð**.
bregða (brá) *sv.* to move, put, draw (with dat.); ~ *í hagldirnar* thread (the rope) through the buckles 2/130; ~ *hendinni* slip one's hand, move one's hand quickly 2/169; ~ *saxi* to draw a sword 2/526. Impers. *e-m bregðr mjök við* one is much taken aback by 2/305. Md. *bregðast við* to jerk o-self away, pull back quickly 2/506; †*bregðast e-m* to fail s-one, be unable to save s-one 2/337.
†**breiðr** *a.* broad 2/208.
brenna (brann) *sv.* to burn (intransitive) 2/304.

brenna (d) *wv.* to burn (transitive) 2/529.
breyta (tt) *wv.* to alter, change; ~ *orðum við e-n* to speak to s-one in different ways, try various approaches on s-one 1/236.
brjóta (braut) *sv.* to break 2/497; wreck (a ship) 2/577; ~ *upp hurð* break down a door 1/392; ~ *e-n á bak aftr um e-t* 2/516, see **bak**; ~ *hlið á* break down an opening in (a wall), break a hole in it 2/126. Md. *brjótask á hurðina* hurl o-self at the door, hammer on the door 1/387; *brjótask út* try to break out 1/391.
bróðir (*pl.* **brœðr**) *m.* brother.
brotna (að) *wv.* to break (intransitive), be broken 2/50.
brott (**á** ~, **í** ~) *adv.* away; *vilja á* ~ to want to get away, to want to get out 1/388.
brottu (**í** ~) *adv.* away, off 2/64; gone away 1/329.
brún (*pl.* **brýnn**) *f.* brow, eyebrow.
†**brýna (d)** *wv.* to sharpen 2/406.
†**brynpálmr** *m.* corslet-palm (tree) (kenning for sword) 2/406.
brögð *n. pl.* trick, device, stratagem; *ef aungra bragða væri í leitat* if they did not find some way out of the difficulty 2/96.
brögðóttr *a.* crafty, cunning, wily 1/343.
bú *n.* household, farm; *setja* ~ *saman* set up house; *setjast í* ~ settle down 2/617.

búa (bjó, bjuggum, búinn) *sv.* (1) prepare 1/9; equip; ~ *sik* fit o-self out (*at* with), clothe o-self, attend to one's personal appearance 1/223. (2) live, dwell 1/462, 466, 2/19, 85, 197. (3) pp. *búinn* ready 1/33; *munu* ~ will be ready, eager 1/453; *þeirrar farar* ~ prepared to make that journey 2/242; fitted out, dressed 1/123; *vel* ~ finely attired 2/443; *vel at afli* ~ gifted with great strength 1/6; *vel at íþróttum* ~ good at sports, highly accomplished 2/31; *við svá búit* thus, without more ado, while matters stand thus 1/422. (4) Md. *búast* prepare o-self, get ready 2/437; ~ *til* get ready for, set out on 2/537.
búð *f.* hut, temporary dwelling (used during the sessions of the Alþingi by those attending it); *vera í* ~ *með e-m* to be in s-one's hut, to stay with s-one for the period of the assembly 2/154.
búningr *m.* outfit, dress; *skipask margir menn vel við góðan búning* decent clothes often change a man for the better 1/223.
†**burr** *m.* poetical word for son; *Stórólfs* ~ kenning for Ormr 2/365.
burt(u) *adv.* = **brott(u)**.
búsifjar *f. pl.* relations between neighbours, neighbourliness; *veita e-m þungar* ~ to be a bad neighbour to s-one, to make

being a neighbour a misery for s-one 2/451.
byggð *f.* settlement; district, neighbourhood 2/97, 106; †dwelling 2/369.
byrðr *f.* burden, load 2/118, 144; *hann skyldi hafa byrði sína* he could have as much as he could carry 2/105.
byrgja (**gð**) *wv.* to shut in, lock in 1/374.
†**byrhestr** *m.* 'wind horse', kenning for ship 2/209.
bæði, báði *n.* of **báðir** *as conj.* both.
bœr (*gen.* **bœjar**) *m.* farm 1/360, 2/85; town, city 1/35.

dagr *m.* day; *um daginn* during the day, later in the day 2/140, 163; *seint dags* late in the day 2/296; *til annars dags* until the next day 2/476; *í dag* today, at the present day 2/83; in pl. days, lifetime, reign 2/247.
dáit *pp.* of **deyja**.
dála *adv.* very, very well, completely; *ekki ~ er þat* not all that well 1/108.
dauðr *m.* death; *rífa til dauðs* tear to death 2/308.
dauðr *a.* dead; *ætla e-n dauðan* think that s-one is dead 2/424; *Hakon jall ~* earl H. (was) dead 2/428; *geingr af henni dauðri* leaves her lying dead 2/498.
detta (**datt**) *sv.* to fall, drop; *hvórt þegar dettr líf ór mér* whether I shall immediately drop dead 2/241.

deyja (**dó**) *sv.* to die.
digr *a.* thick.
digrð *f.* thickness; *báði at leingd ok ~* see **leingd**.
dimmr *a.* dim; *e-m er dimmt firir augum* it is too dark for s-one to see, s-one's eyes are not used to the darkness 2/312.
dó see **deyja**.
dofna (**að**) *wv.* to go numb; *e-m dofnar hǫndin* one's hand goes numb 1/78.
Dofrafóstri *m.* fosterling of Dofri 2/5 (see note).
dóttir *f.* daughter.
draga (**dró**) *sv.* to draw, pull: *~ undir* to pull underneath 2/129; *~ (boga) firir odd* to pull the bow past the point of the arrow, i.e. draw the arrow back until the point is behind the bow 2/597; †*nú mun segg á síðu sverðs egg dregin verða* now the edge of the sword will be drawn against (i.e. will pierce) the warrior's side 2/353; *~ á sik* put on, pull on (gloves) 2/481; *~ af e-m* take away from s-one, deprive s-one of 1/20. Impers. *er í tók at ~ skúrirnar* when the storm clouds began to gather, when the rain became imminent 2/42; *tók at ~ at heyjum hans* his stocks of hay began to diminish 2/94. Pp. *dreginn mjök* half starved 2/102. Md. *dragask* to go on, to turn out 1/307.

dráp *n.* slaughter, killing; *af drápi Hildiríðarsona* because of his killing the sons of H. 2/5.

dreingiligr (**dreng-**) *a.* valiant, heroic; *hversu . . . dreingiliga vörn* what a valiant defence 2/551.

dreingskapr (**dreng-**) *m.* manliness, nobility of character 2/418; *með litlum dreingskap* with little manhood 2/528.

drekka (**drakk**) *sv.* to drink; *sitja ok ~* to sit drinking 2/271.

drepa (**drap**) *sv.* to strike, kill 1/326, 415, 2/309; *~ at ferligu* see **ferligr**.

drykkja *f.* (1) drinking, the act of drinking: *sitja í drykkju* to sit drinking, sit over one's drink 1/378. (2) drinking feast, banquet 2/269.

duga (**ð**) *wv.* to be of use; pull one's weight 2/44; *~ vel e-u* to be of benefit to s-thing 2/136.

dylja (**dulða**) *wv.* to conceal, deny 1/383.

dyrr *f. pl.* doorway, entrance, opening; *ór dyrunum* away from the entrance 2/483.

dœma (**ð**) *wv.* to judge, decide (a case) 1/53.

†**dökkr** *a.* dark 2/374.

eða, eðr *conj.* or; and 1/221; but 1/99, 192; *þó at . . . ~* even if . . . or if 1/273.

ef *conj.* if; provided that, as long as 2/201; in case 2/463.

efni *n.* material (to work with) 1/372.

eftir see **eptir**.

†**egg** *f.* edge 2/353.

eggja (**að**) *wv.* to urge on 2/43; to goad 2/52.

†**ei** *adv.* not 2/347.

eiga (**átta**) *pret.-pres. vb.* (1) to have; *hann átti sér* (refl. pron., pleonastic) *bróður* he had a brother 1/4; to own, possess 1/110; *ef þú átt þetta eigi* if you do not possess these qualities 1/167; †*gramir eigi* may the trolls take 2/279; *~ bardaga* to fight a battle 2/267; to have as wife, to be married to 2/20, 23; to get, beget (a son) 2/29. (2) *~ við* to have to do with, to have dealings with; *at því at ~ við hann* from his company 1/238; *at þér muni þvílíkt við mik at ~* that your relationship with me will be the same 1/268; *við fjándr slíka at ~* to have dealings with such fiends 2/258. (3) Impers. *átti með þeim illan enda* things came to a bad end between them 2/89. (4) With inf. to be obliged to; *ef hann á at ráða* if it is left to him to decide (what will be your fate), if he has to decide 1/458; *~ at ráða firir* to be ruler (governor) over 2/183; *~ at mæla eftir* see **mæla**.

eigi *adv.* not; *~ er þat* that is not so 2/563.

einart *adv.* continually, on and on; *gekk* ~ kept going on his own, went right on 2/343.

eing (**eng**) (*pl.* **eingjar**) *f.* meadow, hayfield 2/58 (see note).

eingi see **engi**.

einhamr *a.* single-shaped; *eigi* ~ having more than one shape, able to change one's shape by magic 2/27 (see note), 87; *sá er* ~ *hefir verit* of those who have not had supernatural powers 2/181.

einkum *adv.* especially, particularly.

einn (*f.* **ein**, *n.* **eitt**) *a.*, *num.* and *pron.* (1) one, a certain 1/374, 2/8; ~ *dag* one day 2/37; *í einu* all together, at once, at the same time 2/161; *í einum stað* in the same place 1/257. (2) only one 1/172; single 1/112; *þat eitt* only that, that alone 1/222; *þat eina* only that 2/141; *þik einn* only you 2/462. (3) alone, on one's own 1/64, 275, 2/323, 360, 568, 612. (4) Pl. *þær einar eingjar af Stórólfshvóli* only those fields at Stórólfshvóll, those (are) the only ones of the fields at S. that 2/81; *aurskór einir* a set of (four) horseshoes 2/156.

einnhverr *a.*, *pron.* some, a certain; *eitthvert sinn, einhverju sinni* on one occasion, at some time, once; *þat er sagt einnhvern dag at* it is said that one day 2/57.

einrænligr *a.* singular, odd; *með einrænligu móti* of a peculiar kind 1/445.

eira (**ð**) *wv.* to spare (with dat.); impers. *hversu honum eirir* how he would get on 1/275.

ekki (**1**) *adv.* not.

ekki (**2**) *a.*, *pron.* (*n.* of **engi**) no, nothing, none 2/146, 298; *varð* ~ *af ferðinni* nothing came of the expedition, the expedition was abandoned 2/259; with partitive gen. ~ *vópna* no weapons 2/581.

elda (**ld**) *wv.* to heat, smelt; ~ *grátt silfr* to quarrel 2/88 (see note).

eldaskáli *m.* living-room, kitchen; *ekki lagðist Ormr í eldaskála* O. did not lie about in the kitchen (like the idiot boy of popular tales), he was not an idiot 2/35.

eldr *m.* fire; *bera eld at* to light a fire 2/529; in pl. flames 2/304.

elli *f.* old age; *til* ~ until old age, all the rest of his life 1/466, until he became an old man 2/197.

ellidauðr *a.* dead from old age.

elligar *adv.* otherwise.

ellri *a. comp.* older; *sem hann var þá* ~ as he got older 2/179.

en *conj.* but, and; *after comp.* than.

enda *conj.* and indeed, besides, moreover 2/34.

endi *m.* end 2/612; conclusion; *illr* ~ a bad end 2/89; *á enda* right to the end, completely 2/343.

engi, **eingi**, **øngi**, **aungi** *a.*, *pron.* no, none; no one 1/148, 2/333,

583; *at øngu* by no means, in no way 1/377; *með øngri sætt* without reaching agreement 1/352; *vildi við aungan af standa* would part with it to no one 2/98.

enn *adv.* still 2/83; longer: †*vera* ~ continue to be 2/277; even so; further, also 2/57; ~ *þótt* even if 1/384; †again, once again 2/372; with neg. yet 1/132; with comp. still, even (more) 1/329, 412.

eptir, eftir *prep. and adv.* (1) with acc. ~ *þat er* as conj. after 2/291. (2) with dat. after; in pursuit of 1/419; *senda* ~ *e-m* send for s-one 1/119. (3) with dat. according to 1/463; in accordance with 1/346; ~ *því sem segir* as is related, according to what is written 2/292. (4) as adv. †behind 2/385 (see **liggja**); back 1/26; *vera* ~ to be left behind; *þat eina* (*var*) ~ only that remained 2/141; *fara* ~ to follow 1/67; *koma* ~ come up, catch up 1/82; *frétta* (*spyrja*) ~ enquire 1/379, 2/601; *hér* ~ afterwards, in a moment, now 1/446.

er *rel. particle* and *conj.* who, which, that; when 1/26, 242, 344, 2/72; since 1/37, 394; where 1/59, 61 (2); while 1/67, 234, 302; as; now that 1/131; ~ *svá er* that it is so 1/190; after comp. as, in proportion as 1/61 (1), 441 (1), 464 (2) (see **betr**).

era see **vera**.

erfiðr *a.* difficult, hard; *nokkut erfitt* something unpleasant 2/518.

erriligr *a.* of lively appearance, spry, virile, athletic 2/443.

ey (*dat. sg.* **ey** or **eyju**, *pl.* **eyjar**) *f.* island.

eygr *a.* having eyes (of a certain kind); *eigi var hon vel eyg* she did not have very nice eyes 2/305.

eykr *m.* beast of burden or draught animal; horse 2/39, 47.

eyra *n.* ear.

eyrendi (cf. **ørendi**) *n.* (1) mission, purpose; ~ *þitt* your purpose in coming, reason for coming 2/453, 546. (2) the fruit of an errand: *skaltu* ~ *hafa* you shall have something for your pains, you'll get what you came for 2/319.

eystri *a. comp.* more easterly.

fá (**fekk**) *pp.* **fenginn, feinginn**) *sv.* (1) to get, take; receive 2/146; *hey* (acc.) *kunni hvergi at* ~ hay was nowhere to be obtained 2/97 (see **kunna**); ~ *e-t af e-m* get s-thing from s-one 2/101; ~ *vald yfir* conquer 2/267; ~ *sér e-t* provide o-self with s-thing, get o-self s-thing 2/64; ~ *e-n hǫndum* take hold of s-one 1/322; ~ *e-n til* to find s-one for s-thing, get s-one to do s-thing 2/575. (2) ~ *e-m e-t* give s-one s-thing, provide s-one with s-thing 2/61; *er Hreiðari fenginn hestr* H. is provided with a horse 1/277; to give back 1/372 (2). (3) with pp. to be able to, manage to (do s-thing); *ekki fær þú mik lattan* you cannot stop me, dissuade me 1/64; *at hann fekk unnit* in managing to defeat (see **at (1)**) 2/553.

faðir *m.* father; *systkin at föður* see **systkin**.

faðmr *m.* (a measure of length) fathom, *c.* six feet; *annarr fjögurra faðma* one four fathoms long 2/110.

fága (að) *wv.* to clean; ~ *sik* to clean o-self up 1/231.

fagna (að) *wv.* (with dat.) to greet; ~ *e-m vel* to welcome s-one; impers. *var e-m vel fagnat* s-one was made very welcome 2/194.

fala (að) *wv.* to ask to buy; *falaði af honum hey* asked to buy some hay from him 2/103.

fall *n.* fall.

falla (fell) *sv.* to fall; fall in battle, die 1/350; ~ *á kné* kneel down 1/124. Impers. to suit, agree; *fell vel á með þeim* they got on well together 2/231.

fallinn *a.* (*pp.*) (with dat.) suitable, a good thing (for s-one) 1/15.

fang *n.* the breast and arms, the chest; *framan í fangit* straight into his chest, against the front of his body 2/489.

far *n.* means of transport, ship; passage: *taka sér fari* (dat.) get a passage (*með e-m* on s-one's ship) 2/227, 434.

fár (*f.* **fá**, *n.* **fátt**) *a.* few; n. as subst. little; *kvað fátt verra* said there was not much that was worse 2/258; *fátt veit sá er søfr* (proverb) a sleeping man notices nothing 1/42; coolness: *var heldr fátt með þeim* they were not on friendly terms 2/98; *finnask fátt um* see **finna**; with partitive gen. *fátt manna* few men 1/204.

fara (fór) *sv.* (1) to go; with suffixed pron. †*færik* I would go 2/275; travel 1/31, 2/199; sail 2/363; ~ *á sæ*, ~ *á skipi* sail; †~ *fjörð* sail (down) a fjord 2/356; ~ *yfir land* travel around the country 2/190; to move, be passed around 1/407, 2/158. (2) leave, go away, depart 2/280; *fari hann eigi* let him not go 1/281; go forward, carry on 1/77, 286; ~ *burt með e-t* to go away taking s-thing, take s-thing away 2/530. (3) ~ *með* to handle, interfere with 2/602; ~ *at* to go by, take notice of: *at því fer ek meir sem nú er* I consider what is now more important, I am more interested in the way things are now 1/106; ~ *verr* see **verr**. (4) Impers. ~ *fram* to happen, be carried out 1/321; *hvernug farit hefir* how things have gone, what has happened 1/425; *hversu ferr* how things will go 1/296; *hversu þat ferr* how that will turn out 1/452; *er svá hafði fram farit* when things had gone on like this 1/312; *e-m ferr vel* things go well with one, one gets on well; *má honum vel vera farit* he may be a fine person, he may have good qualities 1/103.

fáskiftinn *a.* taking little interest in things, aloof, quiet 2/548.

fast *adv.* firmly, hard 2/43; energetically 2/507; insistently, strongly 2/104; very much, exceedingly, quickly 2/94, 514.

fastr *a.* firm; *vera ~ fyrir* stand firm 1/306; held fast, stuck fast 2/504.

fatla see **fetill**.

fé (*gen.* **fjár**) *n.* property, money.

feðgar *m. pl.* father and son.

feigð *f.* the state of being about to die, the approach of death; fate, doom; *~ kallar at e-m* fate is calling to s-one, one's death is imminent, one's hour has come 2/331.

feigr *a.* fey, on the point of dying, doomed; †*færik á feigum fæti* I would go on doomed feet, i.e. my steps would lead me to my doom 2/274; *comp. at ek sé eigi þar feigari en hér* that I shall be no closer to my death there than I am here 2/203.

feinginn, feingu, fekk see **fá**.

feldr *m.* cloak.

fella (**d**) *wv.* to cause to fall; kill; *~ fénað* to kill off cattle 2/95, 137.

felldr *a.* fitting, suitable, a good thing (*e-m* for s-one) 1/260; *betr ~* more suitable; *ek em þér vel ~* I am a very suitable person for you (to employ) 1/398; *ekki vel felld* not wise, not sensible 1/456.

fémætr *a.* worth money, valuable; *þat sem meira var fémætt* everything else of value 2/532.

fénaðr *m.* cattle, livestock.

fenginn see **fá**.

ferð *f.* (1) journey, expedition 2/259; *vera kominn á ~* to be started on one's way, to be off 1/278; *gera ~ sína* to set out 1/354; *eigi heptir þetta ferðina mína* this will not stop me going 1/283. (2) †a group of men travelling, an army (cf. Old English *fierd*) 2/379 (dat. sg.).

ferligr *a.* monstrous; n. as subst. *drepa at ferligu* to make into something monstrous, give excessive importance to 1/210.

fernir *distributive num.* (Latin *quaterni*), but often used as a cardinal num. four 2/39 (v.l. *iiii*).

fet *n.* pace, step 2/613.

fetill *m.* strap (by which s-thing is carried); *í fatla* into harness (referring to the ropes tied round the hay) 2/131.

fimm *num.* five.

fimmtán *num.* fifteen.

fimmti *ord. num.* fifth.

fingr *m.* finger.
finna (fann) *sv.* to find; discover, realise 1/237, 242, 334; notice 1/172; ~ *til* mention, bring forward, suggest 1/169; ~ *at e-m* find fault with s-one, find s-thing wrong with s-one 1/181; *máttu nokkvot at* ~ can you find any fault 1/160. Md. *finnask* to meet each other 1/249, 292; *vér finnumk* we (i.e. Magnús and Haraldr) are bound to meet, cannot help meeting, we continually meet 1/343. Impers. *e-m finnsk fátt um* one is little pleased, one thinks little of 1/320; *fannsk honum mikit um* he was very impressed by this 2/134.
firir see **fyrir**.
firna (að) *wv.* to blame; ~ *e-n um ef* to say s-one will be doing wrong if 1/31.
fjall *n.* mountain; *milli fjalls ok fjöru* from the mountains to the shore.
fjándi (*pl.* **fjándr**) *m.* fiends, devils.
fjándligr *a.* devilish, fiendish.
fjándskapr *m.* hostility, hatred.
fjár see **fé**.
fjara *f.* shore, beach.
fjárskakki *m.* unequal share of money 1/19.
fjórði *ord. num.* fourth.
fjórðungr *m.* quarter 2/64 (see note).
fjórir *num.* four.
fjúka (fauk) *sv.* to be driven, to fly, be blown; ~ *fyrir* to give way before s-thing 1/305.
fjölkunnigr *a.* having knowledge of many things, especially of magic; skilled in magic 2/28.
fjǫlmenni *n.* crowd, host of people; following, band of supporters 1/420.
fjǫlmennr *a.* crowded, with many people; well attended 2/151; *n. as adv. er fjǫlmennt væri* where there were a lot of people about 1/61.
fjörðr *m.* fjord; †*fara fjörð* to sail a fjord, by fjords 2/357.
fleinn *m.* weapon with a long thin point or blade; javelin 2/501.
fleiri *a. comp.* (of **margr**) more.
flestr *a. sup.* (of **margr**) most; *sem flestir menn* as many people as possible 1/59; *flestir allir menn* nearly all the men 2/579.
fletta (tt) *wv.* to strip; ~ *e-n klæðum* to strip the clothes off s-one 2/322.
fleygja (gð) *wv.* to throw, fling; *fleygir þegar í brott* immediately flings it down 1/413; ~ *e-u af sér* to throw s-thing (clothing) off 1/176.
†**fleyskip** *n.* warship 2/356.
fleyta (tt) *wv.* to lift just off the ground, to raise slightly (with dat.) 2/165.
flokkr *m.* company, troop.
flytja (flutta) *wv.* to carry, convey; take (s-one on a journey) 1/32,

109. Md. *flytjast* travel, get (to a place) 2/426.

†**forðum** *adv.* formerly, in days gone by 2/359.

forlög *n. pl.* fate, destiny, fortune 2/198.

†**forma (að)** *wv.* to create, bring about, achieve; ~ *kólfi* do things with an arrow, use (aim) arrows 2/383.

forn *a.* old, ancient; *at fornu* in ancient times 2/181.

forræði *n. pl.* management, business management; *kunna engi* ~ to know nothing of money-matters or business 1/21.

forspá *f.* prophecy, prediction 2/196.

forvitni *f.* curiosity; *e-m er (mikil)* ~ *á* one is (very) curious (about s-thing); *mun þér ok* ~ *á at vita* you will also be eager to know 2/455.

fóstbróðir *m.* fosterbrother, sworn brother, sworn comrade.

fóstbræðralag *n.* fosterbrotherhood, sworn brotherhood, sworn friendship.

fótr (*pl.* **fœtr**) *m.* foot; *fara undan við fót* take to one's heels 1/80; †*á feigum fæti* see **feigr**.

frá *prep.* (with dat.) from 1/295, 467; off 1/307; ~ *því er* from the time when 2/301; about, concerning 1/1, 159, 2/536; *absol.* about it, about what had happened 1/426; away 2/225.

fráleikr *m.* speed in running, fleetness of foot 1/71.

fram *adv.* forward, on (of time) 1/464; *leggja hest* ~ to race a horse (*hjá* against) 1/286; *fara* ~ see **fara**.

framan *adv.* in front, from the front, on the front side; *firir* ~ as *prep.* (with acc.) in front of.

framaverk *n.* deed bringing fame, distinguished deed 2/200 (see **vinna**).

frammi *adv.* forward; *leggja hest* ~ to race a horse 1/289.

frár *a.* swift, fast-running; *sup. manna frávastr* the fastest of men 1/6.

frétta (tt) *wv.* (1) to ask; *var völvan frétt at forspám sínum* the prophetess was asked to make her predictions 2/196; ~ *eptir* to enquire 1/378. (2) to learn by asking, to hear 2/287.

fríðendi *n. pl.* good things, fine things; *nokkvot til fríðenda* something good (about s-one), a redeeming feature 1/185.

fróðr *a.* wise, learned.

frægr *a.* famous, renowned; *comp.* 2/263.

†**frækn** *a.* valiant, brave 2/365.

frændi (*pl.* **frændr**) *m.* kinsman, relative; *Haraldr* ~ my kinsman H. 1/343.

frændsemi *f.* relationship, kinship; *var betr í* ~ *þeirra* relations were better between them 2/138.

fúlga *f.* a pile of hay (originally a

thin covering or layer of hay, cf. *fela* to hide); the pile of hay waiting to be thrown up onto the haystack 2/46.

fullr *a.* full (*af* of) 2/531; full up 2/136.

fundinn *pp.* of **finna**.

fundr *m.* meeting, conference 1/290; *beiðask fundar e-s* to ask to meet s-one 1/122; *á fund e-s* to see, speak to s-one 1/251, to meet 1/417; *á yðarn fund* to meet you, into contact with you 1/115; *hans fǫr á konungs fund* his interview with the king 1/218; *bera saman fundi* see **bera**.

furða *f.* wonder, miracle; *e-m þykkir ~ í* one thinks it amazing, one is amazed.

fúss *a.* eager; anxious (to do s-thing) 2/257; sup. *þess var ek fúsastr at* what I wanted most was to, my greatest desire was to 1/337.

fylgja (**lgð**) *wv.* (with dat.) to accompany; keep up with 1/285, 290; *fylgi* (3rd pers. sg. or pl. optative) *Hreiðari heim* let s-one take H. home 1/281; *fylgir sú náttúra* this quality pertains to them, they have this quality 2/467.

fylgjusamr *a.* closely following; *vera e-m ~* to stick close to s-one 1/294.

fylla (**d**) *wv.* to fill; *~ upp af e-u* to fill up with s-thing 2/164.

fyrir, **firir** *prep.* (1) (with acc.) in front of 1/125, 402, 411; in the presence of 1/209; before, up to 1/124, 396; to the attention of 1/54; *ganga ~* go before, go into audience with 1/87; *~ sik* into his presence 2/560; in return for, in payment for 1/24, 351, 460; *draga ~ odd* see **draga**; *~ þetta* for this reason 1/290; *~ margs sakir* for many reasons, in many ways 1/399. (2) (with dat.) in front of 2/596; *verða ~* see **verða**; *~ munni sér* see **munnr**; off, off the coast of 1/447; *norðr ~ landi* off the coast to the north 2/249; *norðr ~ Mæri* in the north off the coast of Mærr 2/212, northwards along the coast of M. 2/296; for, because of 2/256; *~ sǫkum* (with gen.) because of 1/5 (see **vit**); *~ því at* as conj. because 1/241; *mikill ~ sér* important, influential 1/463. (3) Absol. as adv. in front 1/121; in the way, within range 2/584; *þar ~* already there, in the way 1/420; previously, first 2/133; *segja ~* prophesy, foretell 2/191; in exchange, in payment 1/454, 2/117. (4) In prep. or adv. phrases of place: prep. (with acc.) *~ neðan* below 2/287, *~ framan* in front of 2/326, *~ útan* on the outside of, on the west side of 2/11; adv. *~ sunnan* on the south side, on the south coast 2/7.

fyrirgera (**ð**, *pp.* **-gǫrr**) *wv.* to

forfeit; ~ *sér* forfeit one's legal rights (to compensation for injury or death) 1/349.

fyrr *adv. comp.* earlier, before 2/225; before now 1/172; on a previous occasion 2/594; ~ *en* as conj. before, until, right up to the moment when 2/522; *eigi ~ en* not until 2/422; *ekki mun ek ~ upp gefast en* I shall not give in before 2/572.

fyrri *a. comp.* former, earlier 1/466.

fyrst, fyst *adv.* first 2/113; at first, in the first part (of the poem) 1/440, in the beginning 1/445; most of all 1/59.

fyrsta, fysta *f.* beginning; *í fyrstu* at first.

fyrstr, fystr *a. sup.* first.

fýsa (t) *wv.* to urge; md. to be eager; *fýstist norðr* became eager to go north 2/294.

fyst(-) see **fyrst(-)**.

fœða (dd) *wv.* to give birth to 2/14; rear, bring up; md. *fœðask upp* be brought up, be alive 1/182.

fœra (ð) *wv.* to bring, carry; move 2/482; convey, send 1/318; put 2/464; ~ *niðr* throw down 1/323, 2/314; ~ *e-t í* let s-thing in, fix s-thing on 2/66; ~ *saman í múga* pile up in heaps 2/78; ~ *hey saman* pile hay up, make haystacks 2/38; *fœrðr í reikuð* see **reikuðr**. Md. *fœrast undir í* put o-self down into, get down into, put on 2/130; *þegar at aldr fœrðist yfir hann* as soon as he came of age 2/217.

fœri *p. subj.* of **fara**.

fœrr *a.* able (to do s-thing); *til þess ~* capable of this, having the power to do this 1/148.

fœti *dat. sg.* of **fótr**.

fǫðurarfr *m.* inheritance from a father, patrimony.

fǫr *f.* journey 1/65; expedition 2/242; going 1/218 (see **fundr**), progress 1/92 (see **ógreiðr**); *í ~ með* with, along with 1/94; *þar er bróðir minn í ~* I've got my brother with me 1/96; *leyfa þér þessa fǫrna* permit you to go there 1/259. In pl. (1) expedition, travels 2/423, 431; *hafa sik í fǫrum* to spend one's time in travel 2/218. (2) trading voyages: *vera í fǫrum* to be engaged on trading voyages, 'in trade' 1/7 (cf. *farmaðr* merchant); *hafa í fǫrum* to have invested in trade 1/17.

fǫruneyti *n.* company; *eigi í hans ~* not in company with him 1/273; *koma annars staðar til fǫruneytis* fall into the company of others 1/274.

gagn *n.* gain, profit, booty 2/262; advantage, use; *koma e-m at gagni* to be of use to s-one, help s-one out 2/106.

gamall *a.* old, *tólf vetra ~* twelve years old 2/36.

gaman *n.* pleasure, fun; *honum*

GLOSSARY

þætti it mesta ~ at he thought it the greatest fun 1/311; *ekki at minna ~* no less fun for that 1/91; *henda ~ at e-u* to get fun out of s-thing 1/238; *hafa e-t at gamni* treat s-thing as a joke, do s-thing in fun 1/210.

ganga (gekk) *sv.* to go; walk, go about 1/120; go on 2/311, 479; *gátu líta hvar Hreiðarr gekk* got to see where H. was, saw H. walking about 1/301; †*nú er ek geinginn* now I am come 2/361; *svó at hvergi gekk* so that it would not move at all 2/504; *láta ~ e-m e-t* strike (let fly at) s-one with s-thing 1/308; absol. *geingu* were being used, were in use 2/38; as aux. †*gekk at veita* went and gave, did give 2/372. With preps. and advs. *~ á e-t* to walk into s-thing 1/120; *~ e-n á bak* bend s-one over backwards 2/496; *~ at* go up, approach 2/165; *~ firir* to give ground, give way 2/515; *~ inn í* to enter 2/126; *~ með* to accompany; *gekk hér með holdit* the flesh went with it, this took with it the flesh 2/510; *~ með e-t* walk with s-thing, take, carry s-thing 2/133, 613; *~ til* go up, approach 1/392; *~ til Róms* make a pilgrimage to Rome 2/493; *~ undir* to help to lift (s-thing), put one's shoulder to (s-thing) 2/609. Impers. *e-m geingr* things go for one, one gets on 2/74; *e-m geingr lítt* one is getting on slowly, one is not getting on very well 2/59.

gapa (t) *wv.* to gape; *með gapanda ginit* with mouth wide open 2/486.

garðr *m.* (1) an enclosure; yard, farmyard, hay-yard (cf. **heygarðr**) 2/109. (2) In Norway and Denmark usually refers to a house or premises in a town 2/229.

gat *n.* hole, opening 2/325.

gaungumannliga (gǫngu-) *adv.* like a beggar, meanly; *þetta er ~ til látit* that is a beggarly offer 2/116.

gefa (gaf) *sv.* to give; *svó mikit var gefit sem ek bæra* as much was given as I could carry, i.e. the offer was for as much as I can carry 2/121; *sagði . . . (sc. at honum væri) meir gefinn vöxtr en afl eðr harka* said . . . that he was more gifted with size than strength or endurance 2/45; *~ á* press forward, exert o-self to the utmost, make an extra effort 2/515; *upp ~* give up, leave off 2/79; *~ mik upp sjálfan* surrender my independence, lose my security 1/19; *~ sik við* to show concern, show signs of distress; submit, beg for mercy 2/522. Impers. *nú gefr vel til* now it has turned out well 1/281. Md. *upp gefast* give o-self up, give in 2/572; *gefask*

ekki at grandi take (s-thing) in good part, take no offence 1/242; impers. to turn out 1/288.
gegnum, í ~ *prep. with acc.* through.
geil *f.* glen, small valley; the narrow passage between adjacent buildings or between two haystacks 2/49.
geinginn, genginn *pp.* of **ganga**.
gera, gøra (ð; *pp.* **gǫrr, gerr)** *wv.* to make 1/403; do; cause to be 1/465; treat 1/308 (see **harðleikinn**); perform, carry out 1/399, 2/178; *verða at hlœgi gǫrr* to be made a laughing stock 1/225; *svá er nú gǫrt* this is now done 1/230; *skal gera* there shall be made, we shall make 2/568; *illa gerðir þú þat* that was an evil thing to do 2/523; *gera sér* make for o-self; *gerði sér* (sc. *orfit*) *mátuliga hátt* made the handle the right height for himself 2/66; *gera e-m veizlu* to make a feast for s-one 1/377; with suffixed pron. *gerik aðra óvísu þeim er* I perform some other act of hostility against those who 1/22. Impers. of the weather *gerði jarðbönn* 2/93, see **jarðbann**. Pp. *gǫrt* finished 1/375. Md. *gerask* (1) happen, come about, come to be, arise 1/247, 2/231; take place 2/423; *hvat í hefir gǫrzk* what had happened 1/418. (2) get, become 1/462, 2/43, 101, 257, 590; begin to be 2/40.

gerla see **gǫrla**.
gervibúr *n.* store-house 2/123.
gestr *m.* guest; *vera ~ e-s* to stay with s-one 2/546.
geta *f.* guess; prophecy 1/463.
geta (gat) *sv.* (1) to say, mention 1/376; (with gen.) *hǫfðu heyrt getit hans* had heard about him 1/301; *~ um e-t* mention, speak about s-thing 1/27. (2) guess; *at því er ek get til* according to my guess 1/195; *eigi getr þú allnær at* your guess is far from the mark (if you think) that 1/226. (3) with pp. to be able (to do s-thing) 1/290, 2/75. (4) with inf. to come to do s-thing, to get to do s-thing 1/300.
geysihagliga *adv.* extremely skilfully 1/428.
gin *n.* mouth (of an animal) 2/486.
ginna (t) *wv.* to make a fool of 1/148.
ginning *f.* deception, fooling 1/146 (see **virða**).
†**gjalda (galt)** *sv.* repay; *~ e-m e-t* repay s-one for s-thing, take vengeance on s-one for s-thing 2/415.
gjöf *f.* gift; parting present 2/216.
†**glaðr** *a.* glad, happy 2/278.
gleði *f.* merriment, festivity, merry-making 2/269.
gleypa (gleyfta) *wv.* swallow 2/307.
glíkligr *a.* likely, probable.
glíkr *a.* see **líkr**.
glíma (d) *wv.* to wrestle 2/514.

glófi *m.* glove 2/467.

gnógr *a.* enough, plentiful; n. dat. as adv. *gnógu mart* quite enough, quite a lot 2/243.

goði *m.* chieftain, priest 2/21 (as a nickname).

góðr (*n.* **gott**) *a.* good, fine; n. as adv. *er gott at senda þik* you will be a good person to send 1/408; *e-m er gott at heyra* it will be pleasant for s-one to listen to 2/198.

gómr *m.* palate; in pl. gums; *e-m berr mart á góma* many things spring to one's lips, one brings up all sorts of things 1/208.

†**gráðugr** *a.* greedy 2/372.

gramir *m. pl.* fiends, trolls 1/394; *gramir eigi* may the trolls have (take) 2/279.

grand *n.* injury; *gefask at grandi* to take offence at 1/243.

grár *a.* grey; *grátt silfr* drossy silver, impure silver 2/88 (see **elda**).

gras (*pl.* **grǫs**) *n.* grass; vegetation, plants, pastures 1/448.

grasgóðr *a.* having a rich crop of grass 2/70.

greiðr *a.* clear, free from obstacles, easy; n. as adv. *þat gekk þeim ekki svó greitt sem* they did not get on with this as well as 2/74.

greip (*pl.* **greipr**) *f.* grip, grasp; *ganga í greipr e-m* to fall into s-one's clutches 1/260.

greppliga *adv.* fiercely, horribly 2/511.

gretta (**tt**) *wv.* to make a face, screw up one's face; *grettir vaskliga* (he) screws up his face in manly fashion 1/233 (see note); md. *grettast greppliga* to screw up one's face horribly, frown fiercely, pull a horrible face 2/511.

griðkona *f.* female servant, farm-girl 2/71.

†**grimmliga** *adv.* horribly, terribly, cruelly 2/414.

grimmligr *a.* fierce-looking 2/303.

grípa (**greip**) *sv.* to grasp, seize; ~ *upp* snatch up, seize 2/47; ~ *í móti e-u* grasp at s-thing, snatch, catch s-thing 2/502. Md. *grípast til* to get to grips, take hold of one another 2/513.

gripr *m.* a thing of value.

grópasamliga *adv.* (not recorded elsewhere, meaning uncertain) boastfully or energetically, uncouthly (v.l. in A and H: *kappsamliga* vehemently) 1/287.

guð *m.* God.

gull *n.* gold.

gyltr *f.* sow 1/413.

gylla (**d** and **t**) *wv.* to gild 1/403.

gæði *n. pl.* good things; advantage, profit, income 2/255.

gæfa *f.* luck, good fortune 1/115.

gæfir *p. subj.* of **gefa**.

gægjast (**gð**) *wv.* to peep, bend the head over s-thing to see, stick the head up 2/504.

gæta (**tt**) *wv.* (with gen.) take care

of, guard; *at þín verði gætt* that you will be safe 1/342.

gæti *p. subj.* of **geta**.

göfugr *a.* noble, of high rank; sup. *göfgastr* highest in rank, most distinguished 2/22.

gøra, gǫrr, &c. see **gera**.

gǫrla, gerla *adv.* fully, completely; clearly 1/133; exactly 1/194.

háð *n.* mockery, insult, *til háðs var gǫrt* it had been done as an insult 1/413.

hadda *f.* handle (of a pot or cauldron) 2/168.

háðung *f.* insult 1/429.

haf *n.* open sea, ocean.

hafa (ð) *wv.* (1) to have, take 1/16, 2/112; accept 2/107; receive 2/33; get 2/255. (2) to put; ~ *sik at e-m* set on s-one, attack s-one 2/488; ~ *í* put in 2/132; ~ *sik í* spend one's time on, engage in 2/218; *hǫfðu þeir hann til skógar* they took him off to a wood 1/303; ~ *e-n sendan* cause s-one to be sent, send s-one 1/401. (3) as aux. with pp. 1/36, 48, 72 &c.

hagldir *f. pl.* buckles (for fastening harness in which hay was trussed) 2/124.

†**hagliga** *adv.* skilfully 2/383.

hagr *a.* skilful; *vera* ~ to be a craftsman, be an artist 1/197.

haka *f.* chin 2/509.

halda (helt) *sv.* (1) to hold, keep; ~ *vel trú sína* remain a good Christian 2/618; *helt á* he held on (to them) 2/159; ~ *e-m eptir* hold s-one back, stop s-one from going 1/25; ~ *e-n fyrir e-m* protect s-one from s-one 1/341; md. *at þeir haldisk á* that they should continue holding on to each other 1/79. (2) to set one's course, steer, sail, make one's way 2/259, 261, 296, 310, 475, 477; ~ *eptir e-m* give chase to s-one 1/421.

hálfr *a.* half; *hann á allt hálft við mik* all we own is our common property 1/110; *hálfu meiri* twice as much 1/17.

hamingja *f.* luck; sometimes personified, a guardian spirit 2/461 (see note).

handfár *a.* short-handed; *handfátt varð upp at bera* there were not enough people to pass it up 2/39.

handkrœkjask (kt) *wv.* to join hands, link arms 1/76.

hár (*n.* **hátt**) *a.* high.

harðleikinn *a.* playing a rough game; *gera e-m hardleikit* treat s-one roughly 1/308.

harðr *a.* hard; strong, mighty 2/553; n. as adv. *hart* fast 1/67; heavily 2/315. Comp. tougher, having more endurance 2/328.

harka *f.* toughness, endurance 2/45

harmdauði *a.* lamented, causing sorrow by one's death; *var hann fám mönnum* ~ his death did not break many hearts 2/289.

harmkvǫl *f.* torment, torture; *með svó miklum harmkvölum* in such great agony 2/320.

hátta (að) *wv.* to arrange, dispose; *hversu bogi hans var til háttaðr* what had been done to his bow 2/601; impers. with dat. *þar var svó háttat landslegi at* there the lie of the land was such that 2/69.

háttr *m.* manner, kind; *kvæðit mun vera með þeim hætti sem ævi þín* the poem is similar to your life, your life will go like the poem 1/444; *þess háttar menn sem hon er* people like her, her sort of person 2/243.

háttung *f.* danger, risk; *~ er ǫðrum á* there is a danger to others in this, others are in danger 1/166.

haust *n.* autumn.

hefja (hóf) *sv.* to lift; *~ upp* to begin.

hefna (d) *wv.* to avenge, take vengeance for (with gen.) 1/428; *hvórr skyldi annars ~* each was bound to avenge the other 2/235.

heiðr *f.* heath, moor; *firir neðan heiði* below the heath, on the coast at the foot of the moor (i.e. Mosfellsheiðr) 2/287.

heilagr *a.* holy; *hinn heilagi Petrus* St Peter.

heili *m.* brain.

†**heill (1)** *n.* or *f.* (good) luck 2/340.

heill (2) *a.* whole, in good health; *mæl ~, seg ~ sǫgu* speak in health, say what you say in health, i.e. well said, bless you for saying that 1/192, 196.

heilsa (að) *wv.* (with dat.) to greet.

heim *adv.* (towards) home 2/351; *sækia ~* see **sækia**.

heima *adv.* at home; living at home, not away (although not necessarily in the house) 2/595; *var hann ~ jafnan* he always stayed at home, he never travelled, i.e. he was inexperienced (cf. the nickname *inn heimski* 'the foolish', sometimes applied to Hreiðarr in late manuscripts and modern editions) 1/7.

heimill *a.* free, at s-one's service; *~ er (þér)* you are welcome to 1/203.

heimta (mt) *wv.* to claim (*e-t at e-m* s-thing from s-one) 2/145.

heita (hét) *sv.* (1) intransitive (pres. tense *ek heiti*) to be called; *Þórðr hét maðr* there was a man called Þórðr 1/2; *Ingunn hét kona hans* his wife was called I. 2/14. (2) with dat. (pres. tense *ek heit*) to promise; *því hét hann* he promised this 1/29; *~ e-m at* to promise s-one that 2/350; *~ á* to invoke; *~ á guð at* to invoke God and vow, to make a vow before God (to do s-thing) 2/492.

heituhús *n.* brew-house, brewery 2/164.

hel *f.* the abode of the dead; *færa e-n til heljar, koma e-m í hel* to kill s-one 1/319, 2/456.

heldr *adv. comp.* (1) rather, instead; rather than this 1/276; *ek mun vera þér í sinni* I prefer to be on your side (i.e. than on Brúsi's) 2/470; *ek mun ~ borit fá* (sc. *byrðina*) *en þú* I will be better able to carry it than you (i.e. I will be able to carry a larger load than you) 2/118. Intensifying a comp. *frægri ~ en þeir* more famous than they 2/263. (2) somewhat 1/102, 2/40, 303; rather 1/212.

hellir *m.* cave.

hellisdyrr *f. pl.* opening or mouth of a cave 2/464.

helzt *adv. sup.* most of all, especially; probably, most likely 1/194; *þat ~* that in particular, that more than anything else 1/170; *þar . . . sem þá er hann ~* wherever he is, wherever he goes 2/200.

henda (nd) *wv.* to receive, get (*at e-u* from s-thing); to catch 2/488.

hentr *a.* having hands (of a particular kind); *maðrinn ~ mjǫk* the man had huge hands, was large-handed 1/177.

hepta (pt) *wv.* to hinder, prevent 1/283.

hér *adv.* here; now, on this matter, in this case 1/348, 2/117; *~ er* there is here 1/447; *~ eptir* in a moment, now 1/446.

herbergi *n.* room, chamber; *konungs ~* the king's quarters, the king's antechamber 1/224.

herða (rt) *wv.* to press; *~ at* to insist, press one's case hard 2/104. Reflexive: exert o-self; *hertu þik* buck yourself up 2/122.

herðar *f. pl.* the shoulders 2/131.

herja (að) *wv.* to harry, to make raids.

†**Herjan** *m.* a name of Óðinn 2/381 (see note).

hernaðr *m.* plundering, viking raid; *fara (halda) í hernað* to go on a viking expedition 2/261; *vilja í hernað* to want to go on a viking expedition 2/284.

herra *m.* master, lord, (used in addressing a king or jarl) my lord, sire.

hestr *m.* horse; a load (as much as a horse can carry); *reip á tíu hesta* ten harness-ropes (for tying loads of hay onto horses' backs) 2/124.

hey *n.* hay 2/38, 74, 129, 146; haystack 2/43, 48, 49, 84; *~ hans bæði* both his haystacks 2/14; in pl. stocks of hay 2/94.

heygarðr *m.* enclosure for haystacks; wall round haystacks 2/126.

heykleggi *m.* haycock; used (perhaps ironically) of large haystacks 2/109.

heyra (ð) *wv.* to hear, listen 1/30; listen to 2/198; with suffixed

pron. *heyrðak* I heard 1/43;
~ *sagt* hear it said 1/119; ~ *hans getit* hear tell of him 1/301.

heyverð *n.* the price of the hay, payment for the hay 2/145.

†**Hildr** *f.* the name of a valkyrie; *Hildar stormr* the storm of H., a kenning for battle 2/371.

hingat *adv.* here, to this place.

hinn (*f.* **hin**, *n.* **hitt**) *demonstrative pron.* the other 2/235; the opposite 1/211; *hitt sagða ek* what I said was (not that but) this 2/563; *hitt veit ek at* but one thing I do know is that 1/452; *hitt fann ek* I realised one thing 1/334.

hinnug *adv.* elsewhere 1/213.

hirð *f.* the king's court, the king's men; *með hirðinni* with the court, living with the king's men 1/235; *fara til hirðarinnar* to go and lodge with the king's men 1/215.

hirðmaðr *m.* courtier, (sworn) retainer.

hirðvist *f.* stay, lodging at the king's court; *fara til hirðvistar* to be the king's guest, lodge with the king's men 1/95.

hitta (**tt**) *wv.* to meet, go to see, visit; *hittask* (reciprocal) to meet each other 1/424.

hituketill *m.* cauldron (for brewing ale) 2/163.

hjá *prep.* (with dat.) with, close to; ~ *þeim er* near s-one who 1/211; next to 2/198; near, just outside 2/163; against, in competition with 1/286; with, at the home of 2/222; *sitja* ~ stay with 2/260; *vera* ~ to live with 2/449.

hjálpa (**halp**) *sv.* to help; *til* ~ to lend a hand 2/41.

†**hjarta** *n.* heart, mind; courage 2/339.

hlaða *f.* barn 2/136.

hlaða (**hlóð**) *sv.* (with dat.) to pile up; ~ *heyi* to work on top of a haystack piling it up 2/39.

Hlaðajall *m.* jarl of Hlaðir 2/248.

hlass *n.* load (on a horse or a cart) 2/47.

hlaupa (**hljóp**) *sv.* to run; pounce 2/306, 485.

hlið *n.* gateway, opening in a wall; *brýtr* ~ (*á*) knocks down an opening (in it) 2/126.

hljóta (**hlaut**) *sv.* to receive, get as one's lot; †*bana* ~ to meet death 2/213; *lítit ætla ek þik af honum hafa hlotit* I don't think you have been gifted with much of that 1/72.

hluti *m.* part, share; advantage; *gera sér e-t at mestum hluta* make the greatest capital out of s-thing 1/465.

hlutr *m.* lot, part, share; thing 1/112; matter 2/192; *sá* ~ *er* there is s-thing 1/253; *inn fyrra hlut ævinnar* in the earlier part of his life 1/466; *hlut í at eiga* to become involved 1/22; *hvern Haraldr konungr vill þinn hlut* what King Haraldr wishes your fate to be 1/458.

hlýða (dd) *wv.* to listen to; *at þér hlýddið* that you should listen to 1/437; *~ á* to listen 1/217.

hlœgi *n.* laughter, a source of laughter; *er ~ þykkir í* that is thought amusing 1/207; *verðr síðr at ~ gǫrr af* one is less likely to be made a laughing stock by 1/225.

hlæja (hló) *sv.* to laugh (*við* at) 1/311; pres. p. *hlæjandi* laughing 1/239, with a laugh 1/126.

hóf *n.* moderation, measure; *nær hófi* almost enough, nearly well enough 1/140; limit, bounds; *ætla sér ~ um* see **ætla**.

hóf *p.* of **hefja**.

hógværr *a.* gentle (of character) 1/6.

hold *n.* flesh, skin.

hólmr *m.* small island, islet.

horfit see **hverfa**.

horn *n.* corner; direction; *þá skýtr í tvau ~ með okkr* (idiomatic expression) then we are shooting in two directions, our ideas are very different, we are not in agreement 1/60.

hornblástr *m.* blowing of a trumpet, trumpet-call, fanfare 1/48.

hraustr *a.* valiant, brave.

hreysti *f.* valour, courage 2/418.

hreytispeld (or **-speldi**) *n.* 2/582, see note.

hríð *f.* time, period; *um ~* for a while.

hrífa *f.* rake.

hrinda (hratt) *sv.* (with dat.) to push (about or around) 1/304.

hringr *m.* ring, circle; *þar í hring um* round it in a circle 2/343.

hrjóta (hraut) *sv.* to fly, be flung, bounce 1/307.

hryggr *m.* backbone, back; *taka um hrygg e-m* to take hold round s-one's back 2/496; *brjóta í e-m hrygginn* to break s-one's back 2/497.

hræða (dd) *wv.* to frighten; *vera hræddr um e-t* to be afraid of s-thing, be concerned about s-thing 1/262.

hræra (d) *wv.* to move (transitive) 2/75.

hugi *m.* mind, heart; courage; †*stórr í huga* courageous 2/336.

hugkvæmr *a.* ingenious, perceptive 1/145, 430.

hugr *m.* mind, heart; *~ segir mér (um)* my heart tells me, I have a feeling (about s-thing) 1/295, 2/517.

hurð *f.* door.

hús *n.* house, building, room (the different apartments of a medieval dwelling were often different buildings close together) 1/374.

húskall (-karl) *m.* servant, farm labourer; dat. pl. *húskörlum* 2/59.

hvar *adv.* where; *sá hann ~ kettan hljóp* he saw the cat pouncing 2/485; *~ er* wherever 2/262; *~ ... af* where from 2/107.

hvárt, hvórt (*n.* of **hvárr, hvórr**) *as interrog. adv.* whether 2/240, 327; pleonastic, introducing direct questions 1/56, 107.

†**hvass** *a.* keen, sharp 2/380.

†**hvassliga** *adv.* keenly, sharply 2/407.

hvat *pron. n.* what; ~ *sem (er)* whatever; ~ *er þú ætlar* whatever your opinion is 2/205; (interrog.) with partitive gen. ~ *þeira manna* what men 1/93; with dat. what sort of: ~ *látum var* what sort of noise it was 1/46.

hvé *adv.* how.

hverfa (**hvarf**) *sv.* (1) to turn; *er fyrr var frá horfit* where we left off (the story) 2/225. (2) to vanish 2/473.

hvergi *adv.* nowhere 2/96; as intensive neg. not at all, absolutely not (cf. **aldri**) 1/62; *svó at* ~ *gekk* so that it would not move at all 2/504.

hvernug *adv.* how; ~ *þat er* what it is like 1/332; ~ *þótti þér* what did it feel like 1/334; ~ *skulu vit nú þá* what shall we do now then 1/134.

hverr (*f.* **hver**, *n.* **hvert**) *pron.* each, every, everyone 1/30, 163; each man 2/337; ~ *í byggðinni* each man in the district 2/106; *milli hverra múga* between each of the heaps, from one heap to another 2/83; ~ *at öðrum* one after the other 2/307; *hverjum manni kurteisari* the most courteous of men 2/188; ~ *sem firir yrði* whoever got in the way, i.e. for anyone that got in the way 2/583; interrog. who, which, what 2/139, 452, 601; *hverju var líkast?* what was it most like? 1/44.

hversu *adv.* how; ~ *stóra byrði* how great a load 2/144; ~ . . . *dreingiliga vörn* what a valiant defence 2/551; ~ *seint at* how slowly 2/552, see **at (1)**; ~ *margr* however many 2/253.

hví *pron.* (*dat. sg.* of **hvat**), as adv. why.

hvíld *f.* rest.

hvirfla (**að**) *wv.* to turn s-thing over (hay, so that it dries in the sun) 2/74.

hvóftr (**hváptr**) *m.* jaw; *með hvóftunum* between the jaws 2/488.

hvórgi (**hvárgi**) (*n.* **hvórki**) *pron.* neither (of two things) 2/63; after neg. either; *ór hvórigri eyjunni* from either island 2/256; n. as adv. *hvórki . . . né* neither . . . nor 2/75.

hvórr (**hvárr**) *pron.* each (of two) 2/611; ~ . . . *sá er leingr lifði* that one of the two who outlived the other 2/235.

hvór(r)tveggja (**-tveggi**) (**hvárr-tveggja**) *pron.* each (of two things), both 2/61, 250; *þótti þetta mikil aflraun hvór-tveggja* these were both considered great feats of strength 2/162.

hvórt see **hvárt**.

hyggja (**hugða**) *wv.* to think; *at því er ek hygg* in my opinion 1/410; ~ *at e-u* to consider s-thing, examine s-thing closely 1/412; ~ *um e-n* to feel concern for s-one, have s-one's interests at heart 1/211.

hæð *f.* a small hill, rise 1/80.

hœgr *a.* easy; comp. *eigi er þat enn hœgra* that is no easier, that is not the easier course 1/329.

hæll *m.* peg, handle (of a scythe).

hængr *m.* a nickname 2/3, see note.

hætta (**tt**) (**1**) *wv.* to stop, leave off (with dat.) 2/578.

hætta (**tt**) (**2**) *wv.* to risk; *vill eigi þar ~ honum* refuses to risk his being there 1/461.

höfðingi *m.* chief, man of rank; prince, ruler; man of authority 2/220.

höfðingjaskifti *n.* change of ruler 2/428.

hǫfuð *n.* head; *at hǫfðinu* head first 1/324.

†**högg** *n.* blow; *veita ~* deal blows, fight 2/380.

höggva (**hjó**) *sv.* to strike, cut; ~ *höfuð af e-m* to cut off s-one's head 2/520; ~ *upp* to break up, demolish (a ship) 2/608; absol. †~ *sárt* to deal hard blows 2/376.

hǫnd *f.* hand, arm; *báðum höndum* with both hands 2/506; *milli handa sér* in his hands, with his hands 2/63; *fá hǫndum* 1/322 see **fá**; *með manna hǫndum* from hand to hand 1/407; *á höndum* on one's hands, on 2/468; *á aðra hǫnd mér* on one side of me, at my side 1/294; *í hendr þér* into your hands, over to you 1/386; *af þeira hendi* on their side, as far as they were concerned 1/313.

hörzkr *a.* from Hörðaland; nickname, *hörzki* the Hordlander.

í *prep.* (1) with acc. in, into 1/33; towards 1/60; to 2/126, 259; at 1/245; ~ *dag* today, at the present day 2/83; ~ *sumar* this summer 2/59. (2) with dat. in; on (an island); on, by (a river) 2/228; in place-names, at 2/85 (see note); *Véseti ~ Borgundarhólmi* V. of B. 2/185; ~ *honum* in his body 2/50 (see **rif**); dressed in 1/123; ~ *því* at that moment, just then 2/47; *en ~ þessu er* than is involved in this, than is implied in this (action) 1/429. (3) absol. *þar ~* into it, onto it 2/67.

iðjumaðr *m.* hard-working man; ~ *mikill* a very hard-working man 2/37.

ígjarn *a.* (with gen.) eager for s-thing; *verks ~* keen on work, hard-working 2/37.

illa *adv.* badly; ~ *gerðir þú þat* that was an evil thing to do 2/523; *at* *þú mundir ~ reiðr verða* that when you got angry it would turn out badly 1/339.

illr *a.* bad; *illt er lítill at vera* it is a bad thing to be tiny 1/70; *þykkja e-m illt* see **þykkja**.

†**ímun** *f.* poetical word for battle 2/408.

inn *adv.* in.

inna (t) *wv.* to speak of; *md. innask til um e-t* to discuss, consider s-thing together 1/144.

innar *adv. comp.* further in, towards the inside 2/306; *~ at* further in towards (it), in closer 2/500; *~ at þar er Ormr lá* further in to where O. was lying 2/444.

†**inni** *adv.* inside, indoors 2/354 (see note).

íþrótt *f.* sport, game of skill; feat; accomplishment 2/223; strength, ability; †*sinni ~* one's own strength 2/334.

já *adv.* yes.

jafn *a.* equal; *vóru á allar jafnir* they were equal (just as good as each other) in all of them 2/233.

jafnan *adv.* always 1/7, 53; continually, all the time 1/239, 311.

jafnframmi *adv.* at the same time, simultaneously; *kvað þá vísur þessar ~* he spoke these verses as he went (i.e. the poem lasted as long as his entrails) 2/344.

jafnhátt *a. n.* as *adv.* to the same height as, as high as (with dat.) 2/168.

jafnmæli *n.* fair play, equality; *nú skal ~ með okkr* now we shall be quits 1/173.

jafnröskr *a.* equally brave; *at pína hann svó mjök, jafnröskvan mann* to torment such a valiant man as him so much 2/524.

jafnt *adv.* exactly, precisely 1/338; *svá mun vera ~ þegar er þú segir þat* it is bound to be so if you say so 1/201.

jafnungr *a.* equally young; *~ maðr* such a young man 2/54.

jafnvel *adv.* equally well, so well.

jall (jarl) *m.* earl, ruler either independent or subject to a king; a viceroy.

jarðbann *n.* 'earth-ban,' when the earth is frozen or snowed over so that cattle cannot graze; *gerði jarðbönn* the pastures were snowed over 2/93.

járn *n.* iron.

járnmikill *a.* made of solid iron, solid 2/157.

járnsúla *f.* iron pillar 2/325.

jörð *f.* earth, ground; *við jörðina* near the ground 2/129.

jötunn *m.* giant; *aungvar jötna þraungvar* narrow straits of (i.e. among) the giants 2/361.

-k *first pers. pron.* as verbal suffix I; pleonastic with the second of two co-ordinated verbs having the same subject *gerik* I do 1/22, *heyrðak* I heard 1/43, *mælik* I speak 1/210; in a verse *ek færik* I would go 2/275 (see introduction, p. 18 above).

kaf *n.* plunge, dive (into water); *slá í ~* to sink (transitive) 2/577.

kall (karl) *m.* man (as opposed to woman) 2/154; old man; *Stórólfr ~* old S. 2/49.

kalla (að) *wv.* to call, cry out, shout 1/388; summon 2/560; *~ á* call on, call to 2/40; *~ at e-m* call to s-one 2/331; *~ megi þér svó* you can call me that 2/545; *vera kallaðr* to be said to be, considered, reckoned 1/104, 2/22, 82; *eru þeir landnámamenn kallaðir* they are counted as settlers 2/16; *var kallaðr* was called, was known as 2/24, 86, 189, 191.

kanna (að) *wv.* to explore; †get to know, become acquainted with 2/369.

kápu *f.* cloak 2/169.

kapp *n.* zeal, eagerness; *leggja ~ á* show eagerness (to do s-thing), act with eagerness 2/318.

kappi *m.* hero, champion; *konungs kappar* the picked warriors of the king, comitatus 2/551.

kasta (að) *wv.* to throw 2/48; *~ saman* lay together, fasten together 2/124.

kaupa (keypta) *wv.* to buy (*at e-m* from s-one) 1/453.

kaupmaðr *m.* merchant 2/426.

kemba (d) *wv.* to comb; †*~ e-m svardar láð* to comb s-one's head 2/347.

kenna (d) *wv.* to recognise 1/85.

keppa (t) *wv.* to contend, dispute; *eigi þikki mer þú þar mega um ~* I don't think you are in a position to argue about the matter 2/243.

kerti *n.* candle 2/161.

ketta *f.* she-cat 2/254.

kikna (að) *wv.* to bend over backwards (intransitive); *~ við* to give way by bending backwards 2/490.

kippa (t) *wv.* to snatch, pull sharply; *~ e-u at sér* jerk s-thing towards o-self 2/503.

kirkja *f.* church; *at kirkju* attending church 2/596.

kirkjudyrr *f. pl.* doorway, entrance of a church 2/596.

kista *f.* chest, box 2/531.

kjaftr *m.* jaw; *kjaftarnir báðir* the skin from both upper and lower jaws 2/509.

kjósa (kaus) *sv.* to choose; *sik ~* to choose o-self to be 1/163.

kleggi *m.* cock of hay; stack (cf. **heykleggi**) 2/132.

kló (*pl.* **klær**) *f.* claw.

klæða (dd) *wv.* to clothe; *~ sik* to get dressed 2/299.

klæði *n. pl.* clothes.

knáleikr *m.* prowess, strength 2/149.

knáliga *adv.* energetically, hard 2/422.

kné *n.* knee; *falla á ~* kneel down 1/124.

knýta (**tt**) *wv.* to fasten, tie (*um e-t* round s-thing) 2/342.

†**kólfr** *m.* arrow, bolt (properly a blunt-headed arrow) 2/382.

kolsvartr *a.* coal-black; *sú in kolsvarta ketta* that coal-black cat 2/448.

koma (**kom**) *sv.* (1) (intransitive) to come, arrive 1/36; get to (a place) 2/241; *þar er kominn Brúsi* B. was there 2/316; *at vóri komnu* when spring was come, at the beginning of spring 2/261. (2) (transitive) with dat. to bring; ~ *skipi* bring a ship, sail 2/286; *at ek skyldi aungri vörn firir mik* ~ that I should not manage to put up any resistance 2/331; ~ *sér í skip* to get o-self a passage 2/425; ~ *e-u í brott* remove s-thing 2/466; ~ *e-m í hel* cause s-one to go to Hel, kill s-one 2/456. (3) (intransitive) with preps. and advs. ~ *á* reach, get to, arrive at 1/85, 345; go to 2/201; *kominn á þrítögsaldr* arrived at the age of thirty 2/226; *láta* ~ *á sik* let o-self be dressed in, put on 1/227; *kominn af* descended from 2/221; ~ *at* arrive (at) approach, come to land 2/8, come up 2/47, reach 2/311; ~ *at gagni* see **gagn**; ~ *eptir* come up, catch up 1/82; *vera kominn frá e-m* to be descended from s-one 1/467; ~ *fram* to happen, come to pass 2/519; ~ *í land* come to the country 2/429; *e-t kemr e-m í hug* one has a feeling, a premonition, about s-thing 1/338; *lét þar í* ~ fastened onto it 2/67; *er hann var inn kominn* when he got inside 2/485; *hvar Hreiðarr er niðr kominn* where H. had got to 1/354; ~ *til* to get to, arrive at, reach 1/289, 2/158, come across, find 1/274 (see **fǫruneyti**); ~ *e-m til lítils* to be of little use to one, to be of no avail 1/284; ~ *upp* to get known 1/206; *kemr útar* comes out, is being thrust out 2/501; ~ *við* to come to land at, harbour at 1/34. (4) Md. *komast í* get in 2/465; ~ *með* keep up with 1/72; ~ *undan* get away 2/421; ~ *út ok undan* to manage to get out and away, escape 2/309. (5) Impers. *kom við sem mátti* 1/237, see note; *svó kom at* it turned out that, it came about that 2/234; *er þar komit at* the point is reached at which 1/321; *gerðist tímum mjök fram komit* time was getting on 2/102.

kona *f.* wife 2/14; woman 2/190, 442.

konungr *m.* king.

kostr *m.* choice, chance, opportunity; *kost átta ek* at I could have, it was within my power to 2/172.

kristna (**að**) *wv.* to convert to Christianity, to baptise; md. *kristnast* to become Christian, be baptised 2/441.

krumma *f.* colloquial word for hand; paw 1/176.
krækja (**t**) *wv.* to hook (with dat.) 2/167.
kúgildi *n.* the value of a cow 2/147, see note.
kunna (**kann**) *pret.-pres. vb.* to know how to, to be able; ~ *frá at segja* to know about, be able to give details about 2/424, 456; †*ef hann kynni at líta á* if he were able to see 2/413; *ef þú kynnir at koma* in case you should happen to come 2/463. Impers. *hey* (acc.) *kunni hvergi at fá* it was impossible to get hay anywhere, hay was unobtainable 2/96; *vera kann þat* that may well be 1/27; *kann vera* it could happen 1/208.
kurteiss *a.* courteous, gentlemanly, well bred; comp. *hverjum manni kurteisari* the most courteous of men 2/188.
kveða (**kvað**) *sv.* to say, speak; recite, deliver, declaim (a poem) 1/440, 2/459; often used of the delivery of supposedly impromptu poetry 2/271, 331, 344. Md. *kvazt ekki hafa* said he had none 2/103; *kvóðust ætla* they said they thought 2/423; *hon kvezt heita* she says she is called 2/445.
kveðja *f.* greeting, salute 1/88.
kveðja (**kvadda**) *wv.* to greet; ~ *vel* to greet courteously 1/87.
kveld *n.* evening; *um kveldit* in the evening 2/195.

kverkr *f. pl.* throat 2/496.
kviðr *m.* belly 2/341.
kvóngaðr (**kvángaðr**) *a.* married 2/185.
kvæði *n.* poem 1/437.
kvæðislaun *n. pl.* reward for a poem 1/447.
†**kvöl** *f.* torment, torture 2/412.
kykvendi *n. pl.* animals (as opposed to human beings) 1/45.
kynjalæti *n. pl.* strange behaviour 1/465.
kynligr *a.* strange, extraordinary, odd; sup. *fyrst kynligast* most odd to begin with 1/441.
kynna (**d** or **t**) *wv.* to make known; ~ *sér e-t* acquaint o-self with s-thing 2/218.
kynni *n.* acquaintance; a visit to an acquaintance; *fara á* ~ to go on a visit, to go to visit friends 2/593.
kyrr *a.* quiet, peaceful; *sitja um kyrrt* see **sitja**.
kœja *vb.* trouble, disturb 1/36, see note.
kœmir *p. subj.* of **koma**.
kærleikr *m.* affection (usually in pl.); *með kærleikum* on affectionate terms 2/285; *vera með e-m í miklum kærleikum* to be held in high regard by s-one, to be highly favoured by s-one 2/591.
kømr *pres.* of **koma**.

lá, lágu see **liggja**.
†**láð** *n.* poetical word for land;

svarðar ~ the land of the scalp, kenning for head 2/348.

lag *n.* place, position; *í ǫðru lagi* on the other hand, as far as the others were concerned (i.e. back on the farm) 1/418.

land *n.* (1) land, country 2/6, 202, 429. (2) as opposed to sea, the coast 2/249; *ganga á* ~ go ashore 2/297; *á landi* on the shore 2/440; *upp á* ~ inland 2/300; *undan landi* away from shore 2/310; *frá landi* from the shore 2/574; bank (of a river) 2/9; mainland 2/422. (3) piece of land, property 1/449.

landnámamaðr *m.* land-taker, settler 2/16.

landsleg *n.* the lie of the land, terrain 2/69.

langa (að) *wv.* to long for, desire; ~ *til* to long for 1/262.

langr *a.* 1ong; long-lasting, prolonged 2/147; with gen. *þrettán álna langan* thirteen ells long 2/574; *Ormrinn langi* (name of a ship) the Long Serpent; n. as adv. *langt* far, a long way 1/68; (of time) *hvé langt mun til þess* how long will it be until that happens 1/192.

†**langskip** *n.* long ship, warship 2/399.

láta (lét) *sv.* (1) to lose 2/319, 418. (2) to behave 1/47; *svá* ~ *sem* behave as if 1/310. (3) to let; put; ~ *laust* let go 1/78; ~ *til* offer, contribute 2/116; ~ *saman* place together 2/159; ~ *frá landi* put out to sea 2/574. (4) with inf. to allow 1/230; ~ *kæja sik* to have himself disturbed 1/36; to cause (s-thing to be done), have (s-thing done) 1/308 (see **ganga**), 2/38; ~ *síga brýnnar* make one's brows sink, i.e. frown 2/511; *lætr kalla Orm* has O. called 2/560; *vill skýla* ~ wishes to have protected 1/386; *gera* ~ to have done, to get s-one to do 1/399; make (s-thing do s-thing) 2/207. (5) to say; *lét á sannast* see **sanna**. Md. in acc. (or nom.) and inf. constructions *lézk eigi verðr* said he did not deserve 1/289; *lézt búinn* said he was prepared 2/242; *lézt heita* said his name was 2/542; *lézk vildu* said he wanted to 1/391.

latliga *adv.* 1azily, negligently, inadequately.

latta see **letja**.

látum see **læti**.

laungum (lǫngum) *adv.* for long periods 2/88, 222; †at length, with many words 2/273.

launung *f.* secrecy; *af launungu* in secret 1/359.

lauss *a.* loose, free; n. as adv. *láta laust* let go 1/78.

leggja (lagða) *wv.* to lay, put, place; lay down (on the ground) 2/484. With preps. and advs. ~ *kapp á* act with eagerness 2/318; ~ *ætlun á* see **ætlun**; *at* *ek ~ af mér* that I should take off 1/141; *~ af út* to pull outwards and away, jerk back towards o-self 2/503; *~ at* come to land at 2/296; †*~ langskipum at* sail the warships (in) to 2/366; *~ fram hjá e-m hesta sína* to set one's horses to race s-one 1/286; *lagði hvern þeira fyrir* outdid all of them 1/240; *~ niðr* put down 2/613; †*nær mun þat ~ at* it will bring this close that, that will be imminent that 2/211; *~ til* contribute 2/106, sail to 2/265; *var lagðr til sáttarfundr* a peace conference was arranged to deal with the matter 1/248; *~ til við e-n* offer, suggest to s-one 1/16; *~ upp* pass up 2/41; *~ við* come to land at (on), go ashore at (on) 2/8. Md. *leggjast* lie down 2/35.

leið *f.* way; *á þá ~* in such a way; *um ~* on the way 2/594.

leiða (dd) *wv.* to lead; (impers.) to result; *leiddi af þessu* there resulted from this (with acc.) 2/147; md. *láta eptir leiðask* to let o-self be persuaded 1/231.

leiðask (dd) *wv.* (usually impers. with dat.) to get tired of; *tekr mér at ~* I begin to get tired of it 1/315.

leika (lék) *sv.* to play; to move to and fro; (impers.) *lék á ýmsu* it went various ways, it went now one way, now another 1/305; *~ við e-n* to treat s-one (in a certain way) 1/323.

leikmikill *a.* playful, full of fun, boisterous 1/240.

leikr *m.* game, sport 1/307, 314.

leingd (lengð) *f.* length; *báði at ~ ok digrð* both end to end and side by side (so as to make the rope both thicker and longer) 2/125; gen. sg. (or acc. pl.) as adv. *leingdar* for long, any longer (often emended to *áleingdar*; v.l. *leingr*) 2/433.

leingi see **lengi**.

leingr (lengr) *adv. comp.* longer 2/235, 281.

leita (að) *wv.* to seek (with gen.); *sigla at ~ Íslands* to sail for Iceland 2/6; *~ bragða í* 2/96, see **brögð**; *~ við* to try 1/368.

lemja (lamda) *wv.* to strike, beat; disable; *slegit í kaf sjau skeiðr, lamit ok brotit* sunk, disabled and wrecked seven ships 2/577.

lendr *a.* landed 1/340, see note.

lengi, leingi *adv.* long, for a long time 1/456, 458; *svó ~* for as long a time 2/215.

letja (latta) *wv.* to dissuade, hold back (*e-n e-s* s-one from s-thing); *ekki fær þú mik lattan* you cannot stop me (going) 1/65; *at þat skal aðra ~ at* that it will discourage others from 2/320; †*sjaldan ek latta at* I seldom tried to prevent (s-thing from doing s-thing), I was never unwilling for (s-thing to do s-thing) 2/405.

létta (tt) *wv.* to slacken, leave off.

leyfa (ð) *wv.* to permit, allow (*e-m e-t* s-one s-thing), give permission (to s-one for s-thing) 1/259.

leysa (t) *wv.* to redeem, buy; *at ek ~ til mín* that I should buy it for myself 1/454; *~ e-n í burt* discharge s-one, speed s-one on his way 2/215; *~ af* untie, remove 2/124.

lið *n.* help, support; troop of men 1/359, 362.

líða (leið) *sv.* to pass (of time) 1/353; *at vetri liðnum* when winter had passed 2/260. Impers. *er á leið* as time went on 2/95; *um sumarit er á leið* towards the end of the summer 2/265; *er meir líðr á* the longer it (i.e. your life) goes on 1/446; *er meir líðr fram hans ævi* (acc.) the longer his life goes on 1/464; *nú líðr áfram* now time passed 2/92.

líf *n.* life; *lífit láta* to die 2/319.

lifa (ð) *wv.* to live, survive.

líflát *n.* death 2/425.

liggja (lá) *sv.* to lie; lie asleep 2/444; spend the night 2/440; be situated 2/249; †*~ eftir* remain behind (i.e. lie dead?) 2/385.

líka (að) *wv.* to please; *e-t líkar e-m betr* one prefers s-thing 1/215; *e-m líkar illa* one is displeased 1/422.

líkr (glíkr 1/98) *a.* like; with dat. like s-thing or s-one; sup. *hverju var líkast* what was it most like to 1/44; *er þat líkast* it is most likely 2/331.

linaflaðr *a.* weak, feeble 2/45.

líta (leit) *sv.* to see; *~ á* see, look at, examine 1/404, 2/413; md. to seem, appear; *leizt ómáttuligt nokurum manni* it looked impossible for any man 2/480; *hversu lízk þér á mik* what do you think of me 1/157; *sem mér lízk á þik* which I see in you 1/168.

lítill *a.* small; *~ vexti* of small build 1/3 (see **vǫxtr**); *lítit tillát* a mean offer 2/107; short (of time) 2/46, 309; n. as subst. *lítit* little 2/329; *~ af e-u* little of s-thing 1/71; *~ af þeim skipafjölda* a fraction of the number of ships 2/570; *litlu því ofar* a little bit higher 1/171; *litlu síðar en* soon after 2/294; *koma til lítils* see **koma**.

litr *m.* colour; *at lit* in colour 2/303.

lítt *adv.* little, badly 2/59.

ljá *f.* new-mown grass (before it has dried to become hay) 2/72.

ljár *m.* scythe 2/60; scythe-blade 2/61, 65, 67, 80.

ljóð *n.* verse, stanza (of a song or poem); a poem consisting of one stanza complete in itself (cf. **vísa**) 2/206.

ljótr *a.* ugly 1/4, 39, 101; comp. 1/182.

ljúga (laug or **ló)** *sv.* to lie; *~ at e-m* deceive s-one 1/149.

loðinn *a.* shaggy; covered with thick grass 2/70.

lofgjarnliga *adv.* flatteringly 1/167 (see note).

loft see **lopt**.

lokka (að) *wv.* to entice, coax; ~ *fé af e-m* get s-one to part with his money 1/23.

lopt, loft *n.* air; *á* ~ up into the air, aloft 1/323.

losa (að) *wv.* to loosen; ~ *til* loosen up, pull out 2/129.

lúka (lauk) *sv.* to close; ~ *upp* to open up 1/393; impers. with dat. to end, come to an end; *lýkr hér þessi rœðu* that is the end of this story 1/467; *er lokit er kvæði* (dat.) when the poem is finished 1/441.

lundhœgr *a.* gentle in disposition 1/102.

†**lundr** *m.* tree; often used as the basic word in kennings for man; as a half-kenning: man, warrior (i.e. Ormr) 2/367 (see note).

lungu *n. pl.* lungs 2/527.

lyfta (ft) *wv.* to lift (with dat.) 2/166.

lyndislíkr *a.* alike in character 2/450

læti (*dat.* **látum**) *n. pl.* noise; *hvat látum* what sort of noise 1/46.

†**lǫgr** (*acc. pl.* **lǫgu**) *m.* sea 2/208.

lögsögumaðr *m.* lawspeaker 2/19 (see note).

má (ð) *wv.* to wear (down); *máðr upp í smiðreim* worn right down to the thick edge of the blade 2/80.

má, mátti see **mega**.

maðr *m.* man 1/2; person (without distinction of sex) 2/244; human being 2/481; in pl. *menn* people 1/467, 2/191, 195; †*með mǫnnum* among men, i.e. in the world, alive 2/277.

mágr *m.* male relation by marriage; cousin's husband 2/155; see note on 2/384.

mál *n.* (1) speech; *koma at máli við* to get into conversation with, go to speak to 1/432, 2/57; *þat var allra manna* ~ everyone agreed 2/27. (2) subject of speech, matter 1/145; *á þat* ~ on that subject of dispute 1/347; *hafa sitt* ~ to get one's own way 1/269. (3) legal case 1/249. (4) in pl. business 1/299.

málajárn *n.* ornamented (inlaid) sword (cf. Old English *mæl-, malsweord*) 2/484 (see note).

málugr *a.* talkative.

mannfár *a.* having few people about; *vera mannfátt* to be deserted 1/206.

mannraun *f.* trial of courage, danger; *í mannraunum* involving danger 1/400.

mannskræfa *f.* wretch, degenerate person; in direct address with def. art. *mannskræfan* you wretch! 2/122.

mannæta *f.* cannibal, creature that eats human flesh 2/251.

margr *a.* many; pl. as subst. *margir* many men 1/286; *ekki* *margir* not many people 2/456; *því nær* ~ about the same number (of men) 2/438; *þér eruð margir, Íslendingar* many of you Icelanders are 1/145. Sg. used in collective sense *mart orð* many a word, on many subjects 2/359; *hversu margr væri* however many they were 2/253. N. as subst. *mart* much, many things 1/208, 2/200; ~ *e-s* a great deal of s-thing 2/94; *at mǫrgu* in much, in many ways 1/103; *fyrir margs sakir* 1/399 see **sǫk**; dat. pl. *mǫrgum* many things 1/114.

margvíss *a.* wise about many things, having wide knowledge 2/28.

mark *n.* sign, signal 1/361.

mátuliga *adv.* fittingly, suitably; *sér* ~ *hátt* of the right height for himself 2/66.

með *prep.* (1) with acc. with, taking, carrying 2/261, 531, 613. (2) with dat. with, in company with; as a guest of 1/431; among 2/277, 557; together with 2/48; ~ *jalli* among the jarl's following 2/607; ~ *þeim* between them 2/88, 89; ~ *manna hǫndum* from hand to hand 1/407; *vera* ~ *e-u* to have, contain s-thing 1/448; ~ *ǫllu* see **allr**. (3) as adv. as well 2/233; *þar . . .* ~ with it 1/450.

meðan *conj.* while, as long as.

mega (*pres. sg.* **má**) *pret.-pres. vb.* to be able, may, can; to be permitted 2/471; ~ *meira* to be more powerful 2/461; *þó mætti vera* yet there might be, yet one might still have 1/71; *ekki má* it is impossible to 2/464; *má at gagni koma* it may perhaps benefit 2/105; *kom við sem mátti* 1/238, see note.

†**megin** *n.* strength 2/339.

meginland *n.* the mainland 2/534.

meiða (**dd**) *wv.* to injure, maim 1/24.

meinvættr *f.* harmful creature 2/256.

meir *adv. comp.* more; (of time) longer, further 1/446, 464.

meiri *a. comp.* (1) more; *þat sem meira var fémætt* whatever else was of value 2/532; *mega meira* see **mega**. (2) bigger 2/127; *því meiri sem hann var þá ellri* which (i.e. the feats of strength) were the greater as he got older 2/178.

menjar *f. pl.* souvenir, reminder; s-thing to remind one of s-thing (with gen.) 2/525.

mennskr *a.* human; *af mennskum mönnum* by human beings 2/252; *trautt* ~ *maðr* hardly human, almost superhuman (inhuman) 1/325.

merki *n.* mark, sign; in pl. evidence, remains, traces 2/83.

mest *adv. sup.* most; hardest 1/322; †most of all, especially 2/384.

mestr *a. sup.* most, greatest; greatest in size, biggest 2/22; *þykkja ~ maðr (hinn mesti maðr)* be considered the finest of men, be very highly thought of 2/199, 618.

meta (**mat**) *sv.* to value, esteem (with gen. of the amount or price); *mikils metinn* highly esteemed 2/223; md. (for passive) *mazk vel* was highly thought of 1/8.

miðlung *adv.* middlingly, not very well; *~ segir mér hugr um hversu ferr* I have a feeling that things will not go very well, I am not confident of how things will go 1/295.

miðr (*n.* **mitt**) *a.* mid, the middle of; *á miðjum bálkinum* in the middle of the partition 2/325; *undir mitt trét* under the middle of the mast 2/610.

mikill *a.* (1) big, tall, large, great 1/420, 2/54, 162; strong 2/324; *vetr ~* a hard winter 2/93; *þó at eigi sé mikit* though it is not very big 1/449; important, striking 2/427; *~ fyrir sér* important, influential 1/462. (2) much, a great deal of 1/235. (3) n. as subst. much 2/135, 222; *svó mikit* just as much, the same amount 2/106; *tala mikit um* see **tala**; *miklu sterkari* much stronger 2/233. (4) n. as adv. *mikit* a lot, very much. (5) *mikinn* as adv. much, a great deal 1/165 (see note).

mikilligr *a.* big-looking, impressive, overpowering; *sýndist heldr ~* looked rather on the large size 2/316.

mikilvirkr *a.* working hard, energetic 2/43.

milli (**í ~**) *prep.* (with gen.) between 2/13; *~ handa sér* with his hands 2/62; *þeirra í ~* in their dealings together 2/324.

minni *a. comp.* less; smaller, lesser 2/132, 439; slighter 1/429; *af hinu minna* from the smaller one (sc. haystack) 2/112. N. as subst. *eigi minna* (gen.) *vert en* worth no less than 2/146.

minnka (**að**) *wv.* to lessen; md. *minnkast* to grow less 2/494.

minnstr *a. sup.* smallest; *hinn minnsti fingr* the little finger 2/168.

missætti *n.* discord, disagreement; *verða í ~ við* to get into trouble with, fall out with 2/4.

†**mjöðr** *m.* mead 2/358.

mjǫk *adv.* much, greatly, a great deal 1/90; very much 1/463; very 1/68, 2/62; fast 1/278; loudly 1/46.

móðir *f.* mother.

móðurfrændr *m. pl.* relations on the mother's side, one's mother's family 2/222.

morginn, morgunn *m.* morning; *um morgun snimma* early in the morning 1/356; *um morguninn (morgininn)* the next morning 1/40, 2/299.

GLOSSARY

mót (1) *n.* (1) mark; *svá er þó ~ á manninum* there was such a mark on the man, he was such a strange person 1/234. (2) kind, manner; *með kynligu móti* of a strange kind 1/445; *með því móti sem er* in anything of this kind, (as this is) in its own way 1/406.

mót (2) *n.* meeting, public assembly 1/50; *til móts við* to meet, to see 1/251, 2/100; *í móti* as prep. with dat. towards; *grípa í móti e-u* to grasp at s-thing, catch s-thing 2/502; as adv. *í móti* in exchange, in return 1/380.

múgasláttr *m.* mowing so that the hay lies in long heaps; *hafa múgaslátt* to mow the hay into long lines 2/73.

múgi *m.* heap, pile (of hay, extending down the length of the field) 2/75, 83; *færa saman í múga* to pile up in heaps 2/78.

muna (*pres. sg.* **man**) *pret.-pres. vb.* to remember 2/474.

mund *n.* (but often f. in pl.) time, period of time 1/245; *í þær mundir* in those days 2/190; *til annars dags í þær mundir* until about the same time the next day 2/477.

munnr *m.* mouth; *e-t verðr e-m á munni* s-thing comes to one's mouth, one begins to speak (recite, intone) s-thing (implying that the speech is involuntary, and the sibyl possessed) 2/206; *fyrir munni sér* in a low voice, under one's breath 1/153.

munr *m.* difference; *geri ek eigi þann mun ykkar Magnúss konungs at* I am not going to make such a distinction between you and King Magnús as to, i.e. I am not going to regard your wishes as so much more important than King Magnús's that 1/385; *lítinn mun mundi þat segja um einn mann* one man would not have made much difference 2/566; *sjá firir mun um hvórt* foresee the outcome of whether 2/460.

munu (*pres. sg.* **mun**) *pret.-pres. vb.* as aux. (1) indicating future tense: shall, will; (in pret.) would 2/95; to be going (to do s-thing) 1/434; *mun, muni* (subj.) it will be 1/268, 270; *þú munt reiðask* you will lose your temper 1/191; to be willing to 1/226; *þér munuð ráða* you may do as you please, it is up to you 2/571. (2) indicating probability: *mun vera* is likely to be, is probably 1/444; with suffixed neg. *muna* it will not 1/64; *hvárt mun konungr nú á mótinu* is the king likely to be at the assembly now 1/56; *mun verit hafa* must have been, is likely to have been 1/47, cf. 2/604; *muni valla samr orðit hafa síðan ok áðr* can scarcely have been quite the same man again afterwards 2/614; *er mönnum þótti sem vera mundi* which men presumed to have occurred 2/432; *nú muntu þikkjask gerla sjá mik mega* now I expect you will be satisfied that you can see me clearly 1/137; *hverr mundi farit hafa með* who could have been handling 2/602; *því mundi hann þat segja at hann mundi vita* the reason he said it must have been that he knew 1/369. (3) indicating necessity: must 2/352, 368; *at ek muna* that I shall have to 2/452; *at hann mun brjóta* that he would only break 1/392; *hann mun* he will certainly 1/458; *muntu nú* now will you please 2/519.

mæða (**mœða**) (**dd**) *wv.* to weary, make weary, exhaust.

mæla (**t**) *wv.* to speak, say; with suffixed pron. *mælik* I say 1/210; *mæltum mart orð saman* we spoke of many things together 2/358; *mæla við* to speak to, address 1/167; ~ *eftir e-n* to take up the prosecution in a case concerning s-one who has been killed, to assume responsibility for achieving vengeance for a slain man: *þú átt eftir hraustan mann at* ~ it is a valiant man whose cause you have taken up 2/455.

mælgi *f.* talkativeness 1/241.

ná (**náða**) *wv.* to get, reach; get hold of 2/341; to be able; †*ef hann næði* if he could manage it 2/417; to be sufficient, adequate 1/70 (see note).

naddr *m.* stud, nail, point.

nafn *n.* name; *spyrja e-n at nafni* to ask s-one his name.

nakkvarr, nokkur *a.* and *indefinite pron.* a certain 1/80; some, a quantity, a little 1/365; *nokkura stund* for a time 2/159; *nokkura vetr* for a few years 2/616; after neg., any 2/480. N. as subst. something 1/169; *nokkut erfitt* something unpleasant 2/518; anything 1/160; *er nokkvot* is there anything 1/184; *nokkut af heyi* some of the hay 2/101; *nokkut svó* just a little while 2/301. N. as adv. somewhat, a little 1/144; rather 2/312; at all, in any way 1/197; *nokkut svó* just a little way 2/325; with comp. *nokkut harðari* any tougher 2/327.

nálægr *a.* near, close by (with dat.).

nátt *f.* night; *um náttina* for the night, overnight 2/298.

náttúra *f.* magic or innate property or power 2/467.

Naumdælajall *m.* jarl of the men of Naumudalr (Namdalen in northern Norway).

nauðsyn *f.* need, necessity; *eiga* ~ *at tala við e-n* to have important business with s-one 1/128.

né *adv.* (*conj.*) nor.
neðan *adv.* from below, up; *firir ~* as prep. (with acc.) below, on the coast at the foot of 2/287.
nefna (**d**) *wv.* to name; *í nefndan tíma* at the appointed time, inside the arranged time 2/534.
nema (**1**) (**nam**) *sv.* to take; *~ land* to settle land 2/12; *~ stað* (*staðar*) to stop 1/80, 2/444; *~ í e-u* to touch, strike, catch against s-thing 1/309. As aux. with inf. †*nam höggva* did strike 2/376; †*nam at forma* did aim 2/383.
nema (**2**) *conj.* unless; except 2/581; *eigi ~ ørendit væri* (I would) not (have come) unless there had been a reason 1/12; *veit ek eigi ~ þú* I do not know but that you 1/146.
nestlok *n. pl.* the end of the provision-bag, the bottom of the bag; metaphorically *at nestlokum* towards the end (of the poem) 1/443.
neyta (**tt**) *wv.* to use, make use of (with gen.); make good use of, do s-thing with 2/44.
niðr *adv.* down; *~ at* down as far as 2/175.
niðri *adv.* below, at the bottom.
njóta (**naut**) *sv.* to use, have the use of, enjoy; *njót sjálfr* keep it for yourself 1/373; md. *njótast* to enjoy one another, become lovers, marry 2/471.
nokkur see **nakkvarr**.

nokkvor *adv.* somewhere 1/118.
nokkvot *n.* of **nakkvarr**.
norðan *adv.* from the north; *~ frá Myrká ór Hörgárdal* from Myrká in the north in Hörgárdalr 2/152; *~ ór Nóregi af Hörðalandi* from the north, from Hörðaland in Norway 2/220.
norðarliga *adv.* in the northern part, somewhat to the north 2/435.
norðr *adv.* in the north, up north 1/462, 2/212; to the north 2/238, 275; *~ þaðan* northward from there 2/201; *~ firir landi* north(ward) off the coast 2/249.
nú *adv.* now; but now 2/352, 360, 368; and so 1/146; then, next 1/299, 407.
nýkominn *a.* newly arrived, just arrived 1/37.
nýr *a.* new 2/61, 67; *at nýju* in modern times 2/181.
nytjar *f. pl.* use, advantage, profit; *hafa ǿngar ~ e-s* to have no profit from s-thing, to make no use of s-thing 1/111.
nýtr *a.* useful; *þau er nýt eru* which are any good, any help 1/21; *vettugi nýtr* good for nothing, useless 2/142; *~ bóndi* a worthy member of the community 2/197.
nær (**1**) *adv.* nearly, almost 1/121; *því ~ margir* almost as many, about as many 2/438; †*leggja ~* see **leggja**.

nær (2) *adv. comp.* nearer; ~ *er þat* that is closer (to what I want), that's better 1/229; *er ek geng yðr* ~ the closer I am to you 1/298.

nær (3) *prep.* (with dat.) near; ~ *hófi* see **hóf**.

nær (4) *pres.* of **ná** 1/70 (see note).

nærri *adv.* nearly; *því* ~ *hátt* nearly the same in height 2/111; close, anywhere near 2/583.

nös *f.* nostril 2/304.

óbúinn *a.* unprepared 1/377.

oddr *m.* point (of a weapon) 2/597.

†**oddviti** *m.* leader; ~ *þeirra* their (i.e. the warriors') leader, the man in the forefront of the battle 2/409.

ódæll *a.* difficult to manage, disobedient (*e-m* to s-one) 2/34.

ofan *adv.* from above, downwards, down; *af* ~ off, from off the top 2/127.

ofanverðr *a.* upper part of; *á ofanverðum dögum e-s* towards the end of s-one's life (reign) 2/247.

ofar *adv. comp.* higher, higher up.

ófirirleitinn (-fyrir-) *a.* reckless, headstrong 2/53.

ófriðr *m.* hostility, hostile intentions 2/321.

†**ófrýnn** *a.* frowning; *mundi Ormr* ~ *vera* O. would be displeased 2/411.

ofstopamaðr *m.* an arrogant, obstinate man; *illt er at eggja ofstopamennina* (proverb) it is a bad thing to goad arrogant men 2/52.

ofsǫgur *f. pl.* exaggeration; *segja e-t ofsǫgum* to exaggerate s-thing 1/158.

oft see **opt**.

oftala (að) *wv.* to exaggerate; *at þat væri oftalat þótt* that that would be an exaggeration although (one were to say that) 2/586.

ófælinn *a.* fearless 1/409.

ógreiðr *a.* not straightforward, difficult; *verðr honum fǫrin ógreið* it becomes hard for him to make his way 1/92.

ógurligr *a.* horrible 2/302.

ógæfusamliga *adv.* unluckily; ~ *hefir mér tekizt* things have turned out badly for me, luck has been against me (*at* in that) 2/329.

óheilagr *a.* unholy; outlawed 1/351 (see note).

óhlutdeilinn *a.* taking little part in things, keeping to o-self, quiet 2/549.

ok *conj.* and *adv.* and, also 1/114, 189, 261, 2/142, 240; but 1/139; with subj. if 1/72 (2); *samr . . . ok* the same . . . as 2/614.

okkarr (*n.* **okkat**) *poss. a.* (dual) of us two, our 1/21.

óknáleikr *m.* lack of strength 1/74.

ólatr *a.* unhesitant (*e-s* to do

s-thing); *mun ek þess ~ er* I shall not be reluctant (i.e. I shall be eager) to undertake whatever (mission) that 1/401.

ólið *n.* harm, trouble; *at þér verði at því ~ eða ǫðrum* that trouble should come as a result of this either upon you or upon others 1/261.

ólíkligr *a.* improbable; *til þess þætti ekki ólíkligt* that would seem not at all unlikely 1/200.

ólíkr *a.* unlike; sup. *hvat er ólíkast með ykkr* what is the greatest difference between you 1/100.

ómállatr *a.* not hesitant of speech, talkative (*við e-n* towards s-one) 1/39; quick in repartee 1/237.

ómáttuligr *a.* impossible; *leizt ómáttuligt nokkurum manni þat í brott at færa* it looked impossible for any man to move it away 2/480.

ónýta (tt) *wv.* to spoil, ruin 2/79.

ónýtr *a.* useless; *ef ónýtt verðr smíðat* if what is made turns out to be no good 1/372.

opna (að) *wv.* to open; *~ kvið á e-m* to cut open s-one's belly 2/341.

opt, oft *adv.* often, frequently 2/382, 395; over and over again 1/153; comp. *sem oftar* as usual 2/151.

ór *prep.* (with dat.) out of, from 1/386, 2/6, 152 (see **norðan**); *svó at hann gerir ór eitt* so that out of them (the ropes) he makes a single (rope) 2/125; of (a place) 2/3.

orð *n.* word, phrase, sentence; sg. in collective sense †*mæltum mart ~* we spoke of many things 2/359; *nú mæltir þú gott ~* now you have said a good thing, that is just what I wanted to hear 1/264; pl. speech 1/236.

orðit *pp.* of **verða**.

orðsending *f.* message; *eptir ~ konungs* in accordance with the king's instructions 1/346.

orðvarr *a.* careful of speech, discreet 1/208.

orf *n.* scythe-handle 2/61.

orka (að) *wv.* to achieve, be able to do (with dat.) 2/135.

ort *pp.* of **yrkja**.

ósannligr *a.* unjust, unfair; not right 1/113.

ósyknligr *a.* 1/102 see note.

óttafullr *a.* terrified 2/306.

óttast (að) *wv.* to fear 2/462.

óvanr *a.* unaccustomed (with dat.); *því ~ at* unaccustomed to this, that 1/121.

óvarr *a.* unwary; *koma á óvart* to come unexpectedly 1/357.

óvinr *m.* enemy 2/179.

óvísa *f.* uncertainty, doubtful act, act of hostility (cf. **víss** certain); or foolishness, act of foolishness (cf. *víss* wise) 1/23. Cf. *ÍF* V 202, note 4.

óx see **vaxa**.

óþokki *m.* displeasure, unfriendliness, enmity (*með* between) 2/147.

penningr *m.* coin; in pl. money, property 1/111.

pína (d) *wv.* to torture, torment 2/520.

postuli *m.* apostle 2/493.

prímsigna (d) *wv.* to sign with the cross 2/441, see note.

prófa (að) *wv.* to try, find out by trying; try and see 2/609; *nú skal ~* now we shall find out 2/327.

prúðr *a.* as a nickname 2/189, see note.

pund *n.* a unit of weight, equal to 24 *merkr* or about 12 lb. (5 k.).

ráð *n.* (1) advice; *við ~ e-s* according to s-one's advice 1/230. (2) what is advisable, the best thing 1/314; *þikkir mér ~* it seems to me best 2/117. (3) state of life, lot; *ferr hans ~* his fortunes went 1/463.

ráða (réð) *sv.* (1) to advise (*e-m* s-one). (2) to rule; *~ Nóregi* to rule over Norway; *~ firir e-u* to be master of, own 2/250, 450; *~ þar firir* be ruler there 2/266; *eiga at ~ firir* to be lord over (as steward or governor) 2/183. (3) to decide, have one's own way (with) 1/113, 214; *jötunninn varð einn at ~ þeirra í milli* the giant had all his own way in their dealings together 2/323; *þó at sjálfr mætti ~* if he had the choice 1/164; *muntu eigi ~ því* you will not be the arbiter of that 2/205; *þér munuð ~* it is up to you 2/571; *ef hann á at ~* if it is left to him to decide 1/458.

ráðligr *a.* advisable; comp. *ráðligra ætla ek vera* I think it wiser 1/454.

raka (að) *wv.* to rake 2/71.

rakta see **rekja**.

rammr *a.* strong, powerful; *~ at afli* of great physical strength 1/242.

†**raunmargr** *a.* very many; *raunmargan rekk* many a warrior 2/375.

regnligr *a.* rainy, looking like rain; *regnligt gerast* to begin to look like rain 2/40.

reið *f.* riding; *til reiðar* to ride on 1/277.

reiða (1) *f.* service, accommodation; *kvað honum þat til reiðu* said that was freely available to him 2/547.

reiða (2) (dd) *wv.* to cause to move, carry about; spread about, bandy about 1/209.

reiðask (dd) *wv.* to become angry, lose one's temper 1/322, 2/46.

reiðfara *a. indecl.* in the phrase *verða vel ~* to have a good journey (voyage) 1/33.

reiði *f.* anger 1/262.

reiðing *f.* movement to and fro, rocking; *vera í reiðingum* to be in the balance, to be doubtful, touch and go 1/275.

reiðr *a.* angry.

reikuðr *m.* wandering (cf. *reika* to

walk aimlessly), in the phrase *fœra í reikuð* to force to wander, push around 1/90.
reip *n.* rope, harness-rope 2/123 (pl.).
reisa (**t**) *wv.* to raise, erect; pitch (a tent) 2/297.
reka (**rak**) *sv.* to drive (*at* against) 2/515.
rekja (**rakta**) *wv.* to unwind, wind out; md. *röktust á enda* were completely wound out 2/343.
†**rekkr** *m.* man, warrior; sg. in collective sense 2/374.
renna (**rann**) *sv.* to run, gallop; †*lata byrhest* ~ to make the wind-horse gallop, i.e. sail a ship 2/209; impers. *e-m renn í skap* one is deeply moved, overcome by emotion; one loses one's temper 1/321.
rétta (**tt**) *wv.* to stretch out; ~ *e-t at e-m* to hand s-thing to s-one 2/160.
réttr *a.* straight 2/160; right; *rétt trú* the true faith 2/429.
reyna (**d**) *wv.* to try, put to the test; ~ *íþróttir* to compete in sports 2/232; *þær sem eigi reyndi afl með* those (sports) that did not try the strength as well (sc. as skill), those that did not involve a trial of strength 2/233; *lítit mun þat at reyna* little will that be to test, that will not take much testing 2/329.
ríða (**reið**) *sv.* to ride; ~ *mjǫk* to gallop hard 1/278.

rif *n.* rib; *þrjú rifin í honum* three of his ribs 2/50.
rífa (**reif**) *sv.* to tear 2/308; ~ *af e-m* tear off s-one 2/508.
rísa (**reis**) *sv.* to rise; ~ *upp* to get up 2/299.
rísta (**reist**) *sv.* to cut, carve 2/526.
rjá (**ð**) *wv.* to drive away, chase off 1/117 (see note).
róðr (*gen.* **róðrar**) *m.* rowing; *sækja* ~ see **sœkja**.
†**róma** *f.* poetical word for battle 2/374.
Rómferð *f.* pilgrimage to Rome 2/537.
ryðja (**rudda**) *wv.* to clear, strip, remove (with dat.) 2/127.
rykkja (**rykkta**) *wv.* to pull, jerk; ~ *til* tug, pull towards o-self 2/508.
rœða (**1**) *f.* speech, talk, s-thing said; tale, story 1/468.
rœða (**2**) (**dd**) *wv.* to discuss 1/299.
röktust see **rekja**.

sá 2/72 see **sjá**.
saga *f.* something said, a statement; story; *ǫll* ~ the whole story 2/458; *seg heill sǫgu* see **heill**.
sakir *prep.*(with gen.) because of, for.
sala *f.* sale; *til sölu* for sale 2/104.
sama (**ð**) *wv.* to befit, be proper, fitting 1/222.
saman *adv.* together 2/359, 363; *fǫrum* ~ let us keep together 1/83; *fœra* ~ pile up (into stacks) 2/38; *setja bú* ~ see **setja**.

samdœgris *adv.* on the same day 1/36.

samr (*f.* sǫm, *n.* samt) *a.* same; ~ ... *ok áðr* the same (man) as before 2/614; *n.* as subst. *it sama* the same thing 1/153.

samtengja (ngð) *wv.* to join together, unite 1/450.

†**samtog** *n.* drawing (of swords) together; *at samtogi sverða* where swords are drawn against each other, i.e. in battle 2/404.

samvægja (gð) *wv.* (with dat.) to be of equal weight with, to be a match for 2/31.

sandr *m.* sand 2/165.

sanna (að) *wv.* to prove; md. *sannast* to turn out to be true; *láta á sannast* to admit 2/134.

sannr (*n.* satt) *a.* true; sup. *er þat sannast í* the real truth of the matter is 1/25. N. as subst. *satt segir þú* you are right 1/258; *segir frá it sanna* tells the whole story 1/426; *at sǫnnu* truly 1/167.

†**sárr** *a.* painful; *n.* as adv. *hǫggva sárt* deal hard blows 2/376.

sáttarfundr *m.* peace-meeting, peace-talks; a conference to arrange a truce 1/248.

sáttr *a.* reconciled, in agreement; *verða á sáttir, verða sáttir (á e-t)* to reach agreement (on s-thing) 1/347, 348.

saumlauss *a.* without nails 2/157.

saurigr *a.* dirty 1/176.

sax *n.* sword (usually short and single-edged) 2/526.

sé (**1**) *pres. subj.* of **vera**. (**2**) *pres. indicative* of **sjá**.

†**seggr** *m.* man, warrior 2/376; acc. pl. *seggi* 2/407; dat. sg. *segg á síðu* against the warrior's side 2/352.

segja (sagða) *wv.* to say, tell 2/76, 272; relate 2/148; mention 1/168; *þat ~ menn* it is said 2/440; *þat sagði Magnús konungr mér* King M. told me so 1/367. With preps. and advs. ~ *e-m e-t firir* (*adv.*) to prophesy to s-one about s-thing 2/191; ~ *frá* tell about (s-thing) 1/426; *kunnu ekki frá at ~* were not able to give any report 2/424; ~ *mun um* see **munr**. Md. †*segist þat minni móður* let this be told to my mother 2/346. Impers. *segir* it says, it is told (in a book) 2/292; *þat er sagt einhverju sinni at* it is told that on one occasion 1/363; *þat er at ~* that is to be told 2/421; *þat er nú frá Hreiðari at ~* to return to Hreiðarr 1/330; *svó er sagt at* it is said that 2/307; *var honum sagt* he was told 1/35.

†**seiðr** *m.* magic 2/272, see note.

seinn *a.* slow, late; *n.* as adv. *seint* slowly; *seint dags* late in the day, towards evening 2/296.

seinna *adv. comp.* more slowly 2/556.

selja (ld) *wv.* to hand over, deliver 1/380; sell 2/15.

sem (**1**) *rel. particle* who, which, that; *þar ~* where (to a place where) 2/593 (see note).

sem (2) *conj.* as, like 1/45, 306; like, as if it were 2/582; *réttir ~ kerti* as straight as candles 2/160; as indeed 1/458; in proportion as 1/271, 2/178; as if 2/432 (see **munu**); *mönnum þótti ~* it looked as if 2/174; *er nú ~ ek gat áðr* things were just as I said earlier 1/376; *~ áðr höfðu verit* as they had been before, i.e. back into the shape they had been in before 2/161; *~ þú vilt* as much as you want to 1/155; *~ Þórðr er* such as Þórðr 1/212; *hverr ~* whoever (see **hverr**); *svó . . . ~* 2/337–40 see **svá**; with sup. *~ flestir menn* as many men as possible 1/59.

sém *pres. subj.* of **vera**.

senda (nd) *wv.* to send; *~ eptir e-m* to send for s-one 1/119, 344; *~ e-n til e-s* to send s-one to do s-thing 1/408; *er þú vilt mik til hafa sendan* (a mission) which you want to have me sent on (send me on) 1/401.

senn (í ~) *adv.* at once, together.

sér 1/4 see **eiga**; 2/83 see **sjá**.

setja (tt) *sv.* to put, lay s-thing down 1/402; *~ bú saman* set up home, settle down 2/290. Md. *setjast í bú* settle down 2/617.

sex *num.* six.

síð *adv.* late.

†**síða** *f.* side, flank (of the body) 2/352

síðan *adv.* afterwards, then; later 2/24, 86; after this 2/138, 614.

síðar *adv. comp.* later; *því betra er ~ er* getting better as it went on 1/441; later on, below (in a book) 2/148; *~ en* as conj. after.

síðast *adv. sup.* finally, last of all.

síðasta *f.* the last thing, end; *at síðustu* in the end 2/89.

siðr (*acc. pl.* **siðu**) *m.* custom; *at fornum sið* according to the ancient custom, according to the ancient rite 2/235.

síðr *adv. comp.* less; *því betr er þú kæmir þar ~* the less you came there the better, the further you were away from there the better 1/61; *eigi þá ~* none the less for that 1/267.

síga (seig) *sv.* to sink; *láta ~ brýnnar* to knit the brows 2/511; of hay, to be compressed by its own weight; *þikkir vón at sigit muni* it is probably very tightly compressed 2/111.

sigla (d) *wv.* to sail 1/33.

siglutré *n.* mast 2/608.

sigr (*gen.* **sigrs**) *m.* victory; *hafa ~* to be victorious 2/262.

silfr (*gen.* **silfrs**) *n.* silver 1/364; money 1/460.

sin *f.* sinew, tendon 2/174.

sinn (1) *n.* time, occasion; *eitthvert ~* on one occasion 1/432.

sinn (2) (*f.* **sín**, *n.* **sitt**) *poss. pron.* his, her, its (referring to the subject of the clause) 1/9; *~ maðr . . . undan hvórum enda* one man at a time from each end 2/611.

sinni (1) *n.* fellowship, company, help, support; *vera e-m í* ~ to be on s-one's side 2/470.

sinni (2) *n.* time, occasion; *eitt* ~, *einhverju* ~ on one occasion, once.

sitja (sat) *sv.* to sit; sit at table 2/355; to stay 2/268, 435; to be living (in a place) 2/226; *sátu nú margir af sínum hestum* many had to dismount from their horses 1/291; ~ *hjá e-m* to stay with (at the house of) s-one 2/221, 229; ~ *í drykkju* to sit drinking 1/378; ~ *um* to lie in wait for, plot to get hold of 1/23; ~ *um kyrrt* to remain quiet, live an uneventful life 2/176.

sjá (sá) *sv.* to see 1/130, 131; notice 1/412; realise 1/66, 413; understand, know 1/457; foresee 2/583; *sá hann at kona gekk inn* he saw a woman enter 2/442; *sá hann hvar kettan hljóp* he saw the cat pouncing 2/485; *(hann) þykkisk* ~ he feels sure 1/320; ~ *firir* to foresee 2/460; *er vant við at* ~ it is difficult to beware (of him) 1/344; impers. *sér* there can be seen, one can see 2/83.

†sjaldan *adv.* seldom (i.e. never) 2/405.

sjálfbjargi *a.* able to look after o-self 1/5.

sjálfr *pron. a.* self, o-self 1/349; in person 1/249; on one's own, by o-self 1/107; ~ *guð* God himself 2/492.

sjau *num.* seven.

sjór *m.* sea 2/554 (cf. **sær**).

skaði *m.* harm, loss, cause for grief 2/433.

skálpr *m.* sword-sheath 1/309.

skammr *a.* short; n. as subst. *skǫmmu áðr* shortly before 1/36; n. as adv. *skammt* a short distance 1/303.

skap *n.* character, disposition 1/6; heart, mood, temper 1/321 (see **renna**).

skauttoga (að) *wv.* to pull by the loose parts of the clothing (*skaut*) 1/304; *verða skauttogaðr* to get pulled about by one's clothes 1/90.

skegg *n.* beard 2/505.

skeggstaðr *m.* the roots of the beard, the skin under the beard 2/509.

skeið (*pl.* **skeiðr**) *f.* warship 2/569 (see note).

skeina (d) *wv.* to scratch; *skeinask af* to get scratched by it 1/310.

†sker *n.* skerry, rock in the sea; *í skerjum Elfar* at Elfarsker among the skerries at the mouth of the Göta älv 2/381 (see note).

skera (skar) *sv.* to cut; ~ *vaðmál til* cut out some homespun for it (i.e. for the clothes) 1/228; ~ *e-t frá e-u* to cut away s-thing from s-thing 2/527.

skikkja *f.* cloak 1/141.

skilja (lð, ld) *wv.* to part 1/29, 421, 2/284; *undan* ~ to except, exclude, draw the line at 1/147.

Impers. *skilði með ~ þeim* they got separated 1/88. Md. *skiljask frá e-m* to leave s-one's side 1/295; reciprocal *skilðusk* they parted from each other 1/352.

skip *n.* ship; *á skipi* aboard 2/438.

skipa (að) *wv.* to arrange, settle (with dat.) 1/249; *~ e-m* assign s-one a place, make s-one stand 2/610, assign s-one a seat 2/547; *svó mörgum ok miklum köppum sem þar var saman skipat* when there were so many fine champions ranged there together 2/568. Md. *skipask vel* to change for the better, improve 1/222.

skipafjöldi *m.* multitude, large number of ships 2/570.

skipdráttr *m.* 'ship-dragging', either to launch or beach a ship 1/50 (see note).

skipverjar *m. pl.* crew of a ship; *~ sínir* the crew of his ship 2/15.

skjóta (skaut) *sv.* to shoot (*e-u* (with) s-thing); *skaut þremr örum* shot three arrows 2/487; impers. *skýtr* 1/60, see **horn**.

skjótr *a.* quick; n. as adv. *skjótt* quickly 2/519; soon 2/232.

skógr *m.* wood, forest 1/303.

skólmr *m.* a nickname 2/23.

skór *m.* shoe; horseshoe 2/158.

skorta (rt) *wv.* to be lacking; impers. *e-m skortir ekki til* one does not lack the means for 1/222.

skrúðklæði *n. pl.* fine clothes, fancy clothes 1/227.

skræfa *f.* coward, wretch, weakling 2/604 (cf. **mannskræfa**).

skuggamikill *a.* shadowy; *skuggamikit var* it was shadowy 2/313.

skulu (skal) *pret.-pres. vb.* (1) implying necessity or duty: must, shall 1/372; (p. tense) should; to have the duty to 2/235. (2) implying intention: *at konungr skal fara* that the king is to go 1/250; *er ek skal slá með* which I am to mow with 2/60; *hvat skal þat tákna* what will that have been for 1/49; *skyldi Eyvindr* (it was arranged that) E. should 1/360; p. inf. *kvað sér hvórki skyldu* (sc. *duga*) said neither would be any use to him 2/63. (3) implying permission: *skaltu hafa* you may take 2/112; *at hann skyldi* that he might 2/105; *at þú skylir* that you should (be allowed to) 1/318. (4) impers. *þá skal at vísu fara* I shall certainly go then 1/264; *svá skal vera* I shall do so 1/152; *skal gera* we shall make 2/568; p. inf. 1/297; with ellipsis of vb.: *svá skal ok* and it shall (be done) 1/117; *hví skal eigi þat* why not 1/439.

skúr *f.* shower, fall of rain; in pl. storm 2/42.

skýla (d) *wv.* to shelter, protect 1/386

skyldr *a.* (1) necessary, urgent, important; sup. *skyldastr* of the

slá (sló) *sv.* to strike; to mow 2/58, 60; ~ *á sik* put on, assume 1/466; ~ *af* cut off 2/78; ~ *í kaf* to sink (transitive) 2/576.

sláttr *m.* mowing; *fara til sláttar* to go to mow 2/56.

slegit *pp.* of **slá**.

sléttr *a.* level, smooth 2/82.

slíkr *a.* such, of such a kind; n. as subst. such things (*sem* which, as) 1/53, 63 ; *slíkt er þú vill* whatever you like, want to 1/127; *slíkt verðr mælt* so people say 1/184.

slyttinn *a.* lazy; *sagði hann slyttinn* (sc. *vera*) said he was lazy 2/45.

smár *a.* small.

smíð *f.* (1) making, the act of making s-thing; *vera at smíðinni* to be engaged on the (metal-)work 1/375. (2) a work of art, a piece of craftsmanship 1/412.

smíða (að) *wv.* to build, make; *ef ónýtt verðr smíðat* see **ónýtr**; *trautt hefi ek sét jafnvel smíðat* I have hardly ever seen anything made so skilfully, such fine craftsmanship 1/405.

smiðja *f.* workshop 2/65.

smiðreim *f.* the ridge along the back of a scythe-blade, the blunt edge of a blade 2/80.

snákr *m.* snake; as nickname 2/238.

snara (að) *wv.* to turn quickly, step quickly.

snarr *a.* swift; n. as adv. *snart* swiftly, hard 2/49.

snemma, snimma *adv.* early 1/356; very soon, straight away 2/517; at an early age 2/187.

snemmendis *adv.* at an early age 2/30.

snimma see **snemma**.

snúa (snera) *sv.* to turn; ~ *í brottu* turn away, go off 2/64.

sofa (svaf) *sv.* to sleep; *sá er søfr* a sleeping man 1/42.

sofna (að) *wv.* to fall asleep; pp. *sofnaðr* asleep 2/442.

sonr, son (*pl.* **synir**) *m.* son; dat. sg. †*kemba svarðar láð syni* comb her son's head 2/347.

sóru *p. pl.* of **sverja**.

sótti *p.* of **sœkja**.

†**spá** *f.* prophecy 2/279.

†**spara (ð)** *wv.* to spare; md. *sparast* to spare o-self, hold back 2/403.

spotta (að) *wv.* to mock, make fun of 1/209.

speni *m.* teat (of an animal) 1/412.

spyrja (spurða) *wv.* (1) to ask (*e-n e-s* s-one s-thing); ~ *e-n at nafni* to ask s-one their name 2/445; ~ *eftir* to enquire 2/601; ~ *eptir e-m* to ask after s-one 1/34. (2) to learn, hear (by asking) 1/353, 2/249, 539; *spurði út til Íslands* heard out in Iceland 2/431. Md. *spyrjast* to become known, to spread (of news) 2/426.

staðr *m.* place; *annars staðar*

GLOSSARY

(gen. sg.) elsewhere; *nema stað* (*staðar*) see **nema (1)**; *í öðrum stað* on the other side; for his part 2/506.

†**stafn** *m.* stem, prow (of a ship); *stóð þar upp í stafni* stood up there in the bows 2/364.

stakkr *m.* stack (of hay); as a unit of measure *átta stakka völlr* the amount of meadow providing eight 'stacks' of hay; one *stakksvöllr* is said to be 5400 square fathoms (about five acres) 2/81.

standa (stóð) *sv.* (1) to stand 2/364; pres. optative *standi menn* let men stand 1/415; to be, be situated 2/465; *sjá e-t standa* to see s-thing standing 2/324; *svó at í beini stóð* so that he was pierced to the bone 2/491; *láta örina standa í boganum* wedge the arrow in the bow (i.e. between the bow and the string) 2/598; ~ *upp* to stand up, to get up (from bed) 2/474; *upp staðinn* standing up 1/137; *uppi standandi* (of a ship) beached 2/228; *vildi við aungan af* ~ would part with it to no one 2/98. (2) to weigh 2/157.

starfa (að) *wv.* to work, do; *er hann hafði þetta starfat* when he had done this task 2/530.

stefna (d) *wv.* to call, summon (*e-m at sér* s-one to come to one) 1/359.

sterkr *a.* strong 2/335; ~ *at afli* of great physical strength; as a nickname, *sterki* the strong 2/544. Comp. *sterkari* 2/234; sup. *sterkastr* 2/26, 32.

stíga (steig) *sv.* to step, tread; ~ *í sundr* to break under one's foot 2/63.

stofa *f.* room, living-room 1/387.

stórkostligr *a.* splendid, magnificent; amply made, huge 2/62.

stormr *m.* storm, †*Hildar* ~ the storm of H., kenning for battle 2/371.

stórr *a.* large, great 2/67; †~ *í huga* courageous 2/336; sup. *þau blótnaut at stærst verða* the biggest of sacrificial oxen 2/255.

stórvirki *n. pl.* great enterprises 1/409.

streingr (strengr) *m.* string, bow-string 2/487.

stukku *p. pl.* of **støkkva**.

stund *f.* a period of time, a while; *um* ~ for a while 1/314; *nakkvara* ~ for a time 1/431; *á öngri stundu* at no time 1/358; *á lítilli stundu* in a short time, quickly 2/46, 309; pl. *langar stundir* a long time 1/353.

stundum *adv.* sometimes, now and then; ~ ... ~ on one occasion ... on another 1/305.

styðja (studda) *wv.* to rest, support o-self; ~ *á höndum* to go down on hands and knees 2/128.

stærstr *a. sup.* see **stórr**.

støkkva (støkk) *sv.* to leap, spring 2/513; take to flight 1/325, 2/6; *í brottu ~* to leave 2/452.

suðr *adv.* south, to the south; in the south 2/381.

sumar *n.* summer; *í sumri* in the summer (i.e. this summer) 2/348; *at sumri* on the arrival of summer; when summer came 2/537; *um sumarit* in, during the summer 2/38; *í sumar* this summer 2/59.

sumr *a.* and *pron.* some; *seldi sumum* sold it to some of them 2/15; *sumir . . . sumir* some . . . others 2/307.

sundr (í ~) *adv.* apart, in two 2/63; *í ~ ganga* to be severed 2/174.

sunnan *adv.* from the south; back from the south (from Rome) 2/538; **firir ~** on the south side, on the south coast 2/7.

svá, svó *adv.* (1) so, thus, in this way 1/80, 312, 2/219; as a result of this 1/19, 261; *~ er sagt at* it is said that 2/307; *er ~ at* it turns out that 1/77; *~ var gert* this was done 2/581 (cf. 2/42); *nokkut ~* see **nakkvarr**. (2) also, likewise 2/459; *ok ~ eyna* and the island as well 2/533; *ok ~ til Nóregs* and from there on to Norway 2/281. (3) *~ at* so that, with the result that 1/324, to such an extent that 1/405; *~ . . . at* in such a way that 1/307, 2/69. (4) *~ . . . sem* as . . . as 1/151, 2/254; as if 1/310; considering how 1/287, 317, 2/567; at the same moment . . . as 2/337–40. (5) with adjs. and advs. so, to such an extent 2/135; such 2/50, 319; *~ var þeirra mikill aflamunr at* there was such a great difference in strength between them that 2/322; *aldri er hann ~ sterkr né stórr í huga* he is never strong enough nor courageous enough 2/335; *~ mikit* just as much, the same amount 2/106; *~ snart at* so hard that 2/49 (cf. 2/136, 315).

†**svanhvítr** *a.* swanwhite 2/349, see note.

svara (að) *wv.* to reply, answer (*e-m e-u* s-one s-thing).

sveit *f.* company, group of people, party 2/193.

†**sveittr** *a.* sweaty, bloody; *sveittri ferð* to the bloody host 2/379.

†**sverð** *n.* sword 2/353, 404.

sverðskór *m.* the chape or ferrule of a scabbard (not recorded elsewhere; v.l. *umgjǫrð*; the usual term is *dǫggskór*) 1/309.

sverja (sór) *sv.* to swear, take an oath; md. *sverjast í fóstbræðralag* to swear mutual oaths of brotherhood, enter into sworn brotherhood 2/234.

sviftast (ft) *wv.* to wrestle, pull back and forth, struggle with one another 2/507.

svín *n.* pig 1/403.

†**svinnr** *a.* swift, keen, wise 2/377.

svó see **svá**.

†**svörðr** *m.* the skin of the head, scalp 2/348.

†sylgr *m.* drink 2/373.
sýn *f.* sight 2/305.
sýna (**nd**) *wv.* to show 1/426; display, perform; *vörn* ~ put up a defence 2/551; *af jafnungum manni sýnd* to be performed by such a young man 2/55; *þikkist Ormr þá aflraun mesta sýnt hafa* O. thought that this was the greatest feat of strength he had ever performed 2/483. Md. *sýnask* to look, seem (*e-m* to s-one); *sýndist heldr mikilligr* he looked rather on the large size 2/316.
†syngja (**sǫng, saung**) *sv.* to sing, chant 2/273.
syni *dat. sg.* of **sonr**.
sýni *n.* sight; *til sýnis* for inspection, so that people could see 2/158.
sýnn *a.* clear, evident; dat. sg. n. with comp. *sýnu betri* visibly i.e. considerably better 2/451.
systir *f.* sister.
systkin *n. pl.* brother(s) and sister(s); ~ *at fǫður* children of the same father, half-brother and -sister 2/447.
systkinasynir *m. pl.* cousins (sons of brother and sister) 2/247.
sæa *p. subj.* of **sjá**.
sœkja (**sótta**) *wv.* to seek, go and fetch 2/118; ~ *sér e-t* find o-self s-thing 2/113; ~ *hingat* to get here 2/318; ~ *róðr* work at rowing, work at the oars 2/421; ~ *at e-m* attack s-one 1/322, 2/580; ~ *e-n heim* to attack s-one in their home 2/320, (metaphorically) to come over s-one (of an emotion) 1/262.
sœmiliga *adv.* suitably, decently 1/221.
†sær *m.* sea; *á sæ* on the sea 2/395 (cf. **sjór**).
sæti *n.* seat; *vera kominn í* ~ to be settled down, in one's place 2/195.
sætt *f.* agreement; *með øngri* ~ without reaching agreement 1/352; *taka sættir af e-m* to accept a reconciliation with s-one, accept compensation for a crime from s-one 1/408.
sætta (**tt**) *wv.* to reconcile, settle; *var* ~ *því sætt* that was settled, they had reached agreement about that 1/348.
søfr *pres.* of **sofa**.
sǫk *f.* (1) cause, reason; *fyrir vits sǫkum* because of (lack of) intelligence 1/5; *fyrir margs sakir* for many reasons, in many ways 1/399. (2) a matter of dispute, legal dispute 1/246; *valda ǫllum sǫkum* to be responsible for all the trouble 1/350.

taka (**tók**) *sv.* (1) to take, accept, receive; take hold of 2/159; pick up 2/611; ~ *kveðju e-s* respond to s-one's greeting 1/87; ~ *e-m vel* welcome s-one 2/541; ~ *sér* to take for o-self, get 2/65; ~ *sér* *fari* obtain a passage (on a boat) 2/227. (2) to take, hold (capacity) 2/164. (3) with preps. and advs. ~ *á* to carry on, behave, talk 1/288; ~ *á e-u* to take hold of s-thing 2/482; *tak af mér reiðina* release me from your anger 1/398; ~ *mikinn af* 1/165, see note; ~ *til* to set to work 2/73; *nú er þar til at* ~ *er* now we must take up the thread of the story at the point where 2/225; ~ *um kverkr e-m* take hold of s-one by the throat 2/495; ~ *upp* pick up 1/411, 2/597 ; ~ *við* accept, take 2/161; ~ *við e-m* take s-one into one's protection 1/346; ~ *við e-m allvel* to welcome s-one 2/245. (4) with inf. ~ *at*, ~ *til at* to begin to, get down to (doing s-thing) 2/70. (5) md. *takast vel* to turn out well, go well 2/537; *ógæfusamliga hefir mér tekizt at* I have been unlucky in that 2/330.

tákna (að) *wv.* to signify, mean; to be for (a purpose) 1/49; *hvat táknar mótit* what is the assembly for 1/52.

tal *n.* talk; *ganga á* ~ to enter into conversation, go into conference 1/299.

tala (að) *wv.* to talk, to discuss 1/54, 128; to say 2/561; *talat var til* (impers.) people were talking about, the conversation turned to the subject of 2/550; ~ *mikit um at* make a great tale about how, boast that 2/558; ~ *við e-n at* discuss with s-one that 2/237; md. *talast með* discuss one's plans together 2/283.

tíða (dd) *wv. impers.*; *e-n tíðir* one wishes; *sem þik tíðist* as you like 1/151.

tíðendi *n. pl.* news; *ek veit* ~ I have some news for you 1/42; *þau* ~ *er* the (news of the) events which 2/423, 539; *þessi* ~ the news of these events 2/427.

tigr (*acc. pl.* **tigu**) *m.* a group of ten, a decade; in numerals for multiples of ten *sex tigu manna* sixty men 1/355.

til (1) *prep.* (with gen.) to, towards; to the home of 1/340, 2/193, 592; until 1/466, 2/71, 476; for the purpose of; *út* ~ *Íslands* out to (= in) Iceland 2/431; ~ *móts* to summon to an assembly 1/50; *virða* ~ see **virða**; ~ *þess* until that happens 1/193, that this should be so 1/200; ~ *þess at* in order to, with the result that; *þar* ~ *er*, *þar* ~ *at* as conj. until.

til (2) *adv.* too; *eigi enn* ~ *gǫrla* not any too clearly yet, not clearly enough 1/139.

tilgerð *f.* provocation; *fyrir mínar tilgerðir* because of what I had done (to people) 1/24.

tillát *n.* offer, contribution 2/107.

tilraun *f.* experiment, test.

tími *m.* time; *þat var einn tíma at* it happened on one occasion that 2/550; *í þann tíma sem* at a time when 2/595; *í nefndan tíma* inside the arranged time 2/534; *gerðist tímum mjök fram komit* time was getting on 2/101.

tína (d) *wv.* to pick out; md. *sinn mann tínast undan hvórum enda* one man at a time to let go at each end 2/611.

tíu *num.* ten.

tízka *f.* custom, a common event 2/190.

tjá (téða, tjáða) *wv.* to show; to be of use, avail; *ekki tjáir* it is no use 1/63.

tjald *n.* tent 2/297.

tjalda (að) *wv.* to pitch a tent 2/439.

tjaldsdyrr *f. pl.* doorway or opening in a tent 2/303.

tólf *num.* twelve.

torf *n.* turf (used for thatching 2/128).

torsóttr *a.* difficult to achieve; *þér mun torsótt* you will find it difficult 1/25.

trauðr *a.* unwilling; n. as adv. *trautt* scarcely 1/325; scarcely ever, never 1/405.

†traustr *a.* reliable, trusty 2/384.

tré *n.* tree; mast of a ship 2/610.

treysta (st) *wv.* to rely on (with dat.); *†sinni má eingi íþrótt ~* no man can rely on his own strength 2/334; md. *treystask* to be confident 1/341.

troll *n.* troll 2/251; pl. the trolls 1/415, 2/369.

trollskapr *m.* troll-like nature, supernatural power 2/461.

trú *f.* faith, belief, religion; *rétt ~* the true faith (Christianity) 2/430; *sakir trúar þinnar* because of your religion 2/471; *halda vel ~ sína* remain a good Christian 2/618.

trúa (ð) *wv.* (with dat.) to believe 1/369.

†tryggðir *f. pl.* truce; *tældr í tryggðum* betrayed under truce 2/368.

trylla (d) *wv.* to turn into a troll, enchant, endow with supernatural power 2/87.

†tugga *f.* mouthful, something bitten; *~ Herjans* kenning for sword 2/380 (see note).

tunna *f.* (a unit of capacity) a tun, a barrelful 2/164.

tuttugu *num.* twenty.

tveir (*f.* **tvær**, *n.* **tvau**) *num.* two.

tvítögr *a.* aged twenty 2/150.

†tæla (d) *wv.* to trap, betray 2/368.

tönn *f.* tooth 2/308.

um *prep.* (with acc.) (1) (place) around 2/158, 342; near, in the vicinity of 2/606; among 2/262; over, across 2/507; *~ þveran hellinn* see **þverr**. (2) (time) *~ vetr* during the winter, for the winter 2/229; *~ vórit (daginn)* during the spring (day) 2/137, 140; *~ sumarit (morguninn)* in the summer (morning) 2/38, 1/40. (3) (subject) about, concerning 1/27, 145, 438, 2/431; in, with 1/111, 240; ~ *afl* in matters of strength, in feats of strength 2/32; ~ *þat* on that subject 2/273. (4) as adv. round, over 2/130; *þar (. . .)* ~ over it, round it 2/343, 516, concerning that 2/243; in this matter (i.e. in riding) 1/279.

umbót *f.* improvement, repair; pl. *til umbóta* to help matters, look after things 1/213.

umsjá *f.* supervision, guidance, looking after (affairs); *láta þína* ~ lose the benefit of your guidance 1/20; hospitality 1/203.

una (**d**) *wv.* to be content (with a situation), to be willing to stay; ~ *eigi* to be unable to rest (in a place) 2/280, 433.

undan *prep.* (with dat.) away from; ~ *landi* away from the shore 2/310; ~ *hvórum enda* from under each end 2/611; as adv. away; *fara* ~ go off; ~ *skilja* see **skilja**.

undarliga *adv.* strangely, extravagantly; *láta* ~ behave oddly 1/47.

undarligr *a.* strange 1/371, 443.

undir *prep.* (1) with dat. under, beneath. (2) with acc. (motion) under 2/167, 169. (3) as adv. underneath 2/129, 131.

undrast (**að**) *wv. md.* to wonder at, be amazed at (with acc.) 2/504.

ungr *a.* young.

unna (*pres. sg.* **ann**) *pret.-pres. vb.* (with dat.) to love 2/35.

unnit *pp.* of **vinna**.

unnu *p. pl.* of **vinna**.

unz *conj.* until.

upp *adv.* up; inland 2/8; ~ *á land* inland, away from the shore 2/300; ~ *allt at* right up to 2/510.

uppi *adv.* up; ashore (see **standa**) 2/228.

uppstertr *a.* straight up; n. as adv. *uppstert* with head held high, proudly 1/120.

urðu *p. pl.* of **verða**.

út *adv.* (1) out; off, down 2/49; away from shore 2/475; *standa menn upp ok* ~ men stand up and (go) out 1/419. (2) abroad (to Iceland from Norway, cf. **útan**) 1/461; *vilja* ~ to want to go abroad (west) 2/284.

útan *adv.* (1) 'from out' i.e. abroad from Iceland (cf. **út** to Iceland: both adverbs are used as if from the standpoint of a speaker in Norway) 1/14, 32, 109, 2/228; *fór þar* ~ went abroad from there 2/434. (2) *firir* ~ as prep. (with acc.) on the outside of, i.e. on the west side of 2/11. (3) as conj. except 2/457, 462; except that 2/97.

útar *adv. comp.* further out, outward; *kemr* ~ comes out, is being thrust out 2/501.

útarliga *adv.* near the doors, towards the bottom of the table 2/548 (see note).

GLOSSARY

úti *adv.* out, outside 2/109, 134, 580, 596; knocked out 1/324.
útsker *n.* outlying rock; pl. small scattered islands 2/262.

vaðmál *n.* ordinary homespun woollen cloth, plain serge 1/228.
vaðmálsklæði *n. pl.* clothes made of **vaðmál** 1/231.
vafði, vafit see **vefja**.
vaka (ð) *wv.* to be awake; imp. *vaki þú* wake up! 1/42.
vakna (að) *wv.* to wake up; pp. *vaknaðr* awake 1/40.
vald *n.* power; *fá ~ yfir* to conquer, subjugate 2/267; *gefa e-t í ~ e-m* (or *e-s*) to make s-thing over to s-one 2/470, 532.
valda (*pres.* **veldr**, *pret.* **olla**, *pp.* **valdit**) *irreg. vb.* (with dat.) to cause, be responsible for 1/350.
valla see **varla**.
ván, vón *f.* hope, expectation, likelihood; *þikkir ~* it seems probable 2/111; pl. *vita vánir* see **vita**.
vanbúinn *a.* unprepared (*við e-t* for s-thing) 1/359.
vandamál *n.* difficult case (in law), complicated matter 1/53.
vandliga *adv.* carefully, closely, attentively; comp. *vandligar* 1/412.
vandr (*n.* **vant**) *a.* difficult 1/343; requiring care; comp. *er vandara at búa sik í konungs herbergi en annars staðar* it is more important to be careful of one's appearance in the king's antechamber than elsewhere 1/223.
vangafilla *f.* the skin of the cheek; *vangafillurnar* the skin of both cheeks 2/509.
vápn, vópn *n.* weapon; *taka ~ sín* to arm o-self 2/300.
†**vargr** *m.* wolf 2/375.
varla, valla *adv.* hardly, scarcely 1/5, 2/614; not at all 1/279.
varr *a.* aware; *verða e-s ~* to hear of s-thing, learn s-thing, get to know 1/280, realise 2/315; *verða við e-t ~* to become aware of s-thing; to discover s-thing 2/302; *verða við ekki ~* to notice nothing, see no signs of life 2/298; *hann verðr eigi fyrr ~ við en* the first thing he knew was that 2/314.
vaskliga *adv.* valiantly, in a manly way 1/233 (see note).
vatt see **vinda**.
vaxa (óx) *sv.* to grow (*upp* up) 2/36.
vefja (vafða) *wv.* to wrap; *~ með járni* to bind round with iron 2/67; *~ e-u um hönd sér* to twist s-thing round one's hand 2/507.
vega (vá, vó) *sv.* (1) to lift 1/323, 2/131. (2) to kill 1/3.
veggr *m.* wall.
vegr *m.* path, way; acc. pl. *marga vega* in many ways, variously 1/236.
vegsummerki *n. pl.* the evidence of what has been done, the results of the work 2/140.

veifa (ð) *wv.* to wave, swing (with dat.); ~ *e-u um sik* to whirl s-thing round o-self 2/582.

veita (tt) *wv.* to give 2/373; grant (a request) 1/434; †~ *högg* deal blows, fight 2/379; ~ *atsókn* bring an attack 2/553; ~ *viðrbúnað* make preparations 2/463; ~ *afskipti* see **afskipti**; impers. *e-m veitir* things go well for one; *honum mun eigi* ~ things are going to go badly for him 2/492.

veizla *f.* feast, banquet; *þar var* ~ *hin bezta* a big party was being held there 2/194; an official reception for a king or jarl 1/378; *fara at veizlum* to go round on a state visit 2/606 (see note).

veiztu *second pers. sg. pres.* of **vita** with suffixed pron.

vekja (vakta) *wv.* to wake (transitive) 2/475.

vel *adv.* well 1/6; finely; very 1/398, 456; easily, at least 2/110; *sá maðr mun* ~ *vera* he must be a fine man 1/97; *má enn* ~ *vera* he may still be all right 1/99; *vera* ~ to be well, to be good; ~ *farit* see **fara**.

velja (valða) *wv.* to choose, select 1/447.

velli *dat. sg.* of **völlr**.

venda (nd) *wv.* to turn; ~ *e-u um* to turn s-thing round, turn s-thing over 2/130.

vera (var, *pl.* **várum, vórum)** *sv.* (1) to be; with suffixed neg. *era* is not 1/21, *væria* would not be 1/72; *erþú* you are 2/471; *er ek* (late form of first pers. sg.) I am 2/360; *þú er* (early form of second person sg., normally *ert*) you are 1/371; pres. subj. *sé* 1/24, 161; *at ek sé* that I shall be 2/203; p. subj. *væri* 1/12, in reported speech *hann væri* he was said to be 2/251; imp. *ver* be, stay 1/294. (2) to be true; *eigi er þat* that is not so 2/563; *enn þótt þat sé* even if that were true 1/384. (3) to come about, happen 2/270, 432 (see **munu**), 550; *þat var þó eigi* but it did not turn out that way 1/357. (4) to stay 2/11, 297; *vera hjá* to live with 2/448; *vera með e-m* to stay with s-one 2/282, 616; †*vera mun ek enn með mönnum* I shall stay longer among men, i.e. I shall continue to live, I shall not die yet 2/277. (5) with inf. *nú er at* now it is necessary to, now one must 2/225. (6) as aux. forming passive 1/117 (cf. note), 167 (impers.), 2/80, 314. (7) as aux. of p. tense with vbs. of motion 2/302, 316.

verð *n.* worth, price; payment 2/117.

verða (varð, *pp.* **orðinn, vorðinn)** *sv.* (1) to be, become 2/614; to come to be, turn out to be (*e-m* for s-one) 1/92; to grow 2/255; *urðu þá eigi aðrir menn frægri . . . en þeir* they became more famous than any other men

2/263; *verða varr* see **varr**.
(2) to take place, happen 1/317, 2/539; *þá var orðit* there had by then taken place 2/428; *yrði þat svó* if that should happen 2/468.
(3) with preps. and advs. ~ *e-m á munni* see **munnr**; *verðr ekki af e-u* nothing comes of s-thing, s-thing is abandoned 2/258; *verða at e-u* to become s-thing 1/455; *at þér verði at því ólið* that harm may result to you from this 1/261; *verða fyrir* to get in the way (of) 2/584, to come in for, become the object of 1/235. (4) as aux. with inf. to have to, must 1/58; *varð einn at ráða* see **ráða**; impers. with plain inf. *fara mun verða* they would have to go 1/67. (5) as aux. forming passive 1/89, 184, 342 (impers.), 372, 2/148, 353, 552, 555, 556; *er mælt verðr* which is spoken 1/207.

verðr *a.* worthy, deserving; worth (*e-s* s-thing); *eigi minna* (gen. sg.) *vert en* worth no less than 2/146; *þikkja e-m mikils vert um* one has a high opinion of, one is very impressed with 2/177.

verk *n.* work 2/37.

verr *adv. comp.* worse; *fara e-m ~* to suit one worse: *eigi veit ek mér ~ fara óknáleik minn en þér afl þitt* I don't see that my weakness is any more of a disadvantage to me than your strength is to you 1/74.

verri *a. comp.* worse; *væria þér ~* you would not be worse off with 1/72; *~ viðreignar* worse to have dealings with 2/254.

verst, **vest** *adv. sup.* worst.

verstr, **vestr** *a. sup.* worst; *því sem vest var orðit* that (hay) which was worst rotted (i.e. the hay on the top and round the sides of the stack that had been rotted by rain) 2/128.

vestr *adv.* west, westwards.

vetr (*pl.* **vetr**) *m.* winter; *í ~* for the winter, this winter 2/546; *um ~*, *um vetrinn* for the winter, during that winter 2/230, 269, 435; *at vetri liðnum* see **líða**; *vetr annan* for a second winter 2/535; *~ mikill* a hard (long) winter 2/93; a year: *tólf vetra* (gen. pl.) *gamall* twelve years old 2/36; *sjau vetra* seven years old 2/31; *þrjá vetr* for three years 2/436; *nokkura vetr* for a few years 2/616.

vetrvist *f.* lodging for the winter 1/202.

vettugi see **vætki**.

vexti *dat. sg.* of **vǫxtr**.

við *prep.* (1) (with acc.) with, together with 1/92; in company with 2/295; near, by, on (a river) 2/13; at (in response to) 2/305; to 2/98, see **standa**; according to 1/230; denoting attendant circumstances, with 1/79; *~ jörðina* near the ground 2/129; *~ Svölðr* at (the battle of) Svöldr

2/570; *tala ~ e-n* to speak with s-one. (2) (with dat.) *hlæja ~ e-u* to laugh at s-thing 1/239; *hafa afl ~ e-m* to have the strength to match s-one 2/466.

víða *adv.* widely, far and wide 2/210.

viðarbulungr *m.* wood-pile 2/66.

†viðför *f.* treatment; pl. *vórar (várar) viðfarar* his treatment of me 2/416.

víðfǫrull *a.* widely travelled, experienced.

víðr *a.* wide; *á víðum velli* on open ground 2/581.

viðrbúnaðr *m.* preparation 2/462.

viðreign *f.* dealing (with s-one), having to do (with s-one); *verri viðreignar* worse to have dealings with 2/254.

viðskifti *n. pl.* dealings, conflicts; *í viðskiftum þeirra Dufþaks* in (as a result of) his conflicts with D. 2/288.

víg *n.* fight, battle; *støkkva í víginu* to flee from the fight 1/326.

víking *f.* piracy, being a viking; *frægri í víkingu* more famous in piracy, i.e. more famous vikings 2/263.

vilgis *intensive adv.* very, too 1/456.

vilja (**vilda**, *p. inf.* **vildu** 1/391) *wv.* to wish, want, be willing 1/30; will, shall, be going to 1/147, 339, 2/467; *~ ekki* to refuse 2/34; *ek vilda* I would like 1/59, 116; *er hann vildi at færi* whom he wished to go 1/94; with ellipsis of following inf. to wish to be 1/457; to want to go 2/283; *eigi vil ek þat* I will not do that 2/171.

vinátta *f.* friendship 1/380; *gerðist þar skjótt ~* they soon became friends 2/232; *með (mikilli) vináttu* on (very) friendly terms 2/285, 533.

vinda (**vatt**) *sv.* to twist; *~ í sundr* wrench apart 2/62.

vindli *m.* wisp (e.g. of straw) 1/306.

vinna (**vann**) *sv.* (1) to work 2/34; to do 1/328; *~ mart til framaverka* perform many deeds bringing fame 2/200; *~ skjótt um* finish the job quickly 2/519; *eigi vel at unnit* not well dealt with (referring to the hay scattered on the ground) 2/142. (2) defeat, conquer, overcome 2/224, 253, 469, 552, 554. Md. for passive *ynnist* would have been defeated 2/587.

vinr *m.* friend.

vinveittr *a.* friendly, pleasant, endurable 1/79.

virða (**rð**) *wv.* to value, assess; *~ þetta til ginningar* consider that (to be) a befooling, think you are making a fool out of me 1/146.

vísa *f.* verse, strophe, stanza (often a poem consisting of one stanza complete in itself) 2/271, 331; in pl. of several verses making up a poem 2/344, 459.

víss *a.* certain; *þeir sá vísan bana* they saw that death was certain 2/583; *verða e-s ~* to find out about s-thing, get to know about s-thing 2/192, 603; *n.* as subst. *at vísu* certainly, indeed 1/156; *n.* as adv. *víst* indeed, certainly, for sure, without doubt 1/132, 2/417; *þat ætla ek víst* I think so certainly (or I consider that certain) 1/57.

vist *f.* stay, residence; *~ þín í Nóregi* for you to stay in Norway 1/456; *betr þykki mér þér þar vistin felld vera* I think it would be more suitable for you to stay there 1/204.

vit (1) *n.* intelligence, sense 1/18; perception, knowledge 1/161; *fyrir vits sǫkum* for (lack of) intelligence 1/5.

vit (2) *pron. dual* we two; *~ erum systkin ok Brúsi* B. and I are brother and sister 2/447.

vita (**veit**, *p.* **vissa**) *pret.-pres. vb.* to know; understand 2/243; notice 1/42 (1); to learn, hear 2/455; find out 2/240; foresee 2/276; *eigi veit ek* (with acc. and inf.) I am not sure that 1/74; *má ek því eigi vita* so I cannot tell 1/199; *eigi má ek annat til ~* I can't tell if it is otherwise 1/368; *~ e-s vánir* to see a likelihood of s-thing 1/265; *~ fyrir* to foresee; *Eyvindr þóttisk ~ fyrir* E. thought it probable 1/357.

vitr *a.* wise; comp. *vitrari* 1/271.

vitrligr *a.* wise, sensible; comp. n. *vitrligra* 1/211.

vizkumaðr *m.* a person of intelligence, a bright person 1/104.

vón see **ván**.

vópn see **vápn**.

vópndauðr (**vápn-**) *a.* dead by weapons; *verða ~* to be killed by arms, die by violence 2/236.

vór (**vár**) *n.* spring; *um vórit* in the spring 2/12; *at vóri komnu* see **koma**.

vorðinn *pp.* of **verða**.

vórkunn (**vár-**) *f.* something to be excused; *er þat ~* that is understandable, you cannot be blamed for that 2/454.

vórr (**várr**) *poss. a.* our 2/416.

vóru, vórum *p. pl.* of **vera**.

væla (**t**) *wv.* to deceive, trick; *~ um* to deal with s-thing; *ef hann vælir einn um* if he is left to manage on his own 1/275.

vænleikr *m.* beauty, handsomeness 1/72.

vænn *a.* promising; handsome 1/3, 2/443; sup. n. as adv. *þótti þeim um it vænsta* they were delighted with the prospect 1/302.

vætki (*dat.* **vettugi**) *n.* (*pron.*) nothing, nothing at all 2/276; *vettugi nýtr* good for nothing, useless 2/142.

vǫllr *m.* field, meadow; *átta stakka ~* see **stakkr**; *á víðum velli* on open ground 2/581.

vǫlva *f.* prophetess, sibyl, fortune-teller 2/191.

vǫrn *f.* defence; *þar til varnar* there as a defence, there to defend it 2/588; ~ *sýna, koma ~ firir sik* to put up a defence 2/330, 551.

vǫxtr (*gen.* **vaxtar**, *dat.* **vexti**) *m.* growth, build; size, bigness of body 2/45; *lítill vexti* of small build 1/3.

yfir *prep.* (1) (with acc.) over, across 2/208; ~ *land* around the country 2/190; *færast ~* see **færa**. (2) (with dat.) over; ~ *sér* on (of clothes) 1/123; *sem ~ kykvendum* as with animals, like you hear from animals 1/45. (3) as adv. across 2/125.

yfirkoma (**yfirkom**) *sv.* to overcome, defeat, beat 2/572.

yfirlit *n. pl.* personal appearance 2/443.

ýmiss *a.* various, different 2/218; n. as subst. *á ýmsu* see **leika**.

ynni *p. subj.* of **vinna**.

yrði *p. subj.* of **verða**.

yrkja (**orta**) *wv.* to make, compose (poetry) 1/438.

ýtri *a. comp.* outer; further out to sea; more westerly (cf. **út, útan**) 2/250, 297.

þá *adv.* (1) then 2/124; at that moment, in this action 2/483; by then, after that 2/80, 136; by this time 2/428, 436; on that occasion, that year 2/151; in that case 1/267. (2) after concessive clauses, yet 2/449, 465. (3) pleonastic with comp. 2/179 (see **ellri**), with sup. 2/199 (see **helzt**). (4) ~ *er* as conj. when 1/70 (see note), 2/31, 354, 366, 384.

þaðan *adv.* from there; away, from that place 1/304; of time ~ *af* from then on 2/138.

þangat *adv.* there, to that place; ~ *sem* in the direction of where 1/81; (of time) ~ *til er* until 2/36.

þannug *adv.* thus, like that; ~ . . . *sem þú ert* just like you 1/163.

þar *adv.* (1) there, in that place 1/461; with him 1/269; in this matter 1/305; on this subject, about this 1/144; to that point 1/321; ~ *er kominn Brúsi* B. was there 2/316. (2) with other advs. ~ . . . *frá* about this 2/456; ~ *í* therein, into it, onto it 2/67; ~ . . . *með* by means of it 1/450; ~ *um* over it 2/516; ~ . . . *um* round it 2/342, about that, on that subject 2/243, in this matter 2/460; *fór ~ útan* sailed abroad from there 2/434. (3) ~ *er* as conj. where; ~ *er heitir* in a place called 2/184, to the place where 1/292, 2/444; ~ . . . *er* in a place where 1/204, at the point where 2/225; ~ *sem* where, to where 2/607, to a place where 2/593 (see note); ~ *til er*, ~ *til at* until 2/311, 612.

þarmaendi *m.* the end of the gut or intestine 2/341.

þarmr *m.* gut, intestme 2/344.

þars *conj.* (for *þar es*, older form of *þar er*) since 1/113.

þáttr *m.* a short story, episode 2/1.

þegar *adv.* at once, immediately; at the moment, off hand 1/162; already 1/232. As conj. ~ (*er*) as soon as 2/518, when, if 1/202; ~ *at* as soon as, when 2/217.

þegja (**þagða**) *wv.* to be silent, say nothing 2/214; *þegi þú* shut up! 1/389.

þeir *pron. pl.* they; ~ *Stórólfr* he and S. 2/87; ~ *Ásbjörn* A.'s party 2/438; ~ *Ásbjörn ok Ormr* the two of them, Á. and O. 2/270; ~ *vóru brœðr ok Véseti* he and V. were brothers 2/184.

þeygi *adv. (conj.)* equivalent of *þó eigi* yet not; nevertheless ... not 1/259.

þíðr *a.* thawed, unfrozen; *á þíðum sjó* on the open sea 2/554.

þikkja see **þykkja**.

þing *n.* meeting, public assembly 1/85; referring to the Alþingi 2/151, 152, 176.

þjóta (**þaut**) *sv.* to screech, shrill, bray; *þaut við mjǫk* it brayed out loudly 1/45.

þó *adv.* yet, nevertheless, moreover 2/142; even so 1/99, 2/450; indeed 2/318; but 1/307; with comp. even (more) 2/254; ~ *at* (cf. **þótt**) as conj. though, although; even if 1/163.

þokki *m.* thought, opinion; *mér erþú vel í þokka* you are much to my liking, I am very attracted to you 2/471.

þora (**ð**) *wv.* to dare 2/583.

þorp *n.* village 2/183.

þótt *conj.* although, though; *enn* ~ even if 1/384; (elliptical) although one were to say that 2/586.

þótti see **þykkja**.

†**þraungr** (**þrǫngr**) *a.* narrow; in metaphorical sense 2/361 (see note to 2/360).

þrettán *num.* thirteen.

þreyta (**tt**) *wv.* to wear out, exhaust 1/288.

þriði *ord. num.* third.

þrífa (**þreif**) *sv.* to grasp; ~ *í skeggit á e-m* to grab s-one's beard 2/505; *hann er þrifinn á loft* he is snatched up into the air 2/314.

þrír (*f.* **þrjár**, *n.* **þrjú**) *num.* three.

þrítögsaldr *m.* the age of thirty 2/226.

þrjóta (**þraut**) *sv. impers.* (with acc.) to fail; *þraut hestinn* the horse was exhausted, collapsed 1/279; pp. *þrotinn* exhausted 1/284.

þúfa *f.* mound, hillock 2/78.

þungr *a.* heavy; hard 2/50; harsh, unpleasant 2/451.

þurfa (**þarf**) *pret.-pres. vb.* (1) (with gen.) to need, want, require 1/202, 362. (2) (with inf.) *þarftu eigi dylja* there's no point in your denying it 1/382; *hversu margir þyrfti undir at* *ganga* how many would need to get under it 2/609.

†**þuss** (**þurs**) *m.* giant 2/415.

þvá (**þó**, *pp.* **þveginn**) *sv.* to wash 1/177.

þverr *a.* transverse, lying across; *um þverar hellinn* across the middle of the cave 2/324.

þverra (**þvarr**) *sv.* to decrease; *þvarr þat allt af þeim hirðmönnum* the courtiers left it off completely 1/243.

því *pron.* (*dat. sg. n.* of *sá*); *í ~ at* at that moment 2/47; *frá ~ er* from the time when 2/301; with advs. *~ nær margir* almost as many, about the same number (of men) 2/437; *~ nærri hátt* about the same in height 2/111. With comp. *~ betr er ek geng yðr nær* the better the nearer I am to you 1/298; *~ betra er síðar er* getting better as it went on 1/441; *~ meiri sem* the greater as 2/178. As adv. therefore, for that reason, so 2/6, 179, 258; *~ at* as conj. because, for; *~ . . . at* for this reason .. that 1/369.

þvílíkr *a.* similar; n. as adv. *þvílíkt . . . sem* the same . . . as 1/268.

þýfðr *a.* covered with mounds 2/69.

þykkja, **þikkja** (**þótta**) *wv.* (personal and impers.) to seem; to be considered 2/162, 197, 199; *þótti hinn mesti maðr* was thought a very great man 2/617; *þóttu mikil* they were considered important, everyone was very struck by them 2/427; *þætti* it would seem 1/200; *e-m þykkir* it seems to one, one thinks (often in the form *þykki* when followed immediately by the pronouns *mér* and *þér*) 1/15, 129, 131, 298, 2/242); *þótti honum* he reckoned 2/146; *mér þætti* I should think 1/61; *þykkir e-m gaman* one thinks it fun 1/91, 287; *eigi þikki mér þú mega* I do not think that you can 2/242; *þykkir e-m vel* it seems good to s-one, one is pleased, content; *þykki mér þat illt* I am sorry, I think it a pity 1/189; *illt þótti mér* I did not like it 1/336. Md. *þykkjask* to think o-self, to think that one: *sem konungr þykkisk þurfa* which the king thinks he needs 1/54; *þóttisk þurfa* felt he needed 1/37; *Ormr þóttist heilsa henni* O. thought (in his dream) that he greeted her 2/445; *þykkisk sjá (firir)* (he) thinks he sees (foresees) 1/320, 2/95; *ek þykkjumk sjá* I think I know 1/457; *eigi þykkjumk ek sjá* I do not think I can see 1/132; *þættumk ek þurfa* I was going to ask for 1/102.

þykkr *a.* thick, wide; *tveggja faðma þykkt* two fathoms wide 2/111.

þyrfti see **þurfa**.

þætti see **þykkia**.

æ *adv.* always 2/409, 617.

æðri *a. comp.* higher; *hinn æðra bekk* the higher bench 2/548 (see note).

ætla (að) *wv.* (1) to think, consider 2/252, 586; expect 2/75; intend; *þat ~ ek* it is my opinion 2/203; *er eingi ætlaði at . . . mundi* which no one thought would ever 2/554; *svó leingi sem ætlat var* as long as had been arranged, intended 2/215; *ætlaði sér varla hóf um* did not know his own limits, knew no bounds 1/279; with acc. and inf. *lítit ~ ek þik af honum hafa hlotit* I think you have been gifted with little of that 1/71; *ráðligra ~ ek vera* I think it wiser 1/454; *~ e-n dauðan* (sc. *vera*) to think that s-one is dead 2/424; *þat ~ ek víst* 1/57 see **víss**. (2) with inf. to intend (to do s-thing) 1/30, 356; to be about (to do s-thing), to try (to do s-thing) 2/73, 491; with plain inf. *~ drepa hann* intend to kill him 1/419.

ætlun *f.* thought, opinion; *at því sem þú leggr ~ á* in your opinion 1/185.

ætt *f.* family, family line 2/221.

ættaðr *a.* descended, originating; *móðir hans var ættuð af Hörðalandi* his mother's family came from Hörðaland 2/220.

ævi *f.* life, course of life 1/444.

ökla *n.* ankle 2/169.

ǫkulbrœkr *f. pl.* ankle-length breeches 1/123.

†**ölkátr** *a.* merry with ale 2/355.

øng- see **engi**.

ör (*pl.* **örvar**) *f.* arrow 2/487.

ørendi (cf. **eyrendi**) *n.* errand; business, reason for coming 1/12; *eiga ~ við e-n* to have business with s-one 1/127.

örlög *n. pl.* fate, fortune, destiny; *segja e-m firir ~ sín* to tell s-one their fortune 2/192.

örvamælir *m.* quiver 2/486.

øxarskapt *n.* axe-handle 1/308.

INDEX OF PROPER NAMES

Names preceded by † occur only in the verses

PERSONAL NAMES

Ásbjörn prúði Virfilsson 63–69, 71–73, 75
Bergþórr bestill, cousin of Ásbjörn 65
Bifru-Kári (Áslákr Bifru-Kári Arnarson) 64
Brúsi (a giant) 65, 68, 69, 72–75
Dofri (a troll) 57
Dufþakr (Irish Dubhthach) 60–62, 67
Einarr (þambarskelfir Eindriðason) af Gimsum 78
Eirekr jall (Hákonarson), ruler in Norway 1000–1013 76–78
Eyvindr, lendr maðr 52–55
Eyvindr snákr, cousin of Ásbjörn 65
†Gautr, companion of Ásbjörn 70
†Geiri, companion of Ásbjörn 70
†Geitir, companion of Ásbjörn 71
†Geitir (a giant name) 70
†Glúmr, companion of Ásbjörn 70
Glúmr (Víga-Glúmr Eyjólfsson?) 41
†Grani, companion of Ásbjörn 71
†Grímr, companion of Ásbjörn 71
guð (God) 74
†Gunnarr, companion of Ásbjörn 71
Hákon (inn ríki Sigurðarson) Hlaðajall, ruler of Norway c. 974–995 65, 72
†Háma, companion of Ásbjörn 70
Haraldr (Hálfdanarson, hárfagri) Dofrafóstri, king of Norway c. 885–931 57
Haraldr (harðráði, Sigurðarson sýrs), king of Norway 1046–66 46, 49–56
†Haukr, companion of Ásbjörn 70
Helgi Hængsson 57
†Herjan (a name of Óðinn) 70
Herjúlfr Hængsson 57
Herröðr, jall in Gautland 66
Hildiríðarsynir (Hárekr and Hrærekr Björgólfssynir, see note to to 2/5) 57
†Hildr (name of a valkyrie, see Glossary) 70
†Hjálmr, companion of Ásbjörn 71
Hrafn Hængsson 57
Hrafnhildr Ketilsdóttir hængs 57
†Hrani, companion of Ásbjörn 71
Hreiðarr, grandfather of Hreiðarr Þorgrímsson 41
Hreiðarr Þorgrímsson 41–56
†Hrókr, companion of Ásbjörn 70
Hængr Ketilsson (Ketill hængr Þorkelsson) 57
†Högni, companion of Ásbjörn 71
Ingunn, wife of Hængr 57
Jörundr goði (Hrafnsson heimska) 57, 62
Ketill hængr ór Hrafnistu 57
Ketill (Þorkell) Naumdælajall 57
Magnús (Óláfsson helga, inn góði), king of Norway 1035–46 41, 42, 49, 50, 52–56
Melkólfr (Irish Maelcoluim, Malcolm) 62
Menglöð Ófótansdóttir 72, 74, 75
†Miðjungr (a giant name?) 70
†Oddvör (mother of Sámr and Sæmingr) 70

INDEX OF NAMES

Ófótan ór Ófótansfirði (a troll?) 72
Óláfr Tryggvason, king of Norway 995–1000 72, 76
Ormr sterki Stórólfsson 57–63, 65–67, 70–78
Petrus postuli (St Peter) 74
†Sámr Oddvararson, companion of Ásbjörn 70
Skólmr (cf. Þorbjörn skólmr: the nickname is used as a personal name) 62
†Starri, companion of Ásbjörn 70
†Stefnir, companion of Ásbjörn 71
Stórólfr Hængsson 57–62, 65, 67, 69, 72
Sumarliði Herjúlfsson 57
†Svanhvít (Ásbjörn's mother) 69, see note to 2/349
†Sæmingr Oddvararson, companion of Ásbjörn 70

†Sörkvir, companion of Ásbjörn 71
†Teitr, companion of Ásbjörn 71
†Tóki, companion of Ásbjörn 70
†Torfi, companion of Ásbjörn 71
Tryggvi (Óláfsson, father of King Óláfr Tryggvason) 72
†Tumi, companion of Ásbjörn 71
Véseti í Borgundarhólmi 63
Vestarr Hængsson 57
Virfill, father of Ásbjörn 63, 66
Þórálfr Skólmsson (inn sterki) 57, 62, 63
Þórarna, sister of Þorbjörn skólmr and wife of Stórólfr 57, 58
Þorbjörn (Þorgeirr) skólmr (cf. Skólmr) 57
Þórðr Þorgrímsson 41–44, 46–48, 50
Þorgrímr Hreiðarsson 41
Þorlaug Hrafnsdóttir 57
Özurr hörzki 65, 67

GEOGRAPHICAL NAMES

Bjǫrgyn (Bergen, Norway) 42
Borgundarhólmr (Bornholm) 63
Danmörk (Denmark) 63, 66, 69, 72, 76
Dufþaksholt (cf. Holt), a farm in southern Iceland 60
†Elfarsker (sker Elfar), the skerries in the estuary of the river Göta (Göta älv) in Västergötland (southwest Sweden) 70
Eyjafjǫrðr (fjord in northern Iceland) 41
†Eyrasund (usually Eyrarsund, modern Øresund, the straits between Denmark and Sweden) 70
†Gautaveldi (poetic name for Gautland) 66

Gautland (provinces of Västergötland and Östergötland in southern Sweden) 65, 66
Gimsar (Gimsan, near Trondheim, Norway) 78
Hlaðir (Lade, near Trondheim, Norway) 65, 76
Hof, a farm on the north side of the eastern Rangá in southern Iceland 57
Holt (í Holti; cf. Dufþaksholt) 60, 61
Hrafnista (Ramsta, an island off the coast from Namdalen in Norway) 57
Hvóll (cf. Stórólfshvóll) 57, 62
Hörðaland (Hordaland, a district in western Norway) 64, 65, 69

Hörgárdalr (a valley near Eyjafjörðr in northern Iceland) 62

†Ífuminni (the mouth of the river Ífa; in Gautland?) 70

Ísland (Iceland) 56, 57, 63, 65, 67, 72, 78

Leiruvógr (a small bay in Kollafjörðr just north of Reykjavík) 67

Markarfljót (a river in southern Iceland) 57

Myrká (a farm on the Myrká river in Hörgárdalr, northern Iceland) 62

Mærr (acc. and dat. Mæri) (modern Møre; cf. Norðmærr, and note to 2/201) 64–67

Norðmærr (now Nordmøre, a district in Norway; cf. Mærr) 64

Nóregr (Norway) 55, 56, 64, 67, 72, 76

Ófótansfjörðr (perhaps the same as Ófótafjörðr, now the Ofotfjord, northern Norway) 72

Rangá hin eystri (Eystri-Rangá, the more easterly Rangá, a river in southern Iceland) 57

Rangá (hin ýtri, Ýtri-Rangá, the more westerly Rangá, a river in southern Iceland) 57

Reyðarfjörðr (a fjord in eastern Iceland) 72

Róm (Rome) 74, 76

Sauðeyjar ('sheep-islands') 65, 67, 72; Sauðey hin ýtri 67, 73; Sauðey hin minni 72

Stórólfshvóll (cf. Hvóll; a farm south of the Eystri-Rangá in southern Iceland) 57, 59, 61, 67, 78

Svarfaðardalr (a valley in northern Iceland) 56

Svöldr (either an island in the Baltic or a river in Vindland, the site of the battle at which Óláfr Tryggvason fell in AD 1000: the site has not been identified with certainty) 77

Upplǫnd (Opland, the inland districts in eastern Norway) 52

Vendilskagi (Skagen, at the northernmost tip of Jutland) 63

Víkin (Oslofjord and the districts round about) 78

Þjórsá (a river in the south of Iceland, Rangárvallasýsla) 57, 65

Þrándheimr (Trøndelag, a district in Norway) 72, 75, 78

OTHER NAMES

Íslendingar (Icelanders) 45

Íslendingaskrá ('The Scroll of the Icelanders', an unidentified book) 67

Menglaðarnautar ('the gifts of Menglöð', the pair of magic gloves) 74

Naumdælir (inhabitants of Naumudalr, modern Namdalen, northern Norway) 57

Ormrinn langi ('The Long Serpent', the great ship on which Óláfr Tryggvason fought his last battle) 76–78

Svöldrarorrosta (the battle of Svöldr) 76